SNAKE BIGHT

ROBERT KING II

This book is a work of fiction.

Names, characters, places, events, locales, and incidents are either the products of the author's imagination or used in a fictitious manner.

Any resemblance to actual persons, living or dead, or actual events is purely coincidental.

ISBN: 979-8-234-08016-5

For Mom

And to the memory of Windham Rotunda and Jon Huber

Prologue

A LEATHER-BOUND NOTEBOOK WITH AN EXQUISITE REPTILE-scale design sat on a stainless-steel desk as a middle-aged man caressed the cover with his fingertips. The man stared at his blurred reflection on the shiny, sanitized desk. His greying hair and tanned skin meshed together in the reflection, almost like an oil painting. He smiled softly, but the distorted face looking back at him gave off a different appearance. Its smile looked angular, a sinister V-shape, as the corners of its mouth seemed to stretch to the top of its cheekbones—it looked *evil*.

He opened the front cover of the leather notebook, and on the very first page it read

PERSONAL JOURNAL OF ABIN MOSES

His signature was perfect; like that of a movie star. It better had been since he'd spent so much time practicing it, waiting for the moment when he won a Nobel Prize and people would no doubt be fighting to get his autograph. Pulling out his rolling chair, he took a seat and began writing. *I fear this may be my last time at the black site. While I've appreciated my time here, I believe they are on to me.*

Abin chewed the inside of his cheek as he wrote the journal entry he didn't think he'd have to for a long, long time. Then, a small beep sounded off next to him. An alarm. He turned his attention to the source of the sound —three computer monitors. Nine squares divided each monitor. The squares displayed the feeds from security cameras that were installed from the entrance to Abin's lab and all throughout the atrium leading up to his main work area. He focused on the first of the squares, the entrance to the lab. The metal door was already open, and two men (one heavy and one skinny) wearing suits were entering. Abin's eyes narrowed, and he grumbled in his thick Southern accent, "Fat Man an' Little Boy."

He reached under the monitors, where a long speaker sat. Twisting a knob on the speaker, he heard Little Boy's voice come through as it turned on. "So, what'd this guy do exactly?" Abin continued watching the men, hoping to find out why they were entering his lab unannounced and uninvited.

Fat Man crossed his arms impatiently as Little Boy closed the first metal door behind them. "Supposedly, he's been using government property for his own experiments. They don't like that."

Little Boy approached the next door, which had a sign above it that read

BIOCHEM LAB

Pulling his suit jacket to the side, he grabbed an identification badge that sat on his belt, next to his gun holster. He waved the badge over the sensor next to the door, unlocking it. "You're telling me this guy works with biochemical weapons and they only sent *us* two to get rid of him?"

Abin peeled his eyes away from the monitor as he felt his stomach twisting into knots. *Shit. I knew it.* He pushed his rolling chair back from the desk and got to his feet, then he rushed over to the side desk where a glass incubator illuminated by red bulbs sat. Embryos inside test tubes filled the incubator; each test tube had a piece of tape on it displaying a number. Abin rested his hand on top of the incubator as he looked through the glass. "I knew this day would come. I just didn't think it'd be so soon." He lowered his head and flipped a switch on the side of the incubator, turning it to the OFF position, and the red heating lamps shut down. Opening the door on the front of the incubator, Abin removed the test tube stand and walked it over to a small grated hatch in the wall. He opened the hatch—the inside charred black—and placed the test tube stand inside. "I hardly knew ya." He shut the grated hatch and returned to his main desk. A big red button labeled INCINERATOR sat on the wall behind the desk. Abin breathed and smacked the button. He heard the *whoosh* of igniting flames next to him as he once again lowered his head. He turned, looking up at the grated hatch that now glowed a bright orange.

The sound of Fat Man's voice coming from the monitor speaker pulled his attention away from the hatch. "First, he doesn't work with biochemical weapons..." Abin turned back to face the monitors. Fat Man and Little Boy had entered the atrium.

Fat Man shut the second door behind them. "He uses small amounts of chemicals on animals to see the effect biochemical weapons *might* have. Second, we're not here to 'get rid' of anyone. We're here to *escort* him to the director to have a talk. See if he can explain himself." A white mouse scurried past Fat Man's shoe, making him jump and yelp.

"Jesus. Calm down," Little Boy said, laughing. "Just 'cause you're the size of an elephant doesn't mean you need to be scared of a little mouse."

Fat Man stared at him with a blank expression. "Ha-ha. Hilarious. Fuck off."

Abin's eyes moved to the next camera feed as Fat Man and Little Boy travelled further into the atrium, approaching waist-high platforms that lined the walls. Three-foot-high glass panels topped the platforms. Behind the glass, someone had planted six-foot-tall trees in moss-covered dirt. Abin grabbed his lab coat from the back of his rolling chair and slung it on before heading toward a door at the back of the lab. He pushed it open and entered the atrium.

As Abin approached the men, Little Boy tapped on the glass. "I thought labs were supposed to be sterile. I don't think moss is sterile." Suddenly, an osprey popped out of the trees and screeched, causing the men to recoil.

Abin chuckled to himself before speaking up. "The part of my lab where I do my research *is* sterile. I like to think of this as my…welcomin' center. It's calmin', bein' surrounded by mother nature, don't ya think?" The two men snapped their heads over to look at Abin. "Hello, gentlemen." Continuing toward the men, he put on latex exam gloves, and when he reached the osprey enclosure, he bent down and picked up a five-gallon pail that sat on the floor. He reached in with one hand. "Can I help y'all?"

"Yes," Little Boy said. "We're looking for Doctor Moses? Doctor Abin Moses?"

Abin pulled a fish out of the pail and tossed it over the glass. "Yer lookin' at 'im."

Fat Man looked at Little Boy with a look of elation,

and then back at Abin. "That's great! If you would come with us, Doctor, the director would like a—"

Abin, looking through the glass pane, cut off the heavy-set man. "Take a gander at that. Marvelous, ain't it?" Inside the enclosure, the osprey hopped down to the moss-covered dirt and stood above the fish, its head flinching as it admired its meal. It pecked at the fish a few times before jamming one of its talons in the fish's underside. It dragged the talon in a straight line, tearing open the fish's belly with an awful ripping sound as its guts spilled out around it. The bird squawked and then feasted on the fish innards.

Abin continued to watch the bird through the glass, almost as if the two men weren't there. "She's a fishin' bird." He set the bucket down beside him. "Normally, they wanna get their prey on their own."

The two men had disgusted looks on their faces as the osprey reveled in the viscera. Little Boy tried to speak again. "That's very interesting, Doctor, but—"

"This one is different, though. Had 'er since she was a baby. She's used to bein' fed by me. Enjoys it, actually."

Fat Man put his hand on Abin's shoulder. "Enough about the bird, Doctor Moses. The director needs to speak with you immediately."

"May I ask what for?" Abin asked, his voice now flat as he continued to stare into the glass. He knew why they were there—he wanted to hear them *say* it.

"I'm afraid I don't have the authority to say anything, Doctor. I just need you to come with us."

Abin broke his gaze from the glass and turned his head toward the men. "Sure. Why don't y'all come to the lab… the main part of the lab, so I can get ready."

Little Boy stepped forward. "I don't think that's really necessary. It's only a few floors up."

"I don't wanna go up in there smellin' like fish guts. I don't think the director would be very keen on that. Do y'all?"

The men looked at each other, and Fat Man spoke up. "He's got a point."

Little Boy rolled his eyes. "Fine. But let's make it quick. We don't want to keep him waiting."

Abin saluted the men and turned to lead the way to the main lab.

A few moments later, the three men arrived at the last door. Abin patted his pants pockets, then the pockets on his lab coat. "Darn it," he said, irritated. "I think I left my ID badge in there. One of y'all wanna do the honors?" He held out his hand, presenting the sensor to unlock the door.

Little Boy once again pulled the badge from his belt and swiped it in front of the door sensor. "Allow me."

"Thank ya," Abin said, smiling as he pushed open the lab door.

Abin led the men to the back of the room. Little Boy elbowed his partner and gestured over to a large glass tank in the corner. The tank contained water, with baby alligators floating on the surface. Both men approached the tank.

"Keep away from the gators, please," Abin said as he washed his hands in a sink at the end of the room.

Fat Man held his hands up defensively. "We're not touching them."

Abin left the water running as he slyly peered over his shoulder to check if the men were watching him. He saw they weren't and opened a waist-level drawer just below the sink. Inside sat a 12-inch-long metal case. Frosty air escaped the case as he cautiously opened it to reveal six vials containing a green liquid. He counted the vials to make sure they were all accounted for, then shut the lid. Taking the case from the drawer, he set it on top of the table, next to the sink.

Abin felt the men approaching him from behind. "We don't have all day," Little Boy said.

Abin exhaled deeply and wrapped his hand around a scalpel inside the drawer.

Little Boy reached for Abin's shoulder. "Hey."

Abin spun around, bringing the scalpel across Little Boy's throat, opening it up as red mist sprayed all over Abin's face. The man brought his hands up and grasped the slice in his neck and then collapsed to the floor.

Fat Man shouted, "What the fuck?!" as he pulled his suit jacket aside and reached for his handgun. Before he could pull it out, Abin spun the scalpel around in his hand and stabbed him in the eyeball. He twisted the small blade in the man's eye, then pulled it back out. Fat Man screamed and covered his eye with one hand and fell to his knees. Abin turned back around to the tabletop and grabbed the metal case.

"Sector B-12…Officer down."

Abin looked back to see Fat Man speaking into his radio. "The suspect is Doc—"

Stomping over to the downed man, Abin kicked the radio out of his hand. He then used the bottom of his foot to push the man down onto his back. Abin set the metal case down on the floor beside him and kneeled over the man. Fat Man stared at Abin's face with his remaining eye. Abin stared back for a moment, breathing heavily. Raising the scalpel high in the air, a friendly smile came over his face, and he then brought the scalpel down into Fat Man's other eye. He kept stabbing until the man stopped moving and his face was an unrecognizable, bloody mess.

Abin stood up and walked back over to the sink at the back of the room. The sound of metal clanging reverberated throughout the room as he dropped the blood-soaked scalpel into the sink. He turned on the water and ran his hands underneath, letting the blood flow down the drain.

Behind him, he could hear a tinny voice through the radio. "Sector B-12. What's going on? Do you need help? Sector B-12?"

Suddenly, a red light in the ceiling's corner began blinking as the building's alarm started blaring. Abin took off his glasses and set them on the table. Cupping his hands under the faucet, he filled them with water, then splashed his face, rinsing the blood off before drying it with a paper towel. He took off his lab coat and let it fall to the floor, then picked up his glasses and put them back on his face.

Returning to Little Boy, he rolled him over and took his handgun from its holster and tucked it into his back waistband. Next, he took the man's ID badge and stuffed it into his pants pocket. Grabbing the collar of the man's suit jacket, he rubbed the material between his forefinger and thumb. He removed the suit jacket and put it on himself.

Passing by Fat Man, Abin bent down and picked up the metal case containing the vials. He walked over to the large tank that held the baby alligators and looked down at them. "I'm sorry, my children. I wish I could take ya with me. I didn't expect this to happen. Yer brothers an' sisters will know the sacrifice all y'all made here." He wiped a tear from his eye and exited the lab.

All the lights in Abin's atrium were shut off, except for the blinking red alarm bulbs, creating an eerie setting. Stopping halfway through the atrium, he placed a hand on the glass osprey enclosure and apologized to the bird before continuing to the exit toward the main building.

He kept his head down as he entered the primary facility and watched closely as crowds of government employees and contractors lined up to prove identification and get searched by the armed guards. Tucking the metal case into the inside pocket of the suit jacket, he walked toward the main exit, making his way through the crowd.

At the exit, he found a long single-file line with a pair of guards waiting at the door, double-checking identification before anyone left the building. Abin begrudgingly got in the line. His stomach twisted in knots as he frantically looked around the building for another way out. He'd not only worked at this site for years, but had also been a part of these security checks plenty of times. He knew there was only one way out, but his rising anxiety made him check anyway. If he didn't get out of there before someone found the bodies of those guards, no one was getting out, whether or not they passed the security check. The line moved forward as he eyed an emergency exit door. The thought of making a break for the emergency door crossed his mind, but reality quickly overrode it. He would run for the door, drawing attention to himself. The guards would yell at him to stop; he would ignore them, and they would fill him with bullets before he reached the exit.

I'm okay, he thought. *I got the guard's badge an' coat.*

The line continued to move forward until Abin was near the door, flanked by two armed guards. "Identification," one guard said.

Abin kept his head down and reached into his pants pocket and fished around. "'Round here somewhere," he said. He pulled the stolen ID badge out and held it out to the guard. He crept his other hand under his jacket, behind his back, and put his fingertips on the grip of the handgun. He began to sweat as the guard held a device in front of the badge to scan it. After a moment, the device blinked green.

"Shouldn't you be part of the sweep?" the guard asked.

Abin wrapped his hand around the gun. "I—"

"Oh, never mind," interrupted the guard as he looked down at the device's screen. "Says here your shift ended forty-five minutes ago. Have a good night, Officer."

Abin released his grip on the handgun, put the ID badge back into his pocket, and nodded at the guard as he exited through the door.

Approaching his car in the parking lot, Abin took the metal case out of the inside pocket of the jacket, then removed the jacket, and dropped it on the ground. He opened the metal case and ran his fingers over the vials containing the green liquid. "Don't worry. We'll find a new home soon." Closing the lid of the case, he got into his car. The engine started, and he drove off, leaving the black site in a trail of dust.

PART ONE: NO KIN

Chapter One

GREG BOYES LEANED ON THE RESTROOM SINK AS HIS disappointed reflection stared back at him from the mirror. *Come on. You got this. You didn't do anything wrong… You have nothing to worry about.* His eyes moved down from his reflection to the Flint Police Department badge on his chest. He covered it with one hand as his eyes moved back up. *You could just tell the truth and save yourself the guilt.* Removing his hand from the badge, he ran it over his buzz-cut. *The truth,* he thought as his memory took him back to that night two weeks ago.

Wipers danced over the windshield, knocking snowflakes off the unmarked patrol car as Greg and his partner, Jake Coleman, sat inside. Greg glanced over at Jake, who was gazing out of the driver's window, examining a normal-looking two-story home. "Are you sure this is something we should take on?" Greg asked. "It doesn't even look like anyone is home."

Jake turned to Greg. "There are people inside. Trust me. We're waiting for a specific car to show up. Quit being a pussy."

Greg sipped his coffee. "I'm not being a pussy. Usually, drug stakeouts aren't the job of beat cops, is all. I'm wondering why *we're* here, just the two of us, with no detectives…no backup."

Greg could tell from his sigh that Jake was losing his patience with him. "You want to get back to detective, right? This is how we do it. Prove to them what kind of officers we are."

"Man, *you're* the reason I'm in a uniform right now. If you hadn't—"

"Hey! Shut the fuck up." Jake turned back to the driver's window. "We said we would never bring that up."

"Yeah, yeah," Greg said. "It's the truth, though."

Jake sounded excited. "There he is, Boyes. In that red Caddy."

Greg leaned forward to look past Jake, out of the driver's window, and saw a dark red Cadillac pull in front of the house. The headlights died out as the engine shut off. A bald man exited the driver's seat, looking around the immediate area. Jake slouched down in his seat and tugged on Greg's coat. "Get down!" Greg slouched down in his seat as well.

After a moment, Jake peeked his head up to look out of the bottom of the window. "Alright, we're clear," he said. Both he and Greg sat back up in their seats as the bald man opened the car's back door and pulled out a satchel. He slung the bag over his shoulder and headed for the two-story house.

"We'll wait for him to get inside and then we'll make our move," Jake said.

"Don't you think we should call for backup?"

"It doesn't matter how many times you ask me, Boyes. We're not calling for backup. You want your shield back, or what? *This* is the way we do it."

Greg looked around coyly. "Yeah. I do want it back. Let's get these fuckers!"

"That's what I'm talking about!" Jake said as he opened the driver's door and got out of the patrol car. Greg pulled his handgun and ejected the magazine to check his ammunition. He slapped the magazine back into the gun and exited the car as well.

Greg joined Jake on the driver's side of the car, and they faced the two-story house. "Alright. It should be a pretty straightforward bust," Jake said. "That guy that just walked in? He's the buyer. That was a big ol' bag of cash he slung over his shoulder. If my informant was right, there should be enough cocaine, molly, and fentanyl laid out on the table when we get in there that they'll give us our shields back *and* suck our dicks."

Greg smiled as he pulled back the slide of his gun, chambering a round. "I think I'll skip the blowjob. The shield is enough."

"Suit yourself. More for me. Let's go." Jake crossed the street toward the house, and Greg followed closely behind.

They arrived at the front door and stood on either side of it with their guns drawn. Greg eyed Jake as he nodded his head, counted to three, then kicked the door open at the handle.

The door swung open, and the two officers quickly entered the house, aiming their weapons around the room. Jake yelled, "Police! Hands where I can see them!"

A group of men stood around a rectangle table filled with bags of drugs, as well as money and guns. The bald man jumped back in surprise. He snatched up his shoulder bag and ran for the staircase leading upstairs. Greg pointed toward the bald man and yelled, "Shit!"

Jake turned toward the bald man as he disappeared up the stairs. He pointed at the men surrounding the table of contraband, with their hands up. "Boyes, handle these guys!" He then sprinted up the stairs after the bald man.

Greg put his attention back on the men and aimed his weapon at them. "Alright. Everyone put your hands behind your head. Lace your fingers." One after the other, the men put their hands together and put them behind their heads. "Good," Greg continued. "Now get down on the ground, face down." The men followed Greg's orders. He approached the table. *Holy shit,* he thought as he admired the illegal substances. *Jake wasn't lying. They'll suck our dicks for this.*

Looking toward the stairs, he shouted, "Jake! Everything alright up there?" He turned to the men on the ground, then back at the stairs. "Jake!"

He pressed the button on the side of his shoulder radio and tilted his head toward it. "Dispatch, this is car 21-7. We need immediate backup at 17324 Roy Street. We have six suspects under arrest in need of evac. Bring a wagon."

The dispatcher's voice crackled through the radio. "Copy that, 21-7. Backup is on the way."

Greg grabbed a handful of zip ties from a pouch on his belt. "Okay, everyone. Move your hands down, behind your backs, and put your wrists together. Slowly." Following instructions, the men moved their hands behind their backs, and Greg secured their wrists with zip ties, one by one.

Greg approached the stairs and tried to look up, but the top of the stairs ended at a wall and turned off to the right. He began ascending the steps cautiously. He thought about shouting for his partner again, but didn't want to give himself up in case things with the bald man had taken a turn for the worse.

Arriving at the top of the stairs, Greg peered around the corner. The hallway contained two doors. One door was open at the end of the hallway. Inside, clear as day, was a toilet. The door on the right was also open. Greg couldn't see inside, but he heard voices. He moved to the side of the doorway to listen in.

One voice got loud. It was definitely his partner's. "I came all the way out here in the middle of the night, risking my ass for *this*?!"

"I'm sorry, man! One of my runners must have skimmed a little off the top," said the other voice. Greg figured it was the bald man.

Staying low, Greg peered around the corner to see the bald man sitting on a couch behind a coffee table filled with cash wrapped in bands. Jake stood on the opposite side of the table, holding the man's shoulder bag in one hand and his gun in the other. Jake tipped the bag upside down and shook it. "A little?! Where's the rest of it? Don't bullshit me!"

The bald man trembled in fear, sweat dripping down his brow. "I-I'll talk to my guys. I'll find the rest of it. I-I swear!"

"This isn't the first time this has happened," Jake said as he tossed the bag at the bald man's feet. He raised his gun, aiming it at the man's head. "But it will be the last."

The bald man sat up straight on the couch and leaned forward. "No! Listen, I—"

Bang!

The bald man's head snapped back as blood painted the cream-colored wall behind him. His body slumped sideways on the couch, and Greg jumped up.

Jake turned to see his partner standing in the doorway. "Greg!" Jake had a feigned look of shock on his face. "You got here just in time! He went for my gun!"

Greg stood silent, trying to comprehend what he had just seen.

Jake started toward Greg, and Greg took a step back. "You saw it, right? He looked like a madman!"

Greg continued to stare at his partner in disbelief. "I... I..."

A voice rang out from downstairs. "Police! Everyone stay where you are!" There were a few moments of silence before the voice spoke up again. "Officer Boyes? Officer Coleman?"

Jake and Greg stared at each other, the tension thick in the air. Greg's fingers tightened around the grip of his handgun.

"Greg..." Jake said in a calm, collected voice.

Greg turned his head toward the door and yelled, "We're upstairs. All clear."

Jake nodded as to say thank you, and Greg turned out of the doorway and headed for the stairs.

Greg descended into the living room, where the drug dealers were being led out of the front door. An officer stood in the middle of the room, writing in a small notepad. Jake wasn't very far behind.

"Good bust, gentlemen. Five guys and a whole lot of drugs," said the officer.

"Six," Greg said, flatly.

"Six?"

"There's one more upstairs. Call the coroner."

"Shit. What happened?"

Jake interjected before Greg could say anything else. "Guy tried running off with the money from the deal. I gave chase, and when I confronted him, he lunged for my service weapon. Officer Boyes arrived just as the man came at me, and...I did what I had to. Right, Officer Boyes?"

Greg continued to look at the officer, avoiding eye contact with Jake.

Jake continued, "Right, Officer Boyes? Greg… Greg…"

———

"Greg?" A female voice from the other side of the bathroom door brought Greg back to the present. He glanced down at his badge's reflection in the mirror. *The truth*, he thought.

He turned and shouted toward the door, "Yeah?"

"The captain is ready for you now," said the female voice. He recognized the voice—it was Sandy, the captain's assistant.

"I'll be right out." Greg turned on the sink and splashed cold water on his face. He gave himself one more look in the mirror and took a deep breath.

When he exited the bathroom, Greg passed by Sandy's desk. Wearing a big smile, her eyes followed him. Greg mustered up a smirk and nodded at her. *Sandy's not avoiding eye contact like she usually does when someone is about to enter a shit storm. It can't be that bad.* He arrived at the end of the hall and entered the captain's office.

Captain Stewart sat behind his large oak desk, flipping through a case file; the light on the ceiling shone off of the captain's bald head. Greg considered making a joke about being blinded by the light, but luckily had second thoughts. "You wanted to see me, sir," he said.

Captain Stewart moved his eyes over the rim of his glasses. "Sit."

Greg sat down in the chair in front of the desk, and the captain closed the manila folder in front of him, giving Greg his full attention.

"So," said Captain Stewart. "The drug bust on Roy… tell me what happened. From the beginning."

Greg filled Captain Stewart in on what happened until he ascended the stairs. "So, I went up the stairs with my service weapon drawn. When I got to the top, I heard two men shouting, but I couldn't make out exactly what they were saying. One voice was clearly Officer Coleman's. I…" Greg paused for a bit too long.

"You what?" Captain Stewart asked, lowering his brow.

"I heard a gunshot, so I breached the room with my firearm. I saw Officer Coleman standing over a man… Guy was shot in the head. He said the man attacked him, went for his weapon, and he had no choice. Upon inspection of the scene, it appeared that Officer Coleman's story checked out."

"That's interesting," Captain Stewart said as he stood up from his chair.

"Well, I can't be certain it happened that way, but looking at the evidence—"

"Not that, Boyes. What I find interesting is Coleman's side of the story." Captain Stewart leaned forward on his desk with his fists. "According to him, *you* did the shooting."

Greg sat with his mouth agape, unsure if he had just heard his captain correctly. "He…he said what?"

Captain Stewart stared into Greg's eyes, his jaw clenched. Greg could tell he was trying to stay calm, but wasn't doing a good job. "You and Officer Coleman are both suspended indefinitely pending investigation."

"What?! I didn't shoot anyone!" Greg yelled as he stood up from the chair and also leaned forward on the captain's desk as his body tensed up.

"I don't give a flying fuck if you did or didn't!" Captain Stewart shouted back. "But you two *fuckwads* couldn't be bothered to at least get the same story together, so now the shooting has to be investigated."

"This is bullshit! You want to know the truth?!"

Captain Stewart's eyes opened wide.

For a single moment, Greg considered telling the captain what he *had actually* seen.

His body loosened as he stood up from leaning on the desk. "I told you the truth. I heard shouting and a gunshot, and the man was dead when I entered the room. I didn't fire my weapon even once. Any investigation will prove that." He realized that snitching would only make things worse. He could feel the tears forming in his eyes, not from sadness, but from anger—betrayal.

Greg took his gun out of his holster and slammed it on the captain's desk while looking him in the eyes. Then he grabbed the badge on his uniform shirt and ripped it off, tearing the fabric, and slammed it down next to the gun.

"Internal affairs will be in touch," Captain Stewart said.

Greg turned and headed for the door.

"And if you think you're *ever* getting your detective shield back, think again!" Captain Stewart shouted as Greg exited the room. "It's not gonna happen! Not while I'm in this seat!"

Greg slammed the door closed behind him.

Chapter Two

SNOW CRUNCHED UNDER THE TIRES OF GREG'S FORD pickup as he pulled into the parking lot of The Nightstick —an old cop hangout for as long as anyone could remember. When Greg and Jake first graduated from the academy, they'd gotten so drunk there, they almost got banned for life during their first visit. There used to be a machine that measured the strength of your punch. Jake took one drunken swing at it, missed, and slipped, falling into the machine and slicing his forearm open. They got rid of the machine the next day, and Jake still has the gnarly scar fifteen years later. Meanwhile, Greg stumbled around offering fifty dollars to anyone who would let him shoot a shot glass off their head. Greg's offense was less bloody, but only because nobody was stupid or drunk enough to take him up on his offer.

I should've known, he thought to himself as he parked next to Jake's Chevy. He reached into his glove compartment and pulled out an eight-inch metal rod. He exited his truck and slid the rod up his jacket sleeve as he headed for the front door of the bar.

Once inside, Greg looked around the bar as his eyes adjusted. The contrast between the snow and the dingy haunt was jarring, to say the least. In the corner, leaning against the jukebox, he saw Jake flipping through the song selections. As Greg approached him, Jake turned around and recoiled, almost spilling the beer in his hand.

"Hey, Boyes! What are you doing here?" Jake asked, slurring his words. The alcohol on his breath stank so badly, Greg thought it could blow up the entire block if someone were to light a match.

"We need to talk," Greg said.

Jake slapped Greg on the shoulder as he dismissively walked by him, toward the bar. "Come. Have a seat in my office."

Jake bellied up to the bar, almost tipping over as he sat on a stool. He held up two fingers to the bartender, and in return, she poured two shots of tequila and placed them in front of him. He turned to look at Greg, who was still standing by the jukebox. "Well?"

Greg let the metal rod slide out of his jacket sleeve and into his hand.

Jake's eyes moved down to the rod. "What the hell, man? Is this a joke?"

Greg snapped his arm down, causing the rest of the baton to extend out of the metal rod.

Jake's chuckling softened, then left as his smile dissipated. "Seriously. What the hell?"

Greg stood silently, shaking with anger. All he could hear was Captain Stewart's voice. *According to him, you did the shooting.* He squeezed the baton, his knuckles turning white.

Jake nodded and threw a tequila shot into his mouth before letting out an "Ahhhh!" He threw back the other shot and slammed the glass down on the bar and stood up from the stool, wobbling as he did so. He slowly made his way over to Greg, rolling up his shirt sleeves. "We got a fucking problem, Boyes?"

He picked up his pace as he approached Greg and swung at him. Greg easily moved out of the way of the drunk man's fist, causing the man to stumble past him. Greg swung the baton at the back of Jake's knees, taking him to the ground. Greg grabbed the baton with both hands and stood behind Jake. He moved the baton over Jake's head and down to his neck, then pulled it back against his windpipe. Jake grasped at the baton, trying to slip his fingers underneath it. "Why…don't you…fight…like…a man?" he asked, struggling to breathe.

Greg moved the baton away from Jake's throat and put his knee into his back, pushing him forward. Jake scrambled to his feet and turned to face him. Greg tossed the baton to the side, took his jacket off, and raised his fists.

"There. A fair fight," said Jake, rubbing his throat and panting.

The two men walked toward each other. Jake barely had time to raise his hands before Greg's fist rammed into his nose, staggering him. Jake grabbed an empty shot glass from the bar top and threw it at Greg before charging him and tackling him to the ground. He straddled Greg and punched him a few times. Greg rolled him over and returned the blows.

The bartender shouted from behind the bar, "Hey! You two, take it outside!"

The men ignored her as they kept exchanging punches, when finally—*bang*—both men abruptly stopped fighting and turned to the bartender, who was aiming a revolver at the ceiling with smoke billowing from the barrel. "I said *outside*."

Greg and Jake separated and got to their feet. The bartender put the gun back behind the bar and moved a stack of napkins in front of her. "I know you're both cops, and you're always welcome here," she said. "But not tonight. Whatever shit you've got going on needs to be handled elsewhere. You can come back when you know how to behave."

Jake slapped a fifty-dollar bill on the bar top and then left through the front door.

Greg put his jacket back on and grabbed a napkin from the bar. He ripped a piece off of one and shoved it up his nostril. He started to walk away when the bartender cleared her throat. Greg turned to face her. She moved her eyes to the floor and said, "Your baton."

"Right," Greg said, picking his baton up and collapsing it back into a small, eight-inch rod. He grabbed a few more napkins and left the bar.

Outside, Greg saw Jake sitting on the curb in front of the bar, groaning with his head in his hands. Greg shut the door loudly behind him, making Jake jump before he quickly leaned to the side and vomited into the street. Greg sat down on the other side of him, opposite the vomit, and held out the stack of napkins. Jake sneered at him and took the napkins. He winced as he dabbed the cut above his left eyebrow.

"What's your fucking problem?" Jake asked.

"My problem?! My problem is you're a fucking asshole!" Greg shouted. "How the fuck could you tell the captain that I shot that drug dealer?! And what the fuck *was* that, anyway?!"

Jake looked down at his feet. "I already told you. I was working undercover, but I was doing it rogue, so I couldn't tell anyone. I was just trying to get our shields back."

"That doesn't explain why you blew his brains out all over the goddamned wall!"

"He was a nobody…a small fish. I was making an

example out of him to show the higher-ups I meant business."

Greg looked down at his feet. He knew everything coming from his partner's mouth was bullshit. He wasn't sure what to be the most mad at him about—being a dirty cop, pinning a cold-blooded murder on him, or that he thought Greg was so stupid that he'd fall for his horseshit story. "Cut the shit, Jake. You know I don't believe you for a second." Greg turned to face him. "Why pin it on me? You already told the officers on scene that the guy jumped for your gun. Why tell the captain that I shot him?"

Jake, keeping his head down, moved his eyes over toward Greg. "If I had another shooting on my record, they'd put me on a desk…probably for the rest of my career."

"And you thought getting me suspended and trying to blemish *my* record would be better?! You're unbelievable!" Greg stood up from the curb and started toward his truck. After a few feet, he turned back around and pointed at Jake. "You know, when they finish their investigation, they're going to know it was you, right? And when they find out, I won't be there to have your back this time."

Jake finally looked up from the street and up at Greg. "I'm sorry."

Greg spat in his direction. "Fucking dirty cop." He turned and walked away.

Greg got in his truck and slammed the driver's door behind him, then punched the steering wheel as he yelled, "Motherfucker!"

He started his truck, peeled out of the bar's parking lot, and sped down the street, leaving Jake sitting on the curb.

Chapter Three

GREG SHIFTED HIS TRUCK INTO PARK IN FRONT OF HIS house. All the lights were off inside. *They must be asleep.* He peered down at the truck's clock to see it read 10:29 p.m. He exited the truck and walked to the front door, then entered.

Inside, Greg's home was quiet. It was apparent his wife, Lisa, and his seven-year-old daughter, Sage, had long abandoned the main level of the home and retreated to bed. He made his way to the kitchen, where he saw a piece of paper on the counter. It was a note from Lisa that read:

Kyle Didn't make it in tonight. He's hoping for tomorrow. Dinner is in the microwave.
Love, Lisa

Greg's son, Kyle, was supposed to come home from New York University for winter break. He wanted to take the bus for some reason—something about getting the full experience of a road trip. Greg figured the snow must have slowed down his ride.

He threw Lisa's note in the trash bin and opened the microwave to see a plate of lasagna. He closed the door and set the timer. While his food was heating, he grabbed a bottle of beer from the refrigerator and put it over one of his eyes, where Jake had done the most damage. After a few minutes, the microwave dinged. He took the lasagna out, sat at the kitchen table, and ate while he drank his beer in silence.

The next morning, Greg woke up on his living room couch, covered in a thin blanket. He sat up and stretched when he heard a voice coming from behind him. "Hey, honey. You got home late last night. I didn't even hear you come in." Greg turned to see his wife, dressed in a robe with her hair in a messy bun. She stood in the kitchen, making a pot of coffee. "What are you doing down here?"

"I didn't want to wake you." He yawned as he got up from the couch and met Lisa in the kitchen.

She switched on the coffeemaker and spun around to face Greg. "Oh, my God!" she said. "What happened to your face?!" She moved her hand up to his swollen eye and barely touched it, causing him to wince.

"Ow!" he said. "There was a drug bust last night. Some asshole got the jump on me. Sucker punched me."

"Let me get some ice," Lisa said, opening the freezer door.

"I'll be fine."

Lisa threw some ice cubes in a sandwich bag and held it out to Greg. "At least to get the swelling down." She leaned in closer, examining the puffy skin. "Oh, yeah. That's going to be black and blue."

Greg grabbed the bag of ice from her and held it to his face, then exhaled as he took a seat at the kitchen table.

"So," he said, trying to switch the subject from his eye. "I saw Kyle didn't show up yesterday."

Lisa poured coffee into a mug and set it down in front of Greg. "I guess he got pounded with snow and the bus had to stop for the night."

Greg sipped his coffee. "I figured as much."

"They were talking about even moving the football game down here to play in our stadium." Lisa filled her own mug and sat down at the table across from her husband. "Anyway, he was just outside of Cleveland when I talked to him a few hours ago, so he should be showing up any time."

"That's great."

"Yeah," Lisa said, looking down at her coffee. "Can I ask you to go a little easy on him?"

Greg looked at her, confused. "What do you mean by that?"

"You know how you're always picking on him."

"I'm just joking. He knows that."

"Well, he doesn't take it as jokes and he's been having a hard time being almost ten hours away from home for the first time, so just lighten up, okay? For me."

Greg chuckled as he sipped his coffee again. "Alright, alright. I'll take it easy on the jokes." He stood up and grabbed his mug from the table and pointed at Lisa's. "Refill?"

She smiled. "Sure. Thanks."

He picked up her mug and walked over to the coffeemaker and refilled them. "I took some time off."

"What?"

"From work. I used a few weeks of vacation that I had banked." Greg immediately felt guilty for not telling Lisa about his suspension. She had told him to request a different partner when he first lost his detective shield, and he had made a big deal about how Jake had made a mistake and was a good man. Selfishly, he needed to get away for a while, and telling her now would only start a fight. He would tell her eventually, but he had to find the right time.

"Wow!" Lisa said, impressed.

"What? I never use vacation!" Greg said defensively.

Lisa giggled. "No, I know! Hence the 'wow.' I'm shocked!"

Greg set Lisa's mug back in front of her. "How would you feel about getting out of here? Out of the snow?"

"You're serious?"

"Yeah. I was thinking we could go down to Florida or something," he said, smiling.

"I don't know."

"Come on! You're off from teaching for winter break, Sage is out of school, the boy is coming home; it's perfect timing."

Greg's daughter, Sage, ran around the corner and jumped up on his lap to give him a hug. "Dad!"

"Speak of the devil!" Greg said, wrapping his arms around Sage. He weaved his head back and forth, trying to keep her pigtails out of his face. "What do you say, kid? Want to go someplace warm and get away from all this snow?"

Sage pumped her fist in excitement. "Yeah!"

"See? Sage thinks it's a good idea."

Lisa playfully rolled her eyes. "She agrees with everything you say."

Sage jumped off Greg's lap and ran to the chair Lisa was sitting in. "No, I don't. Just most things. Mom, can you make me eggs?"

"Sure, sweetie," Lisa replied. "You want some eggs, Greg?"

Greg stood up from the table. "No, thanks. I'm going to take a shower."

"You sure? Eggs would go well with your *ice*," she said, glaring at the abandoned bag of ice on the tabletop.

Greg quickly grabbed the small bag and put it back on his swollen eye, and the two of them laughed.

Chapter Four

"HOW MANY DO YOU WANT?" LISA ASKED SAGE AS SHE pulled a carton of eggs from the refrigerator.

"Umm…seven!" she exclaimed excitedly.

"Seven? I don't know if your belly can fit seven. How about we start with two?"

Sage grinned from ear-to-ear. "Sounds good!"

As Lisa cooked eggs on the stovetop, the back door cracked open.

Greg and Lisa's son, Kyle, poked his head in the doorway. With his mop of hair hanging halfway over his eyes, he wore a big smile. Sage looked over, her eyes lighting up when she saw him.

"Kyle!" Sage shrieked as she leapt from her chair and rushed toward the door.

Kyle walked all the way into the house and set his duffle bag on the floor before kneeling down to catch his sister. Sage flew into his arms.

Lisa put two scrambled eggs on a plate and set the plate on the table, where Sage was sitting. Then she walked over to Kyle, holding her arms out. "My baby," she said.

Kyle stood up and hugged Lisa. "Hi, Mom."

Lisa gave him a kiss on the cheek. "My goodness! I can almost wrap my arms around you twice! Sit, I'll make you some eggs! You're skin and bones!"

Kyle patted his above average-sized belly and winked. "Oh, it's still there. I just learned to hide it better."

"Skin and bones?" Greg's voice appeared from behind Lisa. "You looking in a funhouse mirror?"

Kyle's smile vanished, and he pulled out a chair at the table and sat down across from his sister.

"Well, well, well. You showed up." Greg stood in the hallway leading to the kitchen, putting his arms through the sleeves of his green long-sleeved henley shirt.

"Hey, Dad," Kyle said, moving his gaze down to the table.

Greg approached him and ruffled his long hair. "Why the long face? Aren't you happy to be home?"

"Yeah," Kyle said as he stood up from the table. "I think I'm going to take a nap. I couldn't sleep at all on the bus."

"Go for it," Lisa said. "You had a long trip. Your room is just how you left it."

Kyle moved around Greg and headed for the hallway. "Thanks, Mom."

"Oh, Kyle!" Lisa said, and Kyle turned around. Lisa continued, smiling, "Watch your language."

Kyle smirked and then left the room.

Greg looked at Lisa, concerned. "What's his problem?"

Metal clanged as Sage threw her fork down on her plate. "All done! I'm going to go play." She jumped down from the table and ran to the living room.

Lisa placed her hands on her hips. "Greg. Come on."

"What?"

"You weren't exactly easy on him, you know, going to

film school. You weren't very subtle in telling him you wanted him to go to the police academy. Now you're picking on his weight as soon as you see him. I don't get you."

"All I was saying is that I could have had a job for him, and it was a gigantic risk going into filmmaking. And I told you, I'm just *joking* with him! He gets it!"

"You made it sound like you didn't believe in him."

"Well, it's a hard business to get into."

"Sure looked like he was in on your 'joke,' too." Lisa rolled her eyes and left through the hallway, and Greg followed her.

"Okay, that came out wrong," he said. "He could have had a guaranteed paycheck six months out of high school and worked on the movie stuff on the side is all I meant." He grabbed Lisa's arm as she was walking away. "Will you listen to me?"

Lisa snapped around. "Will you listen to yourself? Did it ever cross your mind that Kyle didn't want to be a police officer at all?"

Greg let go of Lisa's arm, and his face dropped. "Well, I...I guess it didn't."

"Sometimes you have to think of how you're saying things before you say them, Greg."

"I'm sorry."

"Don't be sorry," Lisa said. "Just *think*, that's all." She got up on her tiptoes and gave Greg a kiss on the cheek. "Now. How about we watch a movie? Forget this ever happened? Then you can work on a fresh start with Kyle when he wakes up from his nap."

"Yeah, okay."

Lisa smiled. "We can't have all this tension when we're a thousand miles away."

"Is that a yes to Florida?!" Greg asked, excited, his eyes widening.

"Yes."

"Great! I'll throw a movie on and we can plan," Greg said as he started toward the living room.

Chapter Five

THE LIVING ROOM WAS DARKENED, ILLUMINATED ONLY BY the TV mounted on the wall. Lisa lay on the couch with Sage lying on top of her, both of them sound asleep. Greg sat back in a recliner, his eyes fluttering as he fought to stay awake. His bag of ice—now a bag of water—sat, dripping, next to a beer bottle on a side table, butted up against the chair.

The arm of the couch creaked, causing Greg to break out of his half-asleep state. He looked over to see Kyle sitting on the couch's arm.

"Hey, boy," Greg said, clearing his throat.

"Why don't you go to bed?" Kyle asked.

"What? I'm in the middle of a movie."

Kyle laughed. "I saw you on the struggle bus. You were almost out!"

Greg readjusted himself in the chair, trying to hide his smile. "Was not!"

Greg reached over to the side table next to him and grabbed his beer bottle. He took a swig and made a sour face. "Blegh! Piss warm," he said. "So…how's school?"

Kyle stood up from the couch arm. "You don't have to do this."

"Do what?"

"Pretend like you give a shit."

"Hey!"

"Sorry…pretend like you care."

"I'm not your mother; I don't care about you swearing. What do you mean, 'pretending like I give a shit?'"

"Because you never…never mind," Kyle said, trailing off.

Greg sat up straight in his chair, looking irritated. "No. Say it."

Kyle began to walk toward to hallway to leave the room.

"Don't walk away from me," Greg said as his voice got louder, causing Sage to stir.

Her tiny voice sounded like the squeak of a mouse as it entered Greg's ear. "Dad, you're too loud."

Greg turned toward Sage, whose eyes were still closed. "Sorry, honey." He looked back to see that Kyle had made his way out of the room. Greg shook his head and sighed and stood up out of the chair. He approached Sage and brushed her hair with his hand. "Why don't we go to bed, Sage?"

"I don't wanna get up."

"You'll be more comfortable in your bed," he said, smiling. "Come on." He picked her up off his wife and held her in his arms. He whispered, "Lisa…Lisa."

Lisa fidgeted a bit before her eyes fluttered open.

Greg continued, whispering, "I'm putting Sage to bed. Meet you in the room?"

Lisa sleepily nodded her head, and her eyes drifted back closed.

Greg carried Sage to her bedroom and lightly laid her

down on her bed and covered her with a blanket. "Good night," he whispered, then exited her room.

Greg approached Kyle's closed bedroom door. He knocked hesitantly and waited for a response, but there wasn't one. He knew Kyle couldn't have been sleeping again already, as he'd just woken up from a long nap. He knocked again, and again, nothing. Turning the handle, he crept the door open anyway. "Boy?"

Greg entered the room to see Kyle, lying in his bed. He faced the ceiling with his eyes closed, wearing headphones as he tapped his foot to the beat of whatever he was listening to. Metal music, Greg figured. He couldn't stand it. The heavy guitar riffs, double bass drums beating like a barrage of thunderclaps, the screaming vocals—it all sounded like just noise to Greg, but Kyle loved it.

Greg approached him, hoping he would sense his presence, but he must have been too absorbed in his tunes. He reached down and shook Kyle's shoulder. Kyle looked over and recoiled, swatting his headphones off of his head.

"Jesus! You scared the shit out of me!" Kyle put his fingers up to his neck, checking his pulse. "You ever knock?"

"I knocked."

Kyle sat up on the edge of his bed. "Do you need something?"

"I wanted to talk about a while ago. If you thought I was being sarcastic when I asked about school, I wasn't."

"I…I guess I overreacted. I just don't want to play the game where you pretend to be interested in what I have going on just to make Mom happy."

Greg sat down next to Kyle on the bed. "I wasn't pretending. You want me to be honest? Fine. I wasn't happy with your choice to go to film school. Not because I don't believe in you. It's just a hard industry to get into and succeed, and I'm a realist. I thought it would have been smarter to have joined the academy and to have a steady government job almost right out of school. It doesn't mean I'm any less interested in what you have going on or that I'm not proud of you."

"Thanks for being straight with me," Kyle said, looking down at the floor.

Greg stood up from the bed. "Now…why don't you pack a bag?"

Kyle looked up at his dad. "For what?"

"Your mother and I decided we're going to take a family trip!"

"What?"

"Yeah! We thought it would be nice to get out of the cold and snow and head down to Florida for a couple of weeks."

"Florida? Couple of weeks?" Kyle said, standing up. "But I only have a couple of weeks before I go back to New York. What about seeing my friends?"

"You'll have a few days to do that when we get back. Just think, after this year, you're going to be doing internships, and after school, you'll be moving to Los Angeles, and some Hollywood big shot isn't going to want to take any trips with his family. Look at it as one last hoorah."

Kyle smiled, although he tried to contain it. Greg knew that pumping him up about his potential filmmaking career would do the trick. He felt a little bad about manipulating his son, but it was far from the worst thing he'd done.

"I guess I don't really have a choice, now do I?" Kyle asked.

Greg slapped Kyle on the back. "Nope!" He left the

room, then peeked back through the door and looked down at his wristwatch. "And it's past midnight, so you only have a few hours to pack. We're leaving tomorrow." Greg winked and bounced back out of the doorway.

Chapter Six

THE NEXT DAY, JUST AS THE SUN WAS RISING, THE BOYES family walked out of the passenger bridge of their airplane and entered their terminal at Miami International Airport. Still wearing winter clothing, they stuck out like a sore thumb compared to the rest of the airport, where almost everyone around was wearing dresses or shorts and tank tops. Lisa led the way, with Kyle following behind her, typing on his cell phone, and Greg picking up the rear, carrying Sage while she slept.

"Kyle, can you take your sister for a minute?" Greg asked.

Kyle continued to type on his phone in silence.

"Kyle!" Greg repeated.

Kyle looked up. "Huh?"

"Can you take your sister for a minute? You weren't texting your friends for two-and-a-half hours. I think they can wait a little longer."

"You're the one who made me come on this trip. I could have been hanging out with them," Kyle said in a snotty tone as he stuffed his phone into his pocket.

"Cry me a river, you're in Miami," Greg said, handing Sage over to Kyle.

Lisa stopped and turned to face the men. "Can you guys just…behave? At least until we get out of the airport?"

Greg and Kyle both lowered their heads in embarrassment and, in unison, said, "Yes."

"Our hotel is near the beach, not too far from the airport. We could probably walk there if we wanted to since we didn't travel too heavily. We could take in the warm weather after being in below freezing temperatures," Lisa said.

"Um, actually," Greg said. "I made other plans."

Lisa furrowed her brow. "What do you mean?"

Greg moved to the front of the group, wearing a big smile. "It's a surprise! I reserved us a car at the rental place downstairs."

They entered the car rental agency directly next to the airport. Greg pointed at the back wall. "Reception is right over there."

Lisa looked at Kyle. "Why don't you take your sister over there and sit down while we take care of the car, sweetie?" She pointed toward the cluster of chairs at the back of the room.

Kyle took his sister over to the waiting area and sat her in her own chair, shaking her gently to wake her up. "Sage. Wake up. My arms are killing me."

Greg and Lisa continued toward the reception area, where an older woman stood behind a desk. Greg waved as he approached the woman. "Hi! I reserved an SUV under the name Boyes. B-O-Y-E-S."

The receptionist typed on the computer in front of her. "Just give me one second, sir…aaand, found it! I'll be back with your keys." The receptionist walked through the swinging door behind the desk.

"Greg," Lisa said. "What's going on?"

Greg turned to face her. "What do you mean?"

"We spent hours yesterday planning this trip and booking a great hotel on the beach, and now you went behind my back and just…changed the plans? For a surprise?"

"Well, I—"

"Here you go, sir," the receptionist said, popping back out of the door. "It's the blue one right near the door."

"Thank you very much."

"Would you be interested in getting insurance for the vehicle?"

"Not today, thanks." Greg grabbed the keys from the receptionist.

"I hope you and your family have a great stay in Miami, sir."

"Thanks!"

Greg could feel Lisa's eyes practically burning a hole in him. "Greg," she said sternly.

Greg grabbed her arm and took her to the side of the reception desk. He knew he had to think up a lie, and fast. There was no way he could tell her about his suspension right now without ruining the entire trip. "Okay, listen. I really wanted to take a rustic vacation. To get a good sense of the wilderness; to become more in tune with the earth." He couldn't even believe his own bullshit, but it was the best he could come up with out of thin air.

Lisa crossed her arms over her chest. "So you *lied?*"

Greg grabbed her shoulders. "I knew you would never go for it, so yeah, I told a tiny white lie. I just wanted a nice, peaceful last vacation with my family."

"And we *will* have one," Lisa said. "But what does that have to do with switching our plans?"

"After I got sucker punched at that bust, I needed some time away from *people*. I didn't think Miami would be the best place to unwind." He could see the tension in her shoulders loosen. *I knew sympathy would work.*

"Okay," Lisa breathed. She uncrossed her arms and put Greg's hands in hers.

Greg smiled softly. "Thank you for understanding. I'm sorry I didn't tell you the truth."

"Next time, just tell me." Lisa kissed him on the cheek and snatched the rental SUV keys out of his hand. "I'm driving!" She spun around to Kyle and Sage, sitting in the waiting area, and held the keys up, jingling them. "Ready, kids?"

Kyle looked up from his phone and dramatically said, "Thank God!" as he stood up and Sage jumped down from her chair. Lisa, Kyle, and Sage headed for the door as Greg chased after them, yelling, "Wait for me!"

Chapter Seven

GREG WATCHED THE SAW GRASS PRAIRIES PASS BY FROM THE
passenger window of the rental SUV. The combination of
the vehicle's speed and the natural breeze made the stalks
blend in an almost hypnotizing way. His eyes moved down
to the side mirror, where his reflection stared back at him,
his newly formed black eye ever present. The contusion
made his heart hurt as he thought about Jake Coleman—
the man he trusted with his life every day—and how that
man had possibly ruined both of their careers. It wasn't the
first time either.

When they were detectives, Greg and Jake were casing
an abandoned factory where a drug meetup was supposed
to take place. A big-time meetup where there were
supposed to be a lot of drugs and a lot of guns.

Jake sat in the driver's seat of the unmarked Crown
Victoria, while Greg sat in the passenger seat. They'd been
sitting for what seemed like hours, and Jake was getting
antsy. He had a hard-on about making the biggest arrests
and wasn't a proponent of observing until they got enough
evidence to make a bust. It would later be obvious to Greg

that Jake was dirty, which explained his eagerness. Jake would try to convince Greg that they should go in, guns blazing, but Greg would never go for it. At the first sight of someone leaving the factory, Jake jumped at the opportunity to take someone down. Greg tried to stop him, but Jake was out of the car and giving chase before he could even get a word out. Greg fumbled his way out of the unmarked car and followed Jake and the suspect down an alley. Greg had just turned the corner when he heard the shots. He arrived to see Jake standing over a body with a worried look splattered on his face. "Greg," he said.

Greg approached the body. "Did you see a gu—" He stopped when he saw the young teenager, lying dead; his shirt soaked in blood and a bullet hole in his cheek. "He's just a kid…" Greg looked up at Jake.

His partner's eyes were full of worry. "I-I *fucked* up." Something shook his voice. "I'll be right back."

Jake ran back down the alleyway toward the car, and Greg had a moment where he wondered if Jake was going to ditch him with this kid's body, but quickly wiped it from his mind. *He wouldn't,* he thought. He looked back down at the kid and stared at the blood that poured from the entrance wound in his cheek as it pooled around his head. *Tell me he had a reason to shoot this kid.*

Moments later, Jake's footsteps came thundering back through the alley as he ran up to Greg, out of breath. "I… I need you to stick with me on this."

"What are you talking about?" Greg asked.

Jake reached into his jacket and pulled out something wrapped in a white handkerchief. He held it out and unwrapped it, and it was a pistol.

Greg stared at the pistol. "What's that?"

"This kid fired at me…remember? Luckily, he missed."

"I don't—"

Jake knelt next to the body, avoiding the pooling blood. "Yeah, yeah, you remember." He carefully used the handkerchief to place the pistol in the cadaver's hand. He then reached back in his jacket and pulled out a pair of latex exam gloves, putting them on his hands. Wrapping his hands around the kid's hands, he pulled the trigger on the pistol, firing the weapon three times. He stood back up, removing the gloves. "Had to get the gunpowder on his hands." Looking up toward Greg, he said, "You're with me on this, right?"

Greg felt a fire in the pit of his stomach, but what choice did he have? "Yeah… I'm with you. You're my partner."

After the investigation revealed security footage from a nearby business, authorities caught and suspended Greg and Jake. The department allowed them to keep their jobs and placed them on administrative duty, but Jake ultimately caused Greg to lose his detective shield.

That's why Greg is so mad at him. That's why he's afraid to tell Lisa the *real* reason they went on vacation.

Kyle's voice sounded from the back seat, interrupting Greg's moment of reflection. "I can't believe we traded the beach for *this*." Greg spun around in his seat to face his son. Kyle was already looking down at his cell phone. "Great. No service." He sighed, frustrated, and put the phone face down on the seat next to him. He looked over at Sage, who was looking out her own window and humming to herself. "Wouldn't you rather be at the beach, Sage?" She ignored her brother and kept humming. Kyle put his face in his hands. "This is already lame."

Dramatic much? Greg thought as he faced forward again. "Come on, man. We're not even at our motel yet. Look up there ahead of us."

Kyle scooted up to the edge of his seat and leaned

between his mom and dad, looking out of the front wind-shield. "Whoa," he said as his gaze fixed upon the lush green of the horizon. The trees looked like they went on for an eternity.

"Beautiful, isn't it?" Greg asked in a satisfied tone. "Just give it a chance. We'll be surrounded by nature instead of a bunch of strangers. It's not like we can't come back to the beach; we'll just have to take a drive to get to it."

Kyle sat back hard, slamming against the back of his seat, and crossed his arms as he looked back out of his own window. "I guess."

Greg shook his head and scoffed. "That's the spirit."

Lisa looked up in the rearview mirror. "Don't worry, honey. It'll be fun!"

"Whatever," Kyle said.

"We're here!" Greg said, his voice full of enthusiasm.

The SUV slowed down as they approached a big wooden sign hanging between two posts. The sign read

WELCOME TO SNAKE BIGHT, FLORIDA

POPULATION: 32

The pavement turned to dirt as they passed between two massive trees whose branches reached out and meshed together, forming an archway over the road.

"Thirty-two people?" Kyle asked from the back seat. "Where the hell did you bring us?"

"Language!" Lisa snapped.

On the other side of the trees, the SUV pulled into a clearing containing a quaint little town that sat just off the swampland water. Greg admired their surroundings, his face practically glued to the passenger window. "It's like Mayberry!" he said excitedly as the SUV passed by the

Snake Bight General Store on their right and the doctor's office on their left.

Lisa looked around in amazement. "Wow, Greg. It's great!" She craned her neck to the back seat. "Kyle? Isn't it—"

Greg shouted, "Lisa!"

Lisa spun her head back and slammed on the brakes, and the tires came to a screeching halt. A little girl stood in front of the vehicle. She looked through the windshield at Greg and Lisa, expressionless.

"Holy shit," Greg said, trying to stay calm.

Kyle popped up between his parents. "Jesus, you almost hit that little girl!"

The little girl disappeared as she bent down in front of the SUV.

Kyle leaned forward, even further in between his parents. "Where'd she go?"

The little girl popped back up into view, holding a kickball in her hands. She continued to stare into the vehicle, unblinking, showing no emotion. Something seemed off about her, almost as if there was nothing behind her eyes.

"What's she doing?" Lisa asked.

Kyle sounded intrigued. Greg could hear the smile in his voice. "Whoa. She's creepy!"

Sage piped up from her seat. "Maybe she wants to play with me!"

"I'm not sure what to do here," Lisa said.

Kyle shouted, "Go around her!"

Greg and Lisa turned their heads to the back seat, and both said, "Be quiet!"

"Her eyes are funny!" Sage giggled from the back seat.

Greg and Lisa faced back forward. The little girl's face turned into a gleeful smile, and she waved at the Boyes family and ran away.

Greg gave a tiny wave back and watched her disappear into the town.

"That was weird," Lisa said.

Greg pointed ahead to a one-story building with an awning that covered the seven doors lining its face. "It looks like that's our motel." He felt relieved.

"Thank God," Kyle said. "After the flight and this drive, my legs are killing me."

The SUV pulled into a parking spot in front of the nondescript building, and Greg opened his passenger door. "You guys hang tight while I go inside and make sure we're in the right place."

Kyle rolled his eyes. "There's only like four buildings in the whole place… I think you nailed it."

Greg got out of the SUV and headed to the front door of the building. "Smart ass." He entered the front door to find a room containing a reception desk and a few waiting chairs scattered about. Behind the desk was an open doorway. He approached the desk and smacked a bell that bore instructions to ring for service. The ding of the bell dissipated as Greg looked around the room, hoping for someone to appear. He leaned on the desk and rang the bell once more. "Hello?"

A voice rang out from the doorway behind the desk. "Coming!" A few moments later, a pale, bald man with wide eyes popped out of the opening, wiping down the front of his white dress shirt. "My apologies, sir. I was just having a quick bite. I hope you weren't waiting too long."

"Don't worry about it," Greg said. "I really just walked in."

The pale man smiled. "Name's Saul. Welcome to the Snake Bight Inn. How can I help you today?"

"Hi, Saul. I had a reservation for two rooms. It should be under Boyes. Greg Boyes."

Saul swung open the cover of the large ledger in front of him and ran an index finger over the page, looking through names.

There are seven rooms. There can't be that many names, thought Greg.

"Boyes…Boyes… There you are," said Saul. He turned to face the corkboard hanging on the wall behind him that held the room keys.

Greg noticed that the keys for rooms one through four weren't hanging from their hooks. "Pretty busy, eh?"

Saul looked over his shoulder as he grabbed the keys off the hooks labeled six and seven. "Pardon?"

Greg pointed at the corkboard. "I see a few rooms are booked."

"Rooms one through four are, let's say, being remodeled. A couple is in room five, but they're older, so you shouldn't have to worry about noise or anything. The husband just retired, so they're celebrating on vacation." Saul handed the room keys over to Greg. "You'll be in six and seven. I'll just need your deposit for the rooms. So, what brings you to our little town?"

Greg pulled his wallet out of his back pocket, pulled out a credit card, and handed it to Saul. "My son is home from college on winter break, so we're taking a family trip. We're from Michigan, so we needed someplace warm."

Saul smiled. "Well, you've come to the right place for warmth." He ran Greg's credit card and handed it back to him. "I hope you and your family enjoy your stay. If you need anything, I'll be right here, so don't hesitate to ask."

"Thank you very much," Greg said, and he turned and exited the inn.

Outside, Greg approached his family, standing at the SUV. "We're all set," he said. "We have six and seven; the rooms are at the end over there."

He grabbed hold of his suitcase handle and then let go. He patted the front and back pockets of his pants. "Shit."

"What's wrong?" Lisa asked.

"I think I left my wallet in the front office. I'll be right back."

Greg ran back up to the office door.

"Hey, Saul," he said as he hastily entered the office.

Saul was standing in the same spot behind the desk. "Mr. Boyes, can I help you?"

Greg approached the desk and grabbed his wallet off the counter. "Forgot my wa—"

The sound of Lisa shrieking cut Greg off. He turned his head toward the door, and Lisa screamed again.

Greg shouted, "Lisa!" and ran back out the front door.

Chapter Eight

GREG BURST THROUGH THE DOOR, EMERGING FROM THE front office. He snapped his head over to see his family huddled outside one of their rooms with the door open, their luggage still surrounding them. Greg ran over and hugged Lisa as she put her face into his chest. "Lisa, are you okay? What's wrong?"

Kyle pointed at the open door. "Dad! There's a freakin' crocodile in there!"

Greg looked over at Kyle, his eyes almost bursting out of their sockets. "What?!"

"Yeah, check it out!"

"Mr. Boyes!" Saul shouted as he ran out of the office door and toward the family. "Is everything alright?!"

Greg let go of Lisa and turned to Saul. "My son said there's a crocodile in one of our rooms!"

The corners of Saul's mouth slowly turned up, and then he let out a deep belly laugh.

Greg's eyebrows lowered. "What's so funny?!"

Holding his stomach, Saul tried to suppress his laughter. "I'm sorry, sir." He wiped a tear from his eye. "There are no crocodiles here."

Greg looked at him, confused.

"Here. Come with me." Saul put his hand on Greg's shoulder and led him toward the open door. Greg reluctantly walked with him, stopping in front of the doorway, and Saul continued into the room.

Saul's voice carried out of the open door. "How did you get in here?"

Greg slowly leaned forward, peeking into the room. He jumped back when he saw the black scales adorned with white stripes, the rows of sharp teeth, and the black vertical slits in the middle of glassy green eyeballs.

Saul shouted out of the doorway, "It's okay! Come on in!"

Again, Greg peeked through the open door, this time more calm. Saul was standing between two twin beds, holding a two-foot-long alligator in his arms.

"What the hell?" Greg asked. "I thought you said there were no crocodiles here?"

Saul smiled and looked down at the alligator lovingly. "This isn't a crocodile; it's an alligator. A baby too."

"Same difference! Why the hell is it in our room?"

"I'm truly sorry, sir. You see, the path just to the right of the inn leads to an opening in the swamp. This little guy must have made his way into town." He looked up at Greg and chuckled. "I guess he was trying to get a free room."

Greg was looking back at him, straight-faced.

"Right. I'll get him out of here and back into the swamp." Saul carried the alligator past Greg and to the door. "Again, I'm so sorry for the disturbance. This is extremely rare, but every time it has happened, it's only been a baby. Everything will be okay. I promise."

"It's fine," Greg said.

Once Saul and the alligator were out of the room, Greg shouted toward the door, "It's okay, guys. You can come in now."

Kyle entered the room and threw his luggage on one bed before he lay down. Lisa followed shortly after with Sage connected to her hip, still looking frightened.

"It's okay, Sage," Greg said. "The alligator is gone. It's safe."

Lisa sat Sage up on the other bed. "That was terrifying. I wonder how that thing got in here."

Greg opened the mini-fridge in the corner, checked the inside, then shut the door. "The office guy said it made its way up from the swamp."

"How close is the swamp?"

"He said the path right next to us leads down there, but he didn't say how far it was."

"Do you think it will happen again? It's making me feel a little uneasy about this place."

Greg approached Lisa and grabbed her by the shoulders and kissed her on the cheek. "We don't have anything to worry about."

"How do you know that?" Kyle asked.

Greg snapped his head over and gave Kyle a look to shut up. "I just do." Greg moved back to the door. "I'll go to the general store and see if they have something to scare them away. Just in case. The guy said it probably got curious because it's a baby, and the full-grown alligators would never come up here."

Whatever helps calm their nerves, he thought.

Lisa smiled a little, giving Greg a small sense of relief. "Okay. Yeah, that sounds like a good idea."

"Does anyone want anything else while I'm there?" Greg asked.

Sage's eyes lit up. "Candy!"

"Do you want to come with me?"

Sage fell back on the bed, slamming her head on the mattress. "No, I'm tired."

"Okay," Greg said, chuckling. "What kind of candy do you want?"

"Sour Patch Kids!"

"Sour Patch Kids, it is."

Chapter Nine

GREG CLOSED THE DOOR OF THE ROOM BEHIND HIM. HE shut his eyes and took a deep breath through his nose. *You can't beat that fresh air.* Upon opening his eyes again, he saw the little girl from before standing in front of him, holding her kickball. She wore the same emotionless look as she had earlier.

"Hi," Greg said, smiling. He put his hands on his knees and bent forward, getting down to her level. "I'm Greg. What's your name?"

The little girl continued to stare at him blankly, not blinking.

Greg stood back upright. "Okay..." He moved to walk around her, and she quickly turned and ran away, back toward the town. *What a weird little girl.*

Over his shoulder, Greg heard a low, guttural growl, like the sound of a garbage disposal. He slowly turned to look back. It was coming from the path off the right-hand side of the inn—the path to the swamp. He glanced around to see if anyone else was nearby, but no luck. *Maybe*

I imagined it. Creeping over to the edge of the inn, he peered around the corner. Knee-high swamp grass lined the path until it disappeared where the surrounding trees and weeds grew thicker. The growl reappeared again. It sounded as if it were coming from the patch of swamp grass closest to him.

He'd spotted a thin tree branch on the ground and picked it up. Slowly approaching the grass and wiping the sweat from his brow, he carefully split the grass using the branch and jumped back and shouted when he saw a dark figure move. "Shit!"

He wielded the branch like a sword, ready to attack. He felt like an idiot, but had no other choice.

The swamp grass shook as if something was readying to come out.

"Come on, you fucker," he mumbled.

As the grass began to part, Greg held the branch high in the air, and then—a duck waddled out, followed by four ducklings. The ducks quacked as they passed by. He lowered the branch, deflated, and began to chuckle. *A duck,* he thought, smiling, as he threw the thin branch into the long grass and headed back toward town.

As Greg approached the general store, a man leaning against the building smiled at him. "Hello, stranger," he said. "Nice vehicle you've got there." The man wore dirty jeans and a flannel shirt with the sleeves rolled up to his elbows, along with a vertical scar over one eye, from his eyebrow down to his cheek.

Greg raised an eyebrow. "What's that?"

The man pushed himself off the building and extended his hand out. "Sorry. Name's Brent. I saw you and your family pull in earlier. That SUV you rolled up in is pretty slick."

"Oh, thanks," Greg said as he put his hand out and shook with Brent. "It's a rental."

The little girl from earlier ran up to Brent and held her hand out to him.

"Candy *after* dinner," Brent said, looking down at the little girl. He moved his gaze back up to Greg. "I believe you've already met my daughter, Ashley. "

Greg smiled at the little girl. "Yeah, we ran into each other earlier."

"You sure did. You almost ran her over," Brent said.

Greg stared at him, unsure of what to say. His abdomen tightened with nerves.

Brent stared back at Greg straight-faced, and after a few moments, broke into laughter. "I'm just messing with you." He smacked Greg on his back as his laughter calmed down. "You should've seen your face!"

Greg relaxed and let out a nervous chuckle of his own.

Brent ruffled the hair on the top of his daughter's head. "*Someone* needs to remember to look both ways before they cross the street." He then nudged her away with the palm of his hand. "Why don't you go play?"

Ashley looked at Greg, staring into his eyes for a moment before skipping off.

"Cute kid," Greg said. "I saw her just outside, at the inn, too."

Brent looked at Greg as if he had a square head. "What do you mean?"

"Just now. Before I came over here. She was hanging out outside the inn. She moves quickly."

"Nah, she's been with me all day."

From the look on his face, it seemed to Greg that Brent had been offended. Greg knew he'd seen her, though. *Whatever. Not worth arguing over.* "My mistake," Greg said. "Long day of travel, you know."

Brent's expression changed in an instant, turning to a smile. "No worries! I totally get it! So, what brings you to Snake Bight… I'm sorry, I didn't catch your name. My mouth gets running and I forget to stop it."

"It's Greg. Greg Boyes. My family and I are taking a small vacation."

"Ah. Well, you picked a great place! The weather is perfect this time of year."

"So I've heard. We're thinking about driving to Miami tomorrow to hit the beach."

"Oh, I see. You're one of *those*," Brent sounded disappointed.

"One of what?"

"You came to our little town so you could stay for cheap, but spend all your time in fancy-pants Miami with all the other tourists."

"No, no. It's not that!" Greg insisted. "I wanted to stay in the Everglades. They're beautiful. It's just that my family will kill me if we don't go to the beach at least once while we're here."

Brent's eyes narrowed in disbelief. "Yeah…okay."

Greg looked around uncomfortably. "I was actually going to ask the store clerk if there were any nature tours or something available while I was inside."

Why the fuck am I explaining myself to this guy?

"Speaking of," Greg said as he put his hand on the door to the general store. "I have to get running. My family is waiting for me back at the inn."

Brent held up his hands and stepped aside, giving Greg more space. "Don't let me keep you. The last thing you want is an upset family on vacation."

Greg opened the door. "Thanks. It was nice meeting you, Brent."

Brent nodded, and Greg entered the building.

Passive aggressive much? Greg thought as he picked up a small basket from a stock next to the checkout counter. He tilted his head back to look up at the aisle signage and rubbed his chin. "Hm. I guess sandwiches would be good for the beach."

As Greg walked through the grocery aisles of the general store, gathering sandwich ingredients, he was pleasantly surprised to see the townspeople of Snake Bight greet him as they passed. He couldn't help but feel something strange eating at the back of his brain like a parasite, though. The people were...*odd*. They all had the same enormous smiles and wide eyes as Saul, the innkeeper. It reminded him of *The Stepford Wives*.

He stopped at the refrigerated section to have a look at the pre-packaged lunch meats. He opened the refrigerator door and bent down to grab a package of ham. "You don't want any of *that*," said a female voice from over his shoulder. He turned around to see an elderly woman standing nearby, holding a handbasket of her own, smiling at him. She nodded to her right and said, "If you go just around the corner there, there's an actual deli counter. Just passed the soda display. Fewer of those preservatives."

Greg smiled back at her uneasily. "Well, uh, thanks for the tip." He couldn't get used to the looks on these people's faces. He thought they appeared *stretched* out; their smiles forced upon them, like they were in pain.

"No problem!" The woman placed a hand on her chest. "I'm Murial, the town nurse."

Greg shut the refrigerator door and waved his hand. "Nice to meet you, Murial. Don't take offense, but I hope I won't have to see you too much while I'm here."

The woman laughed and said, "Let's hope!"

"Although if I find anymore alligators rummaging

around my room, I might see you sooner rather than later."

Murial smiled. "Oh, they're harmless…mostly."

"I should get going," chuckled Greg. "I have a hungry family waiting for me."

"Please, please. Don't let me keep you! It was nice meeting you!"

After he'd made his trip to the deli counter, Greg arrived at the checkout and placed his basket full of freshly sliced meats and cheeses on the countertop. The cashier behind the counter had his back to him. "Everyone here is so nice," Greg said. "I'm not used to that."

The cashier turned around, and it was Brent's smiling face. "You won't find a friendlier group of people on the planet."

Greg shook his head in disbelief. "Brent?!"

"Oh, don't be so surprised."

Greg thumbed toward the door. "I…I just saw you outside."

Brent began grabbing the grocery items from Greg's basket. "I was on break."

Oh, god. How is he going to make me feel bad now?

Brent began scanning and bagging Greg's items. "You said earlier you were going to ask about tours around the Everglades? Boy, do I have the *perfect* activity for you and your family. I'm sure Saul told you about the swamp just off the inn; he tells everyone, after all. Anyway, there's a boat tour that runs through the whole swamp once a week. It's really cool. The host shows you the most beautiful views of the swamp that nobody else gets to see." Greg opened his mouth to speak, but Brent continued before he could. "I know what you're thinking. 'A swamp? Beautiful?' But you have to see it for yourself to believe it. Plus, you get the entire history of Snake

Bight, and the host is an expert. He founded the damn place."

Greg handed his credit card over to Brent. "Interesting. I'll have to run it by the family."

"Usually you would have missed it since it ran a few days ago, but an older couple staying in town really wanted to go, so they're running an extra special tour. It's tomorrow, though, so you'd probably have to put off the beach a day." Brent handed the card back to Greg.

"Right. Like I said, I'll ask the family." Greg grabbed his bags and started toward the door. "Oh! Do you have Sour Patch Kids?"

"Sure do," Brent said as he turned to face the wall behind him. He turned back with a bag of the sour candy. "Here you go."

"Thanks. I promised my daughter. How much?"

Brent smiled. "It's on the house."

Greg returned the smile. "Hey, thank you!"

"No problem. Remember to ask your family about the swamp tour. I *promise* you won't want to miss it."

Greg pushed open the door to the outside. "Will do."

"If you decide to go, just talk to Saul. He'll call and set it up for you," Brent shouted, leaning over the counter as Greg exited the general store. "Make sure you tell your son about the alligators! The swamp is *full* of them!"

Greg stuck his head back in the door. "Oh! That reminds me! Do you sell anything that would ward off the alligators?"

Brent appeared confused. "What do you mean?"

"Well, we had a baby alligator make its way into our room, and it scared my family pretty good. I wasn't sure if you had some sort of pepper spray or—"

Brent's enormous smile vanished, and his face turned grim. "I'm going to pretend you didn't even ask such a question. The alligators in this town are just as much a part of the population as the people."

"I-I'm sorry. I didn't mean to offend—"

"Don't worry about it. Consider yourself lucky you didn't say that to the *wrong* person."

Too embarrassed to speak, Greg hung his head and left through the door.

Chapter Ten

GREG ARRIVED BACK AT THE ROOM, WHERE LISA, KYLE, and Sage were sitting on one of the twin beds, playing go fish. "Hey, you guys found something to do!"

"My phone is useless, and there's no TV. It's brutal," Kyle said. "Mom, do you have any sevens?"

Lisa smirked. "Go fish."

"Go fish! Go fish!" Sage teased.

Kyle grabbed a pillow from behind his back and lightly smacked it across his little sister's face, causing her to fall back, laughing. Kyle then grabbed a card off the top of the deck. "This is so boring!"

"You're just mad because you're losing," Lisa said, prodding him.

"It's good to have some quality family time." Greg set the grocery bags down on the dresser and looked over at Sage, who was staring at him with big puppy-dog eyes. "Don't worry," he said, reaching into one bag. "I didn't forget." He pulled the Sour Patch Kids from the bag and tossed them onto the bed. Excited, Sage crawled over to the bag and tore it open, and began munching on the sour candies. "Take it easy! You'll get a tummy ache!"

Greg looked down at his feet and saw Kyle and Sage's empty bags strewn about the floor. "So, I guess the kids called this room already," he said, chuckling.

Lisa pushed herself off the bed. "I didn't stand a chance. They were like rabid animals as soon as you left the room. Clothes were flying everywhere!" She leaned over to peer into the grocery bags. "What did you get?"

"Just some stuff for sandwiches for now," Greg said.

"Ah, good beach food."

"That's what I was thinking." Greg then looked up at Lisa. "Although…"

"I don't like when you get that look."

"What look?"

Lisa smiled. "*That* look. Out with it."

"I was talking to the cashier at the general store, and he mentioned some kind of swamp tour. I guess it's a big deal for the town."

Lisa crossed her arms disapprovingly. "A swamp tour?"

"I was wary at first too, but he told me you get to see the most beautiful parts of the Everglades that you won't see anywhere else. I thought it sounded kind of interesting."

"Yeah, I suppose it *could* be interesting. Maybe we'll check it out one day."

Greg turned his head up and looked at the ceiling, avoiding eye contact with his wife. "We'd have to go tomorrow."

Kyle jumped up from the bed. "Tomorrow?! We're supposed to go to the beach tomorrow!"

"I know, I know. But we're here all week. The ocean isn't going anywhere." Greg hunched over and stomped toward the bed, holding his hands up with his fingers curled like claws. "The man said the swamp is full of *alligators*." Kyle stared at him with a blank face, unimpressed. Greg, keeping the same ridiculous pose, spun to face Sage. "What about you, little girl? Do you want to see a bunch of big, scary alligators?"

Sage pulled the blanket up to her chin, and Greg let out a roar. He then leapt onto the bed and began tickling her. Laughing hysterically, Sage finally spat, "Okay, okay! I want to see the alligators!"

Greg rolled over onto his side, looking at Lisa lovingly. "What do you say, honey?"

Lisa rolled her eyes, trying to hide a smile. "I guess the beach can wait an extra day."

Greg and Sage both shouted, "Yay!"

"Great…" Kyle muttered.

Greg got up and grabbed his and Lisa's bags from the floor. "It's getting late. You guys can stay up for a bit, but not too much longer. We should try to get an early start." He focused on Sage, who was still going to town on her Sour Patch Kids. "And you, little lady. Save some of that candy for tomorrow."

Sage looked up at him with a red-tinted, toothy grin.

"Here, baby. I'll keep those safe," Lisa said as she grabbed the candy bag from the bed.

"Good night, kids. Remember, not too late," Greg said as he and Lisa left the room.

Outside, Greg closed the door to the kids' room. "Wow," he said. "That was far less resistance than I thought it would be."

Lisa inserted a key into the lock of the next room. "I think everyone is just happy to be out of the cold."

"Look at that. It's Saul," Greg whispered. "What's he doing?"

A few doors down, Saul was exiting one of the

supposed closed rooms, struggling to carry more bags than he could handle. "Didn't he tell you those rooms were being remodeled?" Lisa asked.

"Yeah. He sure did." Greg moved around his wife and toward Saul. He held his hand up and shouted, "Hey, Saul!"

Saul jumped, dropping the bag that was slung over his shoulder. "Oh, jeez. You scared me!"

"You need some help?" Greg asked, walking closer.

Saul hurried to throw the bag back over his shoulder. "No, no, no. I'm okay. Thank you, sir." He began to shuffle to his office.

Greg followed him, looking at him sideways. "Brent told me about the swamp tour tomorrow. My family and I were interested in going."

"Great, great," Saul said hurriedly, with his back to Greg as he continued walking away. "Meet out here in the morning." He opened the door of his office and walked in.

Greg stopped, scratching his head. After a moment, Saul stuck his head back out of the office door, his smile big and eyes wide, as per usual. "The Hillards will join you. A lovely older couple." He then slammed the door shut.

Greg stood in the walkway, staring at the office door, when he heard the deadbolt click. He walked back to his room, where Lisa stood just outside. "He was acting strangely," Greg said. "It was like he didn't want me anywhere near those bags."

"Weird," Lisa said as she entered the room.

Greg looked back at the office for a moment before following his wife.

Chapter Eleven

Later that night, Sage twitched in her sleep as she heard twigs snapping just outside the window above her head. When the sounds didn't stop, she kicked the blanket off of her and sat up on the bed. Looking over at Kyle, she found him sound asleep in his own bed. "Kyle," she whispered. She tried again, a little louder, "Kyle!" Her brother tossed around a bit before rolling over, putting his back toward her. She slid off the side of her bed and stood beside Kyle's and put her hand on his shoulder and shook him. "Kyle, wake up."

He groaned. "Go back to sleep."

"Kyle, there's something outside." She stared at his back while he stayed silent, then shook his shoulder again.

Kyle sat up and slammed his hands on the bed in frustration. "We're surrounded by trees. It's probably an animal."

"Can you look?"

"No, go back to bed," he said as he slammed his body back down onto his mattress, rolled back over, and pulled the covers over his head.

Sage got back on her bed and stood on the mattress, reaching for the window behind the headboard. She perched on her tiptoes and barely managed to get her eyes over the sill.

The window looked over the entrance to the swamp path, about two hundred feet away. Thin trees and swamp grass mostly obscured the view, but a small portion of the path was visible. Sage's eyes darted back and forth as she scanned the woods for the source of the noise. A bat quickly flew by the window, causing Sage to duck back under the windowsill. As she slowly peered back over, she saw the little girl from earlier standing in the middle of the path, staring into the window. "Kyle," Sage said, her voice trembling. Kyle groaned, and she continued, "That little girl is out there."

The blanket over Kyle's head muffled his voice. "What little girl?"

"The one with the weird eyes…from earlier."

"What are you talking about?"

"She was in front of Dad's car."

"I know *that*. I mean the eye thing. You shouldn't make fun of people."

"But they're weird! She blinks twice, quick."

"I think you had too much candy before bed. Just lie back down."

Sage continued making eye contact with the girl. The emotionless girl blinked. A thin, almost see-through set of eyelids came down from the top of her eyeballs, followed shortly after by her normal eyelids. Sage dropped onto her bed, putting her back up against the headboard, and pulled her blanket up to her chin. "She did it again!"

Kyle's muffled voice once again came from under his blanket. "What?"

"Her eyes did the *thing* again!"

Kyle sighed and angrily threw the blanket off his head. He sat up on the edge of his bed and glared at Sage. Pushing himself off the bed, he approached the window above his sister's bed and peered out.

"Do you see her?" Sage asked.

"There's nobody there." Kyle plopped back down onto his bed, rolled onto his side, and pulled the blankets back over his body. "Go to bed, Sage."

Sage moved the blankets from her face and stood up on her bed, barely raising her eyes above the windowsill to peek out again.

There were no signs of the little girl.

Only wilderness.

Sage spun around and slid back down the headboard to her mattress. She rested her head on her pillow and covered herself.

Once again, twigs snapping sounded outside her window, and she quickly threw the blankets over her head and whimpered.

Chapter Twelve

GREG LEANED OUT OF THE BATHROOM DOOR, BRUSHING HIS teeth. He admired Lisa as she assembled sandwiches on top of a suitcase and stuffed them into little resealable bags. "Awe ooo echitted awou da shwam tou?" he asked through his toothbrush, a mouthful of foamy toothpaste dripping down onto his bare chest.

Lisa burst into laughter. "You know, I couldn't understand a word you just said." She looked up at him and began laughing even harder. "Look at you! You're making a mess!"

Greg held a finger out as if to tell her, "One second," and ducked back into the bathroom. He spat the contents of his mouth into the sink, rinsed his lips and chest, and rejoined his wife in the main room. "I said, are you excited about the swamp tour?"

Lisa put the last sandwich into a bag. "Yeah, it should be fun. It's not me you have to worry about, though."

"What? Kyle?" Greg asked.

Lisa nodded.

"He'll be fine," Greg said as he slid into a T-shirt. "He agreed to it, didn't he?"

Lisa approached Greg, putting her hand on his chest. "He did, but you know as well as I do, the complaining is coming. Just promise me you'll take it in stride."

"What do you mean?"

"Come on, Greg. We don't have to go over this *again*."

Greg pushed Lisa's hand off his chest as his face turned sour. "Say it."

Lisa stared at him with her doe-like eyes. "He knows how to push your buttons, that's all. This is most likely our last family trip, and I want us *all* to have fun."

Greg's sourpuss turned into a soft smile. "Don't worry, Lisa." He grabbed her hand and pressed it back against his chest, then his stomach, then his forehead. "See? No buttons."

Lisa chuckled. "You're an idiot."

Greg moved toward the door. "I'm going to go see if the kids are awake."

When he was halfway outside, Lisa called to him, "Greg?"

He turned his head back to look at her.

"Positive thoughts," she said.

Greg smiled and continued outside.

As Greg closed the door behind him, he heard another door close next to him. He glanced over to see Saul leaving his office. "Hey there, Saul!"

After a moment, Saul turned to face Greg with his patented grin. "Hiya, neighbor. How are you this morning?"

Man, this guy is weird, Greg thought.

Greg took a few steps toward Saul. "Good, good! I'm loving this sunshine!"

Saul took a step back, almost defensively. "Y-yeah, I bet. I heard Michigan winters can be brutal."

"Definitely—"

Saul interrupted Greg before he could finish his thought. "I have to get running. You're going on the swamp tour this morning, right?"

"I was actually going to ask you about that..."

"It's real simple. Just head down that path to the right of the inn and it will take you right to the dock."

"Okay, but—"

"Gotta go!" Saul said as he turned and hurried away.

Greg stood staring at the front of the inn office with his mouth hanging open. *Freakazoid.* He quickly shook off the weird encounter and walked next door to Kyle and Sage's room. He knocked on the door before opening it.

Sage sat on her bed, playing with the deck of playing cards. "Where's your brother?" Greg asked. Without looking up, Sage pointed to the bed next to hers, but it was devoid of any blankets. Greg shrugged his shoulders.

Sage fanned the playing cards out on her bed. "He's on the floor."

Greg walked further into the room and peeked in the small area between Kyle's bed and the wall, where he saw a pile of blankets shaped like a human. "Kyle..."

No answer.

Greg raised his voice a bit. "Kyle!"

Still nothing.

Greg nudged the pile of blankets with his foot, and the pile moved, and Kyle groaned from underneath. "Wake up, sleepyhead!"

The blankets muffled Kyle's voice. "What do you want?"

"Get up! We have to go down to the dock for the swamp tour."

"Ugh. Already?"

Greg ripped the blankets off his son. "Oh, come on. We went to bed early enough. You should be wide awake! Besides, it's not even *that* early!"

Kyle covered his eyes with his forearm. "Yeah, I *should* be wide awake! Ask Sage about that!"

Greg turned to Sage, smiling. "Sage. Why is your brother still sleeping? And why is he on the floor?"

Sage continued looking down at the cards. "I don't know."

"She doesn't know," Greg said, winking at Sage.

Kyle shot up into a seated position between the bed and the wall. "She kept me up half the night talking about spooky girls with weird eyes!"

Greg put his hand up to his mouth, covering his laugh. "You got scared by a seven-year-old's scary story?"

Sage finally looked up from the playing cards and shouted, "It wasn't a story! I saw her! Outside my window!"

Kyle held his hand out toward his sister while he looked at Greg and bulged his eyes. "See?!" He snatched the blanket from the floor near his feet and yanked it back up over his head as he lay back down.

Greg sat on the edge of Sage's bed. "You just had a bad dream, honey."

"But I didn't!" Sage shouted as she swiped the playing cards, sending them flying to the floor. "It was the girl we saw when we got here! The one in front of the car!"

"Okay, okay," Greg said, rubbing Sage's shoulder. "Maybe she was out playing and the dark was playing tricks on you, making her look scary. Now. Please pick up the cards."

Sage's head dropped, and she hopped to the floor.

"Sorry, Dad." As she bent down and began playing fifty-two pickup, she mumbled, "It wasn't a dream."

Greg stood up from the bed and walked back over to Kyle. He once again yanked the blanket off him, this time with more force. "Alright! Let's get a move on!"

Kyle groaned and sat up. "This sucks!"

Greg walked back to the door. "Be ready in ten minutes. We're not missing the tour."

Chapter Thirteen

GREG EXITED THE KIDS' ROOM. LISA WAS STANDING JUST outside the cover of the inn's awning. She was bent over, applying sunscreen to her thighs right at the bottom of her small shorts. When Greg shut the door behind him, Lisa looked up and smiled. She stood up, flicking her long brown hair back. As she moved her arms up to tie her hair back, her breasts lifted in her white tank top, her skin glistening in the Florida sun. Greg could've sworn he felt his pants getting tighter.

Lisa grabbed a pair of sunglasses that hung from her tank top neckline and put them on her face as she approached Greg, still smiling. "Why are you looking at me like that?"

Greg continued to stare at her, practically drooling. "You just look...*sexy*."

"Oh, yeah?" Lisa placed her hand on his chest and put her lips mere centimeters from his.

Her breath on his lips drove him mad. He felt as if he were going to explode.

"What are you going to do about it?" she added as her

hand drifted downward from his chest. Just as she got to his belt, the door behind Greg swung open, and Kyle and Sage exploded out of their room. Lisa quickly removed her hand from Greg's beltline. Greg gave her puppy-dog eyes, and she mouthed, "Sorry."

Greg reluctantly spun around to face his children, feigning excitement as he tried to pump the blood back to his brain. "You guys ready to go?!"

Kyle crossed his arms. "Like we have a choice."

Greg approached Kyle and put his finger in his chest. "Listen. This is our last family vacation. I don't need you to ruin it by being a little *shit*!" Lisa cleared her throat, and Greg glanced back at her. She was raising her eyebrows at him. He turned back to Kyle and removed his finger from his son's chest. "Just…be cool, man. Let's *try* to have fun, okay?"

"Yeah, okay," Kyle said. "Sorry."

Addressing the family, Greg pointed to the side of the inn and said, "Okay, Saul said we take that trail there and follow it all the way down to the dock."

Kyle and Sage started toward the trail. Kyle held his hands out to his sister and wiggled his fingers. "Maybe we'll see your friend with the weird eyes!" he said in a playfully eerie voice.

"No! Stop it!" Sage whined.

"Kyle, leave your sister alone," Lisa said as she and Greg followed the kids toward the trail. She side-eyed Greg. "See how he listened to you when you weren't being mean?"

"I wasn't being mean in the first place."

"Just keep it in mind."

Greg nodded, and they continued onto the mouth of the trail.

In the trail's wilderness, Greg noticed that Sage's pace slowed down. *Her dream must still be freaking her out.*

"Hey! Look over there!" Kyle said as he pointed through the trees beside them. "You can see the window of our room!"

Sage's steps slowed to a crawl. Greg shuffled up next to her, and she jumped when he put his hand on her back. "See, Sage? There's nobody scary out here. Only ducks and bunnies. Nothing to worry about at all."

Sage looked up at her dad, smiling widely. "Bunnies?!"

"Yeah, bunnies! Will you help me keep an eye out for them?"

"Yeah!" she said excitedly.

After fifteen minutes, an opening in the trees appeared at the end of the trail. "I see sunlight!" Greg shouted.

Kyle began to run toward the opening in front of them, with Sage following right behind him. "I thought it was never gonna end!" he said.

Greg reached his hand out. "Guys!"

Lisa placed her hand on top of Greg's, lowering it down. "Just let them go. They're having fun." Greg nodded, and they continued their normal pace, following their kids.

When they emerged out into the open, Greg was almost blinded by the sun. He turned his head and put his hand up to shield himself from the light. Lisa was looking at him, sticking her tongue out and wiggling her sunglasses with her thumb and forefinger. "What the hell was I thinking?" Greg asked rhetorically.

"You're a damned fool," Lisa teased.

Once Greg's eyes adjusted, and he looked back out into the open, his jaw dropped. "Wow…would you look at that?"

"It's beautiful," Lisa said.

Sunlight glistened off the blue river water that stretched as far back as the eye could see, lined on both sides by lush green trees with tufts of swamp grass surrounding the bottom of their trunks. Mottled ducks paddled around in the river water as Great Blue Heron flew in the sky above, swooping down every so often, attempting to scoop up fish.

Greg approached Kyle and Sage, putting his hand on Sage's shoulder. "What do you guys think?"

"It's pretty!" Sage said.

Kyle moved his hand to his brow, shielding his eyes from the sun as he looked out over the water. "Where are the alligators?"

"We have a whole boat tour," Greg said. "I'm sure we'll see plenty." Greg scanned the area, spotting the dock down by the river, where a couple sat on a nearby bench. "I'll be right back."

Greg approached the bench where the older couple sat, admiring the wildlife, just as Greg's own family had. They appeared to be in their early sixties, but both seemed physically fit for their age. The woman was short and had white hair pulled back with bobby pins. Under the man's red baseball cap with white text scrawled across it, one could see the youth still sprinkled into the back of his short haircut; although the wrinkles on his face showed Father Time hadn't *completely* forgotten about him. Greg thought the man's muscular arms looked strange juxtaposed with his belly, which was bigger, yet seemed firm. He sort of had the build of an old-time strongman—all he was missing was a black singlet and a comically large dumbbell.

"Hi, folks. Are you here for the swamp tour?" Greg asked as he extended his hand out to the man.

"What's it to ya?" the man asked, continuing to look out into the water and ignoring Greg's hand.

"Oh, Norman!" the woman said as she lightly slapped the man's knee. She then stood up from the bench and shook Greg's hand. "Yes, we're here for the tour. I'm Betty, and this is my husband, Norman."

"Nice to meet you. I'm Greg Boyes." He pointed to his family in the not-too-far-off distance. "That's my wife Lisa, and my kids, Kyle and Sage. I didn't mean to disturb you. I wanted to make sure we were in the right place."

Norman, a hulk of a man, stood up from the bench and faced Greg. "Norm Hillard. Master Sergeant, United States Air Force, retired."

Greg shook Norm's hand. "Wow. It's an honor to meet you, sir. Thank you for your service."

"Thanks are unnecessary," Norm said. "Just doing what any red-blooded American would to keep the best country in the world safe. What is it you do, son?"

Greg had to stifle his laughter, seeing that Norm and Betty wore matching cargo shorts and safari vests. "I, uh, I'm a police officer in Michigan…here on vacation."

Norm smacked Greg on the back so hard that Greg's upper body jutted forward. "A-ha! A man keeping our country safe from the inside! I love it!"

"Not as impressive as you, but I try," Greg said, still wincing from the blow. He raised his hand in the air, toward his family, and shouted: "Hey! Lisa! Bring the kids over!" Out in the distance, Lisa gathered Kyle and Sage before all three of them made their way over to the dock.

Greg stood next to his family, facing the couple. "Guys, these are the Hillards: Norm and Betty. Norm. Betty. This is my wife and kids."

"It's so nice to meet you," Lisa said. "You're going to be on the tour as well?"

"Yep," Betty said cheerily. "I don't even know how we ended up here, to be honest. Norm retired not too long ago, and we were catching up on all the traveling we'd missed over the years while he was in the service. We just happened upon this little town. We like to keep to ourselves, so it seemed like the perfect place to stay for a spell."

While Lisa and Betty exchanged pleasantries, Greg put his arm across Kyle's back and squeezed his shoulder. He held his other hand out toward Norm, as if he were presenting him to his son. "Now, this is a *real* man, Kyle."

Norm stuck his hand out to Kyle. "Norm Hillard. Master Sergeant, United States Air Force, retired."

Kyle rolled his eyes and limply saluted Norm, ignoring his extended hand.

Norm sneered and grumbled, "At ease..."

Greg moved his hand from Kyle's shoulder and smacked the back of his head. "Show some respect, Kyle!"

"It's fine," Norm said as he meandered back to the bench and sat down. "Same shit with all kids nowadays."

Greg moved to stand in front of Kyle. "What the hell is the matter with you?"

"What? I'm supposed to blow some old guy for probably killing a bunch of innocent civilians?"

"You—"

"I think I see the boat," Lisa said, interrupting Greg and sliding between him and Kyle. Her voice lowered to a whisper. "Why don't you both cool off? You're going to be stuck on a boat together for a couple of hours. I don't need to see either of you getting thrown overboard."

"I was—" Before Greg could finish his thought, Lisa

shot him a glare that looked like she was on the verge of breathing fire if he said anything else.

"Kyle, go gather your sister for the tour," Lisa said, still staring at Greg.

Kyle turned and headed toward his sister, not too far off in the grass. "Whatever."

Lisa turned to rejoin Betty, but she'd already retreated to the bench with Norm. "Great. I'm sure they *love* us."

Greg hung his head. "Sorry."

A loud horn soon broke the tension as an airboat with three rows of bench seating pulled up on the dock. Sitting on a single seat at the back of the boat, positioned right in front of the massive propeller, was a middle-aged man wearing boat shoes, white chino slacks, and a floral Tommy Bahama shirt. He stood up from the chair and approached the edge of the boat, and bowed down to greet the two families. He removed his straw fedora, revealing his grey ear-length hair. While still bent down, he raised his head to look up at his guests. He was wearing a broad, charismatic grin. "Howdy, y'all!" He stood back upright and placed his fedora back on his head, tucking his hair behind his ears. "My name is Abin Moses, and I'll be yer tour guide this mornin'."

Chapter Fourteen

"It's nice to meet you, Mr. Moses," Greg said, approaching the boat.

Abin bent down and came back up, holding a wide wooden board in his hands. "Ah-ah-ah. Abin will do. I want y'all to feel like family on this little trip." He set the board down on the edge of the boat and dock, making a small bridge between the two. When he stood back up, Abin looked sideways at Greg, pointing at his face. "Quite the shiner ya got there. Who did ya piss off?"

Greg moved his fingers up his face and suddenly remembered his black eye. "Oh, that." He chuckled. "Just a work dispute."

Abin smirked. "Well, I hope the other guy looks worse."

Kyle started toward the makeshift bridge, and Greg extended his arm in front of his chest, stopping him. "Manners, Kyle. Let the Hillards go first." Greg turned to Norm and Betty, still seated on the bench, and said, "Betty, Norm, you go on ahead."

"Oh, you're so sweet," Betty said. She gave Norm's thigh a tiny pat. "Let's go, Norm." The old man grumbled, and they both rose from the bench and approached the boat. Abin held his hand out for Betty, and she grabbed hold of it as he helped her across the bridge.

Once Betty was on the boat, Abin held his hand out for Norm, who waved him off. "I can handle myself."

Abin shouted, "Next up!"

Lisa approached the bridge, holding Sage's hand. She shuffled Sage in front of her. "You go first, sweetie."

Sage looked at the bridge uneasily. "Can you carry me?"

"We might fall in if I carry you. We don't want that!"

Greg knelt next to Sage. "It's okay. Just walk slow. Grab Mr. Abin's hand and he'll make sure you'll make it on the boat. Mom will be right behind you."

"Okay," Sage said as she stepped onto the bridge with her wobbly legs and plodded up.

Abin stretched out his hand. "Come on, little girl. I got ya." Sage grabbed hold of his hand, and he pulled her up the rest of the way.

Once Sage was on board, Lisa, Kyle, and Greg made their way onto the boat.

Abin looked at the older couple. "Betty an' Norm... I got yer names." He shifted his body to face the Boyes family. "But I didn't catch y'alls."

Greg stepped forward. "I'm Greg Boyes. This is my wife, Lisa, and my kids, Kyle and Sage."

"Ah, nice to meet y'all," Abin said. "Do me a favor, Greg?"

"What's that?"

"Could ya grab that board fer me an' bring it on the boat?"

"Sure thing." Greg bent down and brought the bridge back onboard and set it on the floor.

"Thank ya kindly." Abin moved back to the rear of the boat. "Alright, everybody. Go 'head an' grab a seat, an' we can get this thing started!"

The Hillards took the bench in the boat's front, Lisa and Sage occupied the middle, while Greg and Kyle sat in the back row.

"Everybody ready?" Abin asked.

Greg craned his neck around to look at the tour guide. "Shouldn't we have headphones? For the fan?"

Abin chuckled as he took his chair at the very back of the airboat. He put one hand on the driver's stick and the other on the control panel and turned the key. The engine kicked on, and the massive propeller behind him began whirling, barely letting out a hum. "The layman term 'fan boat' would have ya believe it's a fan, but this, my boy, is a propeller."

"I thought they were much louder," Greg said.

"Normal airboats are, but this ain't no normal airboat. I built this one myself… Put a twin-chamber stainless steel muffler on the engine to keep 'er quiet an' avoid burnout… an' the prop blades, well, I made those outta carbon fiber… Smooth enough to put ya to sleep."

From the front of the boat, Norm shouted, "Can we get a move on here?"

Abin straightened up in his chair. "Sorry 'bout that, sir! Get me talkin' 'bout my boat, an' I don't ever wanna stop!" Chuckling, he grabbed the throttle lever, pushed it forward, and the boat began to gently travel down the river.

Greg glanced over at Kyle, who was admiring the sparkling blue water as the airboat waded through it. "Pretty cool, huh?" Kyle glanced back at Greg, smirked, and nodded before turning back.

Greg shuddered at the sudden high-pitched hiss of feedback, followed by Abin's amplified voice. "I'd like to welcome y'all officially to the Snake Bight swamp tour!" Greg craned his neck to look back. Abin held a wired CB microphone up against his mouth. "Is everybody ready?!"

The passengers remained silent, except for Sage, who let out a small "Yeah!"

"Oh, *come on*! Y'all can do better than *that*!" Abin shouted into the microphone.

Most of the boat shouted a less-than-enthusiastic "Yeah!" while Norm only grumbled.

Abin continued into the microphone. "I founded Snake Bight fifteen years ago… I'm not gonna sugarcoat it for y'all… I was a pencil pusher. A forensic accountant. *Trust* me, it was as borin' as it sounds. Lookin' at numbers all day, tryin' to find fraud in multi-million-dollar companies… I wanna go to sleep just talkin' 'bout it. But turns out all that humdrum work came with some good, after all." Abin's voice lowered. "I saw the true corruption in the world…all these…*fat cats* that have our country, our *world* in the palm of their hands…they have it all, but they always need more."

Everyone on the boat slowly twisted their bodies around to look at Abin, who was now staring off into the water, speaking as if they weren't even there. "Ya try to live life how *they* want ya… Ya be a good person, pay yer taxes, work yerself to the *bone* for 'em, an' when yer on the cusp of creatin' somethin' different, somethin' *special*…they try to rip it outta yer hands."

Greg raised his hand. "Uh, Abin?"

Abin whiffled his head from side-to-side before turning back to face the boat's occupants, his smile returning. "Heh. Sorry. Got lost in the water's beauty fer a second there."

Greg glanced at Lisa and mouthed, "What the fuck?" and she shrugged her shoulders. He then looked back at Abin, who was readjusting himself in his seat.

"Anyway, where was I?" Abin asked. "Right. So, I got tired of livin' in the corporate world, an' I did somethin' 'bout it. I took all the money I had, packed up my stuff, an' came down to Florida. Not too long after, I bought a little parcel of land an' set up my little swamp tour."

"What about everyone else in the town?" Betty asked. "Did they come with you from…wherever you came from?"

"No, no," Abin replied. "Believe it or not, they were normal tourists, just like y'all. They took my tour, an' when they heard my story…my *beliefs*, they wanted to take up residency in my town. They were more'n welcome, of course."

Kyle suddenly chimed in, "Are we just going to be on this river? Like, is this the entire tour?"

Greg shot a dirty look at his son and snapped, "Kyle!"

Abin let out a small laugh. "Don't worry, Mr. Boyes, it's alright. The history of my town is a little too slow fer the newer generations with their action movies an' their… *Nintendos*." Abin pointed up ahead of the boat to a line of mangrove trees not too far off in the distance. "Look up there, son. That's where we're headed. *That's* where the tour really begins."

Greg used his hand to shield his eyes from the sun and squinted up ahead at the tree line. The tops of the mangroves were vibrant green and full of leaves. The thin trunks of the trees shot straight down into a complicated root system that fed into the water below. The roots were thick and gnarled, giving the appearance of giant monster claws dipping into the river. As the airboat approached closer to the trees, Greg noticed a pathway into the mangrove. "Are we going in *there*?" he asked.

"Yes, sir," Abin replied.

"It looks dark."

"Nah, don't worry 'bout that. It's only the branches of the mangrove trees. They're intertwinin' up top, sort of makin' a…natural canopy."

As the airboat entered the opening in the trees, Greg looked down in front of him to see Sage, shaking and leaning in close to Lisa. Lisa put her arm around Sage's shoulders and pulled her in closer. Greg leaned forward and rubbed Sage's back. "It's okay, sweetie. Like Mr. Abin said, it's just the trees making it look dark."

Once the airboat fully emerged into the mangrove forest, Greg thought the sight was actually beautiful. Although the trees that lined either side of the waterway were sinister at first glance, their lush tops formed a comforting canopy, just as Abin had suggested. Beams of sunlight broke through the leaves, creating a heavenly light coming from above and shooting down into the water.

"Why is the water green here, but not out there?" Kyle asked as he peered over the edge of the boat.

Abin's voice rang out over the small speaker. "Please don't lean over the boat, young man. I don't want ya fallin' in." Kyle sat back up straight, and Abin continued. "That's a good question, though! There's a lot more plant life here in the swamp proper. The green color is on account of the chlorophyll. Do you know what chlorophyll is, little girl?"

Sage was too busy looking up at the leaves to pay attention, so Greg tapped her shoulder. "Mr. Abin is asking you a question, Sage," he said. Sage turned around to face Abin.

"Do you know what chlorophyll is?" Abin asked again.

Sage placed her forefinger on her chin as her eyes looked up toward the sky. "Um…"

Abin smiled. "It's okay. This ain't a test. Chlorophyll is a pigment that helps plants eat the light from the sun to make 'em big an' strong!"

Lisa lightly nudged Sage with her elbow and smiled at her. "Look at that, Sage. We're *learning* something too!"

Greg heard a giddy Betty from the front of the airboat. "I think it's pretty, don't you, Norm?"

Norm, sitting with his arms crossed, mumbled, "Eh. Water's water."

Greg smiled and shook his head. *Stubborn old man,* he thought.

Abin's voice rang out over the speaker again, this time more enthusiastically. "Let me ask y'all another question… specifically the young'uns."

Speaking out of the side of his mouth, Greg sharply said, "Kyle!" and the boy snapped his attention toward the back of the boat.

"Do y'all like dinosaurs?" Abin asked. He then smacked his knee. "Heh. Who am I kiddin'? *Everyone* likes dinosaurs!" He pulled the throttle lever down, bringing the boat to a standstill in the swampy waterway before standing up from his captain's seat. "Well, today, I'm gonna be showin' y'all some *livin'* dinosaurs!" He moved from the back of the boat up to the middle, between Greg and Lisa's benches. He continued through his toothy grin. "I know what y'all are thinkin'…on account of y'all lookin' at me like someone left the porch light on, but no one's home…but it's the truth! Right through there!"

Greg followed Abin's hand as he pointed out in front of the boat where he could see the waterway ended.

"I ain't talkin' 'bout no T-Rex… Nah, that would be silly," Abin said. "I'm talkin' 'bout somethin' else. Coming in…at *eleven* feet long…one *thousand* pounds—I'm talkin' 'bout the *alligator!*" Abin held his hands up like claws as he looked down at Kyle and made a growling noise. Kyle rolled his eyes.

Greg's eyes turned down to see Sage huddled under Lisa's arm. He looked back up at Abin and cleared his throat. When Abin glanced over at him, Greg moved his eyes in Sage's direction. Abin craned his neck to see her, then looked back at Greg and winked.

"But there's nothin' to worry 'bout!" Abin continued, turning around to face the bench behind him. "These gators are my friends!"

Sage's tiny muffled voice sounded from Lisa's torso. "They sound scary."

Abin kneeled down behind Sage's bench. "Oh, I know, but they only *look* scary…as long as ya follow the rules."

Sage peeked her head up to look at Abin. "Really?"

"Yup! An' the rules are simple!" Abin stood back up. "Rule number one, I'm number one." Abin let his words hang for a moment as he quickly looked from person to person, waiting for someone to react. "Okay, that one was just a joke. It's from a movie, one of my favorites. Boy, it's a hoot an' a half!"

I hope the shitty improv doesn't cost extra, Greg thought.

Abin moved back to his driver's seat in the back of the boat. "Maybe it's funnier if ya see it yerself." He pushed the throttle lever, and the boat once again began traveling forward. "The *real* first rule is, do not, under *any* circumstances, put any body part outside the boat. Ya may see a pretty flower within arm's reach. Maybe a cute little bird is sittin' on a log an' ya want it to fly over an' land on yer finger. Nine times outta ten, that bird is actually standin' on a hungry gator. Now, I know I said the gators are my friends, an' they are…but they will not pass up a free meal."

As the boat neared the end of the archway formed by the trees above, and the sun became brighter, Greg thought to himself, *This is going to be a long trip.*

Chapter Fifteen

GREG HUNG HIS HEAD BACK IN BORED AGONY AS THE airboat finally emerged into the open swamp. *Is he ever going to stop?!*

Abin continued barking over the boat's small speaker. "An' *finally*, the last rule. Do not feed the gators. They are apex predators…at the top of the food chain. They ain't meant to be fed. They're meant to hunt."

Greg brought his head back upright. *Thank God he's do—*

The sight of the swamp interrupted his thoughts; his eyes widened at its sheer beauty. He'd imagined a humid, dark place filled with bubbling black water and rot-covered trees. What he'd seen instead was much different—better. The water, a light green reflective pool holding patches of floating moss, remained mostly undisturbed, except for the occasional ripple from a fish coming to the surface or a dragonfly soaring too close. Swamp grass and reeds lined the water's edge; the cicadas and frogs hidden inside created a serene soundtrack. "Wow. It's beautiful," he said.

"Sure is," Abin said from the back of the boat. "Lotta hard work keepin' this place a nice little hidden oasis."

"Where are the monsters?" Sage asked innocently.

Abin's irritation was evident from his tone. "They're *not*…" He stopped himself and took a breath. "They're not monsters, little lady," he said, his voice notably calmer. "Remember what I told ya earlier? About the bird on a log?" He pointed out toward a tiny island where a small swamp sparrow stood on what appeared to be a piece of driftwood. "Look over there."

Sage snapped her head over to look at the bird.

Abin let out a high-pitched, fragmented whistle. Greg figured it was some sort of bird call, but, honestly, he wouldn't know a bird call from a referee's whistle.

Suddenly, the bird began to rise up as a pair of black-speckled green eyes with vertical slits in the middle emerged from the water underneath it. "I see it!" Sage shouted as she stood up and pointed toward the eyes.

Greg started to lunge forward as he snapped, "Lisa!"

Lisa grabbed Sage by the hips, steadying her, then twisted her head back at Greg. "I got her!" she spat, almost offended.

Greg sat back down on his bench. "Sorry. She scared me, is all."

The sparrow took flight as the green eyeballs began to move through the swamp water. Soon, the back scales of the alligator breached the water like one hundred little shark fins, and Kyle recoiled back.

"What's the matter? Scared?" Greg asked, smiling devilishly.

"No!" Kyle insisted. "I was just adjusting myself in the seat."

"Sure."

Disappointed, Lisa said, "Greg…"

Greg glanced over at her and shrugged his shoulders. "I'm just messing around."

"Pretty neat, isn't it, son?" Abin said. Greg looked over to see he was addressing Kyle directly.

"Y-yeah. It's cool," Kyle replied. "So, like, how do they eat something bigger than them?"

Abin once again pulled the throttle down to idle the boat and stood up from his chair. "Good question! Gators have lightning-fast reflexes, ya see. If yer close to it, an' it intends on bitin' ya, ya ain't gon' outmaneuver it." Abin moved back to his spot between Greg and Lisa's benches. "An' once it gets ya…ya ain't gettin' out. Gators can generate a bite of up to *thirty-seven-hundred* pounds per square inch. Compare that to the average human bite, which is a mere one-hundred-an'-fifty pounds per square inch."

"Wow," Kyle said, amazed. "What do they do after they bite? They have tiny arms, right? It's not like they can hold stuff with their hands."

Abin put his hands over his heart, closed his eyes, and dramatically threw his head back. "Ah! Someone get this boy a gold star!" He brought his head back down and looked at Kyle. "Keep askin' questions like that, an' yer gon' be my star pupil!" He moved his gaze over to Greg, almost as if he were *glaring* at him. "Ya got a special boy here, I can tell. I'd cherish 'im if I was you."

The fuck is that supposed to mean? Greg thought, moving his eyes over to Kyle, who was looking up at Abin in what appeared to be admiration. Greg could practically see the stars in his son's eyes. He scoffed and turned back to Abin.

Abin continued. "When faced with larger prey, after clamping down on it with its mighty jaws, the gator simply drags it into the water, where it has complete control over its future meal." He bent down, getting closer to Kyle.

"Once it's in the water with its prey, it rolls at a high speed, spinnin' its food 'round an' *tearin'* it to *shreds*." Abin stood back upright. "That way, it has smaller pieces to eat."

Kyle was smiling ear-to-ear, his eyes full of excitement and wonder.

Christ. I don't think I've ever seen him this excited about anything. "Hey, buddy…" Greg said, pointing at Sage, who looked as if she'd just seen a grisly murder.

Abin glanced over at the little girl and nervously rubbed the back of his head. "Eh, I apologize, sir. I'm not used to havin' children on my tour. I can get a little… carried away."

"You don't say?" Greg said, giving Abin a side-eye.

Norm shouted from the front of the boat. "Are we gonna get going or what?"

Saved by the grumpy old man, Greg thought, relieved.

Abin moved back to his driver's seat and put the CB microphone to his mouth. "Sorry 'bout the delay, folks. Let's get back to the fun, whaddaya say?" He moved the throttle lever forward, but the boat didn't move. He moved the lever to neutral, then forward again, and the fan let out a loud *ker-chunk* before coming to a stop.

"Everything alright back there?" Greg asked.

Abin frantically moved the throttle lever back and forth. "Fine. We're fine."

"Didn't *sound* fine," added Norm.

"It's *fine!*" Abin shouted, slamming his fist on the console that held the lever.

The boat passengers all spun around to look at him, and he quickly painted his smile back on. "Ain't the first time this has happened; won't be the last. Just gimme a minute." He moved the lever forward one more time, and the boat's engine slowly came to a stop.

"First time *that* happened?" Greg asked.

Abin gritted his teeth and turned the ignition key off. He waited a moment, closed his eyes, then turned it back on. The engine made a gurgling sound before dying again. Abin muttered under his breath, "Shit."

Norm was audibly out of patience. "What's going on back there?"

"Uh, *slight* hiccup, folks," Abin said as he made his way back to the middle of the boat. "But don't worry. This is an easy fix."

Norm stood up from his bench. "So, what the hell are you doing talking to us? Fix it!"

Betty put her hand on Norm's arm. "Norm, honey…"

Norm moved his arm away from his wife. "Don't 'Norm' me. We're paying goddamn customers and shit is breaking down?!"

Abin put his hands up defensively. "I assure ya, I can have this fixed in no time, sir. It's just gon' take a little time. We'll have to go back to my home, where I can get 'er outta the water an' get to the engine."

Greg threw his head back. "You have *got* to be kidding me."

Abin began sweating visibly. "Don't—don't worry. The house ain't too far from here. I live in the swamp. A-an' I'll give y'all full refunds."

"What now? How are we going to get to your house?" Greg asked.

Abin walked to the back of the boat. "We're gonna need a tow." He bent down behind his driver's chair, opened a metal footlocker, and pulled out a walkie-talkie. "I'll have my son come get us. Just hang tight."

Greg turned his attention back to Sage, who remained nestled in Lisa's side. He reached out a hand and rubbed her back. "Are you okay, Sage?"

"It's getting closer."

"What?"

Sage pointed out toward the side of the boat. Greg stood up from the bench to look where she was pointing. In the water, right next to the boat, the scaly back of an alligator emerged out of the water before submerging again as it swam by.

Greg sat back down. "It's alright, sweetie. It's just swimming by."

That thing is fucking huge! he thought.

Abin's voice sounded from the back of the boat. "Good news, folks! My son is on his way, an' should be here very soon!"

Two hours later, Greg was bent over, his elbows on his knees and his head in his hands. He moved his eyes up to look at his family. Lisa had moved to the floor of the boat, and Sage was in her lap, sleeping. Kyle was playing on his phone. "You have service out here?!" Greg asked.

Kyle responded flatly, "No. Brick Break. Doesn't need a connection."

Greg stood up from the bench and stretched his back out. He then turned and walked to the back of the boat where Abin stood, looking out into the swamp. "Abin, I don't think your son is coming. We're running out of drinkable water here."

"He'll be here," Abin said, not taking his eyes off the swamp water. "Don't ya worry. He'll be here."

I'll believe it when I see it, Greg thought.

As Greg turned to walk back to his bench, he spotted a red wooden box on the floor near the footlocker that held the walkie-talkie. EMERGENCY FLARE was spray-painted on it in white.

Greg bit his lip to contain his anger. "You have a flare gun?" he asked in a low, monotone voice.

"'Course I got a flare gun. I ain't crazy," Abin said.

Greg's eyes almost bulged out of his head. "Let's use it!"

Abin barely turned his head back. "My son is *comin'*."

Sage's voice sounded from behind Greg. "Daddy, there's more."

Greg ignored his daughter and pleaded with Abin. "I know, but just in case. Maybe it'll help him find us faster."

"My wife! She's claustrophobic!" Norm shouted.

Greg turned back, and Betty was shaking uncontrollably; Norm, with an arm around her, tried to comfort her. Greg snapped back around to Abin. "Betty is freaking out. We need to go. *Now!*"

Abin twisted around and shouted, "My son is on his way!"

Greg backed off before Sage piped up again. "Daddy!"

Greg turned to face his daughter. "What?!"

Sage was pointing out at the water. "T-there's more."

Greg looked at the side of the boat, where his daughter pointed. The water there teemed with alligator eyes—more than he could count.

He mumbled, "Holy shit."

Chapter Sixteen

Greg approached Abin and grabbed him by the collar of his floral button-up shirt. "I thought you said the alligators were friendly."

"T-they are," Abin said, grabbing his straw fedora to keep it from falling off his head.

Greg removed one hand from Abin's shirt and pointed out to the water. "Then explain *that!*"

"They're curious, is all!"

Suddenly, the boat shook.

"Dad!" Sage cried.

Leaning back, Kyle shouted, "It's coming for the boat!"

An alligator with a scar over one eye breached the water, flopping about a third of its heavy body onto the side of the boat before sliding off, back into the water. The boat rocked back and forth, taking on some swamp water. "Abin! What the hell are you going to do?!" Greg shouted.

Abin's eyes darted around nervously. "It's just playin', don't worry!"

Greg heard Lisa call him from over his shoulder.

He spun to face his wife, who was sitting with her arms

around Sage and Kyle. Her eyes welled up as if she were on the verge of crying. Greg's brow furrowed with determination as he turned and stomped past Abin toward the back of the boat.

"What are ya doin'?" Abin asked.

Greg ignored him, and as he approached the red box, kicked open the lid, and reached inside and pulled out the flare gun. He cracked it open and dropped a flare into the cylinder before smacking it shut.

"I told ya my son is on his way! The flare gun is unnecessary!" Abin said.

Greg pushed past him once again and moved to the side of the boat.

"What are you doing, Dad?" Kyle asked from the boat's floor.

"I'm taking care of this," Greg said as he aimed the flare gun off the side of the boat, toward the nearby alligator.

Abin rushed up behind him and quickly put his hand on top of the gun and pushed the barrel downward. "Ya ain't takin' care of *nothin'*!" He leaned in closer to Greg, his voice lowering. "And if ya even *think* 'bout hurtin' one of my gators again—"

"You'll *what*?" Greg interrupted, sneering.

Abin grabbed the bottom of his floral shirt and began picking it up. "I'll—"

A horn sounded off in the distance, cutting Abin off. He let go of his shirt, letting it fall back down, and smiled at Greg. "Why don't ya take a seat, sir. That'd be my son."

Out in the distance, a fishing boat approached the tour group, sounding its horn as the alligators split up and swam away.

Greg stared back at Abin blankly before giving him a

brief nod. He turned to walk back to his bench when he heard Abin clear his throat.

"My flare gun."

Greg looked down at the gun in his hand. "Oh… right." He handed the emergency firearm over to Abin and took his place back on the middle bench. When he sat down, he saw Lisa was still looking at him, worry in her eyes. Greg wanted to comfort her, but didn't know how.

He moved his eyes up to Betty's back. She was still shaking and appeared to struggle to breathe as Norm held her and rubbed her back. "Don't worry, Betty," Greg said. "Abin's son is here to tow us to land. We're going to be okay." Norm turned his head slightly to glance at Greg and nodded, silently thanking him.

Soon, the twelve-foot fishing boat idled up next to the airboat. When it came to a stop, the man who drove it stood up from the driver's seat in the back. *That's a big boy*, Greg thought as he admired the man who stood almost seven-feet-tall and appeared to be made of pure muscle. He wore loose-fitting blue jeans and a dirty white tank top. Long black hair draped down to the pulled-up neck gaiter that covered the lower half of his face, but from what Greg could see, the man didn't seem like he was interested in meeting any strangers.

Abin shouted, breaking Greg's solid gaze on the statuesque man: "My boy! Yer my savior!" The man ignored Abin and began fixing a tow chain from his watercraft to the airboat. Abin continued, "This is my son, Ethan! Say hi to the folks, Ethan!"

Ethan barely looked up from the chain, one eye peeking out from behind his stringy hair, and grunted before going back to work.

"He ain't really the talkin' type. Please take no offense."

"Is he going to be able to pull us?" Kyle asked, still seated on the floor.

Abin smiled. "Of course! Ethan's boat doesn't look that big, but its motor is a monster. I bet he could pull an airplane outta the water with that thing."

Sage pointed at the man's neck gaiter. "What's on his face?"

Lisa put her hand on Sage's arm, lowering it. "It's not polite to point, Sage."

"Ah, ya see," Abin said. "Ethan has terrible allergies. If he don't cover his face, he'll be coughin' an' sneezin' all over the place."

Ethan finished connecting the boats and lumbered back to his chair.

Abin took his spot back in the driver's seat of the airboat. "Looks like we're all set here, folks. If y'all could please return to yer seats, Ethan will take us to land, an' I can get to fixin' my boat, an' we'll be on our merry way!" He waited until Lisa, Sage, and Kyle returned to their bench seats and shouted over to Ethan. "All good over here, son!"

Ethan grunted and turned up the throttle on his boat. As it started forward, the tow chain tightened, jerking the airboat before it took off after Ethan's boat. "Don't worry," Abin said. "That initial jerk is the worst part. Only smooth sailin' from here on out."

Kyle leaned over to Greg and whispered, "That dude is massive."

"No shit. I wonder where he gets it. His mom is probably nine feet toll," Greg said. He and Kyle snickered.

Lisa turned around to glance at them. "What's so funny?"

Greg stifled his laughter. "I'll tell you later."

Abin finally spoke up again about half an hour later. "…
An' there she is."

Greg looked out into the distance to see an island—a
decently sized one at that. "That island up there?" He felt
sick making nice with Abin after the thing with the alligators. He wasn't sure why Abin was lifting his shirt back
there, but brain went to the worst-case scenario and
thought maybe a gun. All he knew was the guy clearly had
a short fuse—and it was his responsibility to get his family
home safe.

Abin stepped up ahead, a twinkle in his eye. "Yes, sir.
My little paradise."

As the two boats approached, a house appeared in the
island's center, surrounded by lush green grass that looked
as fresh as the rough at Pebble Beach. Greg leaned forward
to Betty again. "We're here, Betty. Everything will be
alright." Betty stayed silent, trying to control her breathing
as she nodded.

"Thanks," Norm mumbled, continuing to face
forward.

Ethan drove his boat, with the airboat towed behind it,
up to the long dock that protruded off the island. He
stepped off his boat and onto the dock, the wood beneath
his boots creaking in agony under his sheer mass. He
disconnected the tow chain from the two boats before tying
the airboat off on one dock post. Ethan jumped back into
his boat with a *thud* when Abin called for him. "See the
airboat gets in the boathouse, boy." Ethan grunted, then
took off, driving his boat down one side of the island.

Abin moved the wooden board between the airboat
and the dock. "Okay, folks. One by one, let's go." He stood
by the board, giving the women a hand, as the two families

crossed the bridge onto the dock. "Once Ethan gets my boat onto the back of the island, we'll start on gettin' 'er fixed up to get y'all back into town." Once the airboat was empty, Abin stepped up onto the dock himself and flung the makeshift bridge back onto the boat's floor. "In the meantime, why don't y'all come up to the house? I'm sure y'all are hungry by now."

Lisa held up her bag. "I brought sandwiches."

"Ah, nonsense," Abin said with a grin. "I'll have my wife cook up somethin' warm. Just throw that bag back on the boat." He walked to the front of the group and waved his arm forward. "Come on now."

Greg stopped and watched his family as they began travelling toward the house. He still didn't know what to think about Abin Moses. Was he an actual threat—or was he just frustrated about his boat and misdirecting his anger? Either way, they were stuck there for now.

Sage turned back and shouted to Greg, "Daaad, come on!"

I'll keep a close eye on him.

Greg smiled and jogged up to join his family. "Coming!"

PART TWO: REVIVAL

Chapter Seventeen

THE TOUR GROUP LED BY ABIN APPROACHED THE HOME AT the island's center. Greg came to a halt, Lisa right next to him, and they admired the beautiful log cabin. An expansive, stilted deck surrounded the perimeter of the two-story home. The building had large windows lining its sides, two sliding glass doors on its face, and a deeply slanted roof. Off to the side of the home, a large wooden boathouse loomed in the distance.

"Wow," Lisa said with her hands over her chest. "Abin… It's beautiful."

Abin tipped his straw fedora, then turned to admire the building himself. "Thank ya, ma'am. A lotta hard work. I built 'er myself." He approached the deck stairs, putting a hand on the railing. "Why don't we head inside? Get outta this sun? My home is *yer* home."

Abin climbed the stairs, with Betty, Norm, Kyle, and Sage following him. Greg stood at the bottom and grabbed Lisa's wrist. "Hold on a second, Lisa." Kyle and Sage stopped just a few steps up. "You kids go ahead. We'll be right behind you." Kyle shrugged as he and Sage ascended the steps.

"I want to live in a place like this!" Lisa said cheerfully.

Greg stared into her eyes. "I think there's something *off* about this guy."

"Norm? I mean, he's grouchy, but——"

"No. Abin."

"He seems nice enough to me."

"Didn't you see him back on the boat?"

"Oh, Greg. I think he was just mad about his boat breaking down."

"He threatened me!"

"Threatened?! He lowered the flare gun because you were going to shoot an alligator!"

"Yeah, but you didn't hear him."

Lisa's face turned grim. "What did he say?"

"Well, he didn't get to finish, but there was something about his *tone*."

Lisa pulled back. "Are you sure you're not over-reacting?"

"You wanted me to be more honest, right?"

Lisa's eyebrows raised in agreement.

Greg grabbed Lisa's shoulders. "I…I think he was about to pull a gun on me."

"Oh, come *on*," Lisa said, rolling her eyes.

"I'm serious! He started lifting the front of his shirt. I've been a cop long enough to know that can only mean one thing."

Lisa grabbed hold of Greg's hands and took them off her shoulders. "Do you think it's *possible* that you're looking for a reason to be suspicious of him? This trip was out of nowhere, and it's in your blood to look at everyone sideways. Maybe you just need to settle into vacation mode still."

Greg dropped his head. Disappointment that she didn't believe him mingled with the thought that maybe she was right.

"He's opening up his home to us, Greg." She rubbed the side of his arm. "Forget the boat thing and give him a chance. Please."

Greg nodded slightly. "Okay."

"Okay?"

"Yeah."

"Alright. Let's go have some fun! I'm starving!" Lisa grabbed Greg's hand, and they headed up the deck stairs, toward the sliding glass doors.

I'll play nice…for now. For Lisa's sake.

Chapter Eighteen

GREG HELD HIS HAND OUT, LETTING HIS WIFE ENTER THE cabin before him. "Ladies first," he said, smiling.

Lisa dramatically threw her head back and fanned herself with her hand. "Oh, such a gentleman!"

Greg chuckled and closed the sliding door behind him when he heard a voice in front of him.

"Thought y'all mighta got lost." Abin was standing just inside the cabin's foyer; Kyle and Sage stood behind him, admiring the wall decorations and ceramic vases adorned with alligator paintings.

The home gave off a warm, cozy feeling. Natural pine covered the walls, and a darker-toned wood with a matte finish made up the floor. The rectangular windows on the walls featured dark wood frames similar to the flooring and were large enough to flood the room with natural light while offering a sweeping view of the surrounding swamp.

"I, uh…" Greg said, scratching the back of his head, trying to think of an excuse as to why they were behind.

Luckily for him, Lisa was there to jump in. "We haven't

had any *alone* time since we got to your lovely town, so we were…taking our time."

Abin smirked and winked. "Ah, I get it."

Gross, Greg thought.

"Come on in!" Abin turned from the foyer into the living room, Greg and Lisa following him. "Little Sage and Kyle were just takin' a gander at the home." He approached Kyle and put his arm around him as they both studied the wall filled with photographs. The scattered frames housed pictures of Abin with citizens of Snake Bight; some of whom Greg recognized. Saul, the innkeeper. Brent, the general store clerk—all of them posing with alligators of various sizes. "Yeah…the entire history of Snake Bight is up on these walls," Abin said.

Greg looked sideways at Abin and his son, then glanced over at Lisa, confused, as she shrugged her shoulders.

"Where are Betty and Norm?" Lisa asked.

Abin took his arm off Kyle and spun around. "Oh, don't worry 'bout them. They're bein' *taken care of.*"

Greg raised an eyebrow. "What does *that* mean?"

Abin's eyes moved around the room, almost as if he were trying to think of something to say, and chuckled. "It, uh, means exactly what I said. They're bein' taken care of." His eyes calmed down as he turned his head toward the doorway to his side and shouted: "Candy!"

Greg and Lisa exchanged glances, and Lisa mouthed, "Candy?"

Abin shouted again, "Candy!"

Finally, a shrill female voice sounded from the other room. "Yes?"

"Come on into the livin' room! We got guests!"

A few moments later, a short, older woman appeared through a doorway, removing oven mitts from her hands.

She wore a gleaming smile; her stringy grey hair was tied up in a bun. While they didn't look bad, her clothes gave the appearance that they were homemade. Greg thought she looked to be at least fifteen years Abin's senior.

"There she is!" Abin said, holding his hands out, presenting the woman. "Greg, Lisa…this is Candy, the light of my life."

"Aww, you're so sweet," Candy said as she kissed Abin on the cheek. "It's nice to meet you all."

Abin moved his head around, scanning the room. "Where's Valentine?"

Small footsteps thudded across the wooden floor in another room, and then, suddenly, a little girl carrying something wrapped in a blanket burst into the living room. She ran up to Abin and leaned against one of his legs as if to hug him using only her body.

Abin's face lit up like a Christmas tree. "Well, hey there!"

The little girl looked up at Greg with unblinking, big doe eyes. Her appearance gave him an uneasy feeling—she looked familiar.

"Oh my goodness," Lisa said.

Greg interjected. "Ashley…"

Everyone in the room turned to Greg.

"What did you say?" Abin asked flatly.

Greg looked around the room, confused, waiting for someone to agree with him. "That's Ashley, right? From town? Brent's daughter?"

Abin glared at Greg. "No. No, this is *my* daughter. Valentine."

Greg's mouth hung open, unsure of what to say.

Lisa butted in, failing to hide the trembling nervousness in her voice as she attempted to break the tension. "Oh, wow! They look like they could be sisters!"

Abin only grumbled as he continued to stare at Greg uncomfortably.

Finally, Candy spoke up. "Probably because they're both so *cute!*" She looked at Greg, raising her eyebrows.

"Right, right," Greg said. "They're adorable."

Abin visibly relaxed, and his grin returned. "Ah, well, she gets that from her mama…not that I have to tell ya that. She's right here, after all."

Candy grabbed Abin's hand and smiled up at him. "You're too sweet. Why don't we sit down for lunch? I'm sure our guests are famished, and they don't want to listen to you fawn over me all day."

"That sounds great! Y'all just follow Candy here. I'm gon' go make sure my son made it to the boathouse safe an' sound."

Greg's voice cracked when he blurted, "Aren't you going to work on fixing it?"

Abin's face turned grim once more. "'Course I am…" He smiled. "…After lunch."

With that, Abin left. Disappearing into a doorway, he left the Boyes family with Candy.

"So…" Candy said, clasping her hands together in front of her. "Who's hungry? Follow me!" She spun around and headed back through the doorway she'd entered through.

Greg and Lisa exchanged awkward looks. "See? I *told* you…he's a *nut!*" Greg said.

Lisa's eyes bulged. "What the fuck *was* that? Acting like *that* because you thought his daughter looked like another little girl? Which she *does,* by the way!"

Greg turned and looked at the photos on the wall that his children were still admiring. He honed in on the photo of Abin with his arm around Brent. Either Ashley or Valentine stood in front, in the middle of them, holding a baby alligator in her arms. "Something is weird. I'm not so sure Ashley and Valentine *aren't* the same girl."

Lisa moved next to Greg. "What? Like they're…*sharing* her?"

"I don't know. That sounds crazy, right?"

"It does."

"And where the fuck are Betty and Norm?"

Lisa's eyes began to water. "I don't like this. I want to go home."

Greg and Lisa both recoiled when Sage shouted. "Mommy, why are you whispering?"

"Shhh, honey," Lisa said, glancing down at Sage. "Mommy and Daddy are just talking." She turned her gaze back to Greg. "What are we going to do?"

Greg dropped his head. "There's nothing we *can* do except be normal, cordial house guests until the boat gets fixed and we return to town."

"Then what?"

"We pack our shit and go stay in Miami, like we were supposed to."

"Right. Normal."

Candy's shrill shout sounded from the next room, causing Greg to look toward the doorway. "Helloooo! Come and get it while it's hot!"

"'While it's hot?'" Lisa asked, echoing Candy. "She already had food made for us?"

Greg looked at Lisa sternly. "Normal. For now." He plastered a smile across his face and said, "Come on, kids! Let's go eat!"

Chapter Nineteen

THE BOYES FAMILY ENTERED THE KITCHEN, AS COZY AND welcoming as the living room, with Greg heading up his usual spot at the rear of the group. Candy stood before a large wooden dining table filled with meatloaf, diced potatoes, and vegetables. Already seated at the table, Valentine still cradled the bundled-up blanket.

"Wow," Greg said. "This looks great, right, hon?"

Lisa stood in silence, staring at the table until Greg nudged her with his elbow. "Right, Lisa?"

"Yes! Yeah, fantastic! Thank you so much, Candy."

Candy smiled softly. "It's my *pleasure*. Take a seat!"

"Come on, guys," Lisa said, looking at Kyle and Sage. The kids took their seats at the table, with Greg and Lisa following shortly after.

Greg eyed Candy as she circled the table, setting plates in front of her guests. She even set plates in front of three empty spots. Abin, Norm, and Betty, he assumed. But what about Ethan?

Greg cleared his throat. "Is Abin going to be joining us? Or the older couple…Norm and Betty?"

Candy finished setting the table and calmly sat in her chair. She slowly raised her eyes to meet Greg's. "Abin should be here shortly. He's checking the boat...remember?" She put her attention on her plate, cutting her meatloaf with a knife and fork.

Something about Candy's tranquil voice was *eerie*, causing the hairs on Greg's arms to stand up. In reality, he didn't care if Abin joined them for dinner. He wanted him to fix the damn boat. He wanted to know only about Betty and Norm. "Oh, right...and the other two?" he asked, almost as if they were a second thought.

"Are you sweet on the old lady or something?" Candy asked, cackling. "They won't be joining us. I'm saving some for them...for *later*."

"Where are they?" Greg cleared his throat. "If you don't mind my asking, that is."

Candy stopped her fork just short of her mouth, waited a beat, then moved her eyes back up toward Greg. "Why are you so concerned?"

Greg raised his voice a bit. "Will you just answer the question?"

Lisa grabbed Greg's thigh underneath the table and squeezed. "Greg..." she whispered from the side of her mouth.

He looked over at his wife, his voice defensively rising in pitch. "What? It's just a question." He turned back to Candy. "So...where are they?"

"There's no need to raise your voice," Candy calmly said before putting a piece of meat in her mouth. As she slid the fork out from between her lips, it dragged against her teeth, making an awful scratching sound.

Greg pounded his fist on the table. "I haven't seen them since we docked! I'd just like to know where they are!"

"Dad," Kyle said, trying to get Greg's attention.

"I'm only trying to wrap my head around where they could have gone in the ten minutes from the dock to the house. I—"

Kyle shouted, cutting Greg off, "Dad!"

Greg craned his head over to face his son. "What?!"

Kyle pointed over Greg's shoulder, and Greg spun around to see Norm standing in the kitchen doorway, leaning against the wall.

"I'm sorry to bug you, Candy," Norm said. "Betty was wondering if we could trouble you for a glass of water."

Greg quickly looked back at Candy, who was smiling. She looked back at Greg as she obnoxiously pushed her chair back before standing up. "Of course, Norm. No trouble at all." She walked over to the sink and pulled a glass out of a cabinet and filled it with tap water. She walked it over to Norm and handed it to him.

"Thank you, ma'am. And thank you for lending Betty a bed to lie down on. She should be on her feet in no time."

Candy caressed the side of Norm's arm. "No worries. She can take as long as she needs. Let me know when you get hungry. I have meatloaf and potatoes waiting for you."

Norm put on an un-characteristic smile and left the kitchen.

Lisa snapped her head over to Greg and glared at him. Greg's face felt like it was on fire. He just knew he was beet red. He quietly began stirring his fork in his food—his head down to hide his embarrassment—as Candy returned to her chair and resumed eating in silence.

Lisa continued to glare at Greg, and he *felt* it. After a moment, he finally spoke up. "Listen, I—"

"Don't worry about it," Candy said cheerfully.

"No, there's no excuse for how I acted."

"You were worried about your sick friend. No harm, no foul."

"Yeah…my friend. Well, I *am* sorry. Thank you for being so forgiving."

Candy looked up from her plate, wearing a wide grin. "If I let it get to me every time someone raised their voice at me, I'd have died of a coronary four times over by now. Let's change the subject, shall we?"

Greg opened his mouth to respond, but Lisa injected herself before he could. "I think that's a great idea." She turned her attention to Valentine. "I didn't get to introduce myself to little Valentine. I'm Lisa. It's nice to meet you!"

Valentine gave Lisa a tiny wave.

"How old are you, honey?"

"S-seven," Valentine said, appearing to struggle to get the word out.

"Oh! My daughter Sage here is seven, too!"

"Hi," Sage said in her shy little voice, as she smiled at Valentine.

"What do you have there? In your arms?" Lisa asked.

Valentine looked as if she were in pain as her lips quivered before she spat out her answer. "B-b-*baby*."

Candy reached next to her and ran her hand down through her daughter's hair. "A *doll*…a baby doll. You'll have to excuse Valentine. She has trouble speaking."

"Shy?" Greg asked.

"No. She was born with a brain tumor."

Geez, no need to sugarcoat it, I guess.

"She developed *dysarthia* and has trouble controlling the muscles in her mouth, so she speaks only in short bursts and at a low volume."

"Aww, poor thing," Lisa said. "Does it hurt to talk?"

Valentine shook her head.

"Well, that's good. Does your baby have a name?"

Valentine looked over at Candy as if she were waiting for permission to answer, and Candy nodded at her. Valentine looked back at Lisa and shook her head again. She then looked down at the bundled-up blanket and rocked it like a baby.

"Why is it all covered up?" Kyle asked through a mouthful of food.

Lisa sighed. "Kyle. No talking with your mouth full."

"S-she's sssick."

"What's wrong with her?" Sage asked.

Valentine's eyes opened wide. "H-ead—"

"That's enough about the doll," Candy snapped. "I think I hear Daddy coming in!"

Greg turned in his chair to face the doorway, actually excited to see Abin. *Thank God. I can get my family the hell out of here.*

He could hear Abin grumbling and slamming things around in another room.

A few moments later, Abin appeared in the doorway. He wore a scowl at first, but quickly painted on a smile when he noticed that all the attention was on him. "Well, howdy, y'all!"

"Did you get the airboat fixed?" Greg asked, almost leaping out of his chair.

Abin rubbed the back of his head and looked down at the floor. "Here's the thing... I ran into a *teeny-tiny* problem."

"No..."

"'Fraid the engine is worse'n I thought. I have to take 'er apart an' rebuild 'er."

Greg threw his head back in frustration. "You've got to be *kidding* me."

"I ain't, son. I apologize. I thought it was gon' be a simple fix." Abin approached the sink and began washing his hands.

"Pardon my asking, but how long do you think that will take?" Lisa asked.

Abin dried his hands and approached the table, leaning on the back of a chair. "I ain't gon' lie to ya, ma'am. It ain't gon' be ready today."

Greg grabbed the napkin next to his plate and squeezed it, his knuckles turning white. He wanted to throw his plate at Abin's face, maybe wiping that stupid grin off his face. He wanted to scream. Instead, he only gripped the napkin harder, and in a low voice, grumbled, "What…"

Abin pulled the chair out and sat at the table. "I'll start workin' on 'er soon as I'm done eatin', honest."

Candy leaned forward, placing her hand on top of Lisa's. "Don't you worry, honey. We have a plenty of spare rooms."

Greg looked over at Candy. He took a deep breath, trying to keep his cool. "It's not about rooms. It's the fact that we're stuck here on an island in the middle of a Florida swamp with complete *strangers*."

Candy looked sweetly at Greg. "But we're nice peo—"

"I don't give a *shit*!" Greg snapped, raising his voice slightly.

Suddenly, a steak knife flew by Greg's face and stuck in the wall behind him with a *thunk*. He turned around to see the knife, its handle still wobbling, then spun back around to face the table. Abin was glaring at him, his head half lowered. He said through gritted teeth, "That's enough."

Greg quickly looked back at the knife, then again at Abin; his mouth agape, unsure of what to think or say.

"I understand yer upset, Greg…but I will *not* have ya disrespectin' my wife. Not in my house, not *anywhere*."

Greg struggled to find his words as his mind immediately went to Jake; the things his partner put him through. He was too trusting, and he knew it. But he also knew to trust his instincts when something seemed wrong. Lisa was right when they first got to the island; it *was* in his blood—and her making it sound like a bad thing sort of made him resent her. He wondered if she'd only listened to him in the first place, would they even be in this mess? He could've easily forced them to take his family back on Ethan's boat.

"We opened *our home* to yer family, and yer so…*fast* to raise yer voice at the smallest inconvenience." Abin's eyes shifted between his guests. "Have we done somethin' to offend ya, Greg? Lisa?"

They stayed silent, only staring at Abin as the corner of his mouth twitched.

Greg felt Lisa's hand inch over his thigh underneath the table and grab hold of his hand. *Her hand is so sweaty… and shaking.* Greg moved his hands onto the table. "You know what, Abin? You're *right*."

Abin's head cocked to the side.

"Before we came down here to Florida, I was under a lot of stress at home because of work, so I've been a little on edge. I've been taking it out on you, and that isn't fair." Greg leaned forward. "I freaked out when the airboat broke down and alligators surrounded us; I only wanted to protect my family."

"Now, I told ya they wouldn't hurt ya!"

"You did, but they also showed up right after you got done telling us how they drown their prey and tear them to shreds under the water." Greg chuckled nervously, hoping that would ease the tension.

Abin leaned back in his chair. The corners of his

mouth began to turn upward and, after a moment, he let out a hearty belly laugh. "I guess I did *just* get done tellin' ya that, didn't I?" He continued laughing.

Chortling along with Abin, Greg shifted his eyes over to Lisa, who remained stone-faced. Greg nudged Lisa with his knee under the table, causing her to snap out of her stare. She took the hint and put on a fake chuckle of her own.

Abin's laughing ceased, and his smile vanished in an instant, as if a switch had flipped in his head. "That thing…back there on the boat…ya gotta understand, that wasn't anythin' *personal*."

Greg's eyebrows raised. He was shocked Abin would even bring the whole incident back up.

"I couldn't have ya hurtin' my gators, ya see, an' ya waved that emergency pistol around like ya meant some serious business with it."

So what? You were going to take alligators over me and my family? Greg thought as he continued to wear a fake smile. "I totally understand. My cop instincts just kicked in and—"

"*Cop?!*" Abin interrupted.

Greg noted the hint of disgust in Abin's voice. "Y-yeah. I'm a cop back home in Flint, Michigan."

Abin grumbled.

"I take it you don't like the police?" Greg asked.

Abin's smile returned. "Nah, nah. Nothin' like that. I just find it…*interesting*, is all." Abin abruptly turned his attention toward his daughter. "Valentine!" The little girl looked up from her wrapped-up doll toward Abin. "Why don't ya show Sage an' Kyle their room so they know where they'll be stayin' fer the night?" He moved his gaze back to Greg. "Assumin' this is all swept under the proverbial rug an' y'all will be stayin' the night."

Greg and Lisa looked at each other. "I guess we don't really have a choice, do we?" Lisa said.

"Nope. Looks like you're stuck with us," Greg added. "Let's forget the whole thing happened. Clean slate."

"Good to hear!" Abin said. "Although it's more like *yer* stuck with *us*." His toothy grin almost gave him an alligator-like appearance himself.

Chapter Twenty

VALENTINE JUMPED DOWN FROM HER CHAIR AND WAVED AT Sage and Kyle, gesturing for them to follow her. Lisa looked over at her children. "Go on. Let the grown-ups talk while you go see your room for the night."

"You don't have to treat me like a little kid," Kyle said, getting up from his chair.

"Just listen to your mom," Greg said flatly.

Kyle rolled his eyes and followed Valentine out of the kitchen with Sage. "Whatever."

"Watch your tone!" Greg shouted out of the kitchen doorway.

Abin dug into his meatloaf. "Y'know, y'all got a bright boy there."

Lisa smiled. "Mmm, thank you."

Greg took a sip from the glass of water in front of him. "Yeah… Bit of a pain in the ass, though."

"Sometimes that can be a product of their environment," Abin said. "Poorly treated people act poorly."

Greg set his glass on the table hard, just short of slamming it. "*Excuse me?*"

Suddenly, Candy yelled out. "Oh, there you are! Have you finally worked up an appetite?"

Everyone moved their attention to the doorway, where Norm and Betty entered the room—everyone except Greg, who continued to store daggers at Abin. *I can't believe this cocksucker,* he thought.

Candy scurried to her feet and rushed over to Betty, grabbing her by the arm to help her toward the table. "I already set up plates for the two of you right over here. And the food should still be warm, but if you need it heated up at all, feel free to ask."

The older couple took their seats at the table. "Thank you, Candy…Abin. You're both so generous," Betty said.

Norm reached toward the big tray that held the meatloaf with his fork and skewered a sizable chunk before bringing it over to his plate. "You have any luck with that boat of yours, Abin?" He didn't even bother looking up as he scooped a spoonful of diced potatoes onto his plate alongside his slab of meat.

"It's a sore subject, right, Abin?" Greg said, his voice full of anger.

Abin ignored the snarky comment. "I was tellin' Greg an' Lisa, the airboat's in worse shape than I'd thought."

"What seems to be the problem?" Norm asked as he cut up his meat. The savory, rich aroma coming from Norm's plate made Greg's mouth fill with saliva, although he'd seemed to have lost his appetite.

"Eh, I gotta take the engine apart. I don't wanna bore ya with the details." Abin took a drink from the glass in front of him. "Bottom line is, it ain't gon' be ready tonight."

Candy jumped in. "Don't worry, though! You two already have a room set up, so you can just stay in there for the night!"

Betty put her arm around Norm. "Why don't you have a look, honey?" She then turned to Abin. "Norm was a part-time mechanic."

"That so?" Abin leaned back in his chair with an impressed look on his face. "Ya work on boat engines?" He took another drink from his glass.

"Planes," Norm said, talking around the pile of potatoes he'd just shoveled into his mouth.

"It was in the Air Force," Betty added.

Abin choked on his water. He quickly grabbed a napkin and placed it over his mouth. "Argh." He coughed. "Sorry 'bout that… Air Force, huh?" He patted his chin and placed the napkin back down on the table. "…the *government*."

"Yes, sir," Norm said proudly. "Just retired."

"Retired…" Abin repeated, quietly trailing off while looking at Norm from the corner of his eye.

Thud!

Thud!

A loud noise broke the awkward tension.

"What the hell is that?" Greg asked, looking around.

Thud!

Thud!

Candy also looked around the room. "It's Ethan. He must be in from the boathouse."

"What in God's name is he doing?" Norm asked. "Sounds like a goddamn earthquake!"

"He's, um—"

"He's a *retard*," Abin spat, interrupting Candy.

One could hear a pin drop as the entire table fell silent; Greg and Lisa sat with their mouths hanging open.

Candy's cheeks turned red. "Oh, Abin. You know I don't like that word," she said as she continued to make eye contact with her guests. "Ethan is our special boy. I'm not sure *why* Abin continues to use such language. I assure you, all his mental faculties are there."

Greg and Lisa continued to stay silent, their jaws practically on the floor.

"Not that we would love him any less if they weren't," Candy quickly added, as she nervously fidgeted with her hands.

Thud!

Thud!

"Jesus Christ with the racket!" Abin shouted as he slammed his fist on the table, causing everyone at the table to recoil. Abin seemed to come back to reality rather quickly as he looked around at his guests and calmed down. "I…excuse me." He pushed himself away from the table and stood up from his chair. "I apologize fer usin' the Lord's name in vain. I'll pray on it later." He walked toward the doorway of the kitchen.

"Abin…" Candy whispered.

"I'm just goin' to check on the boy. Make sure he ain't hurt himself by accident. I'll be back shortly." Abin disappeared out of the doorway, leaving the room in stunned silence.

"Just one of those days, I suppose," Candy said, chuckling.

"How did you meet?" Lisa blurted out, her words almost melding together.

"Pardon?" Candy asked.

"You and Abin. How did the two of you meet? Your accents are so…different."

"It's nothing of note, to be honest. I was on a business trip in Utah and stopped at a used bookstore… I always made sure to find a used bookstore whenever I was in a new city. Well, I wasn't looking for anything in particular. Just browsing, you know, and I found myself in the zoological section. Can you believe that? An entire zoological section in a used bookstore in the middle of *Utah*. Do they even have animals in Utah? Just kidding, I know they do."

Holy shit. Lisa unleashed the Kraken, Greg thought as he watched Candy's mouth move a mile a minute.

Candy continued, speaking quickly, like an excited child. "Anyway, someone designed the spine of a reptile book to look like scales, and I was immediately interested. You've heard of judging a book by its cover, but have you ever heard of judging a book by its *spine?*" She had a hearty laugh at that. "Well, me just being a little thing couldn't reach the shelf it was on, and a handsome man just so happened to be browsing the same section of the same bookshop. When he grabbed the book down for me, and saw it was about reptiles, his eyes lit up as bright as the sun. He immediately asked me out, using teaching me about reptiles as an excuse. I had absolutely zero interest in any alligator or lizard, but I sure pretended I did because I wanted to get to know him. His kind eyes are what did it. I felt like I was walking on clouds when he made eye contact with me." Candy smiled; her eyes rolled back and her eyelids fluttered as her own words sent her back in time.

"We're still talking about Abin, right?" Greg asked.

Lisa elbowed him in the ribs. "Stop it! That's so cute!"

Candy looked down at her hands, still smiling. "Yep. That's my Abin. We started seeing each other officially not too long after that. Then, long story short, he ended up leaving his job at the lab to move down here to follow his dream of founding our community. That way, he knew the animals of the swamp would always be safe and always have a home."

Greg leaned back in his chair and put a finger on his chin. "Did you say 'lab?' Abin said he was a forensic accountant."

One of Candy's eyebrows raised up, seemingly to the top of her head, as she appeared puzzled. Then, as if a lightbulb turned on in her head, she blurted out, "Of course! That's what he called the, uh, building he worked in…*the lab*. Makes it sound ominous for accounting, right?"

Greg's eyes squinted with disbelief. "Right…"

"Who cares where he works?" Norm asked, agitated.

"I don't *care*; I was curious," Greg responded defensively. *Shove it, Norm. Someone's lying about something.*

Candy stood up from her chair. "Well, it's getting late, and we have Mass in the morning. Greg, Lisa, why don't I show you the room you'll be staying in tonight?"

"That would be great," Lisa said. "All that sun earlier zapped my energy."

"Mass?" Greg asked.

Candy nodded and smiled. "You're actually lucky you broke down today of all days. The whole town comes in to hear Abin preach."

Yeah…lucky, thought Greg.

"Oh, we'd absolutely *love* for you to join us!"

Greg moved his eyes to the side, avoiding eye contact with his host. "We're not really church p—"

Lisa interjected, glaring at her husband. "We'd be glad to! Attending your mass is the least we could do, right, Greg?" She glared at her husband, waiting for him to agree.

Unconvincingly, Greg said, "Yeah, sure. We'd be glad."

Chapter Twenty-One

Kyle felt his sister leaning in close to him as Valentine, with her wrapped-up doll in her arms, led them down the dim upstairs hallway. Every few steps, Sage would bump into him, making him stumble. "Will you back off?" he asked, frustrated.

"I don't like it here," Sage whispered.

Kyle pointed down at his shoes. "Well, only *one* of us can walk in these." He then moved his eyes around the corridor, examining the surrounding walls. They weren't of a nice, glossy wood like the rest of the home. The wallpaper that coated the walls instead had a yellow tint to it—one could barely tell that it was once white—and it had little pictures of saw grass patches strewn about. *Really trying to keep up the swampy look,* he thought.

"H-here," Valentine stammered, stopping in front of a thick wooden door.

Kyle's eyes widened as he admired the door. "Wow." The wood at eye level displayed an extremely detailed carving of an alligator head.

Valentine's cheeks puffed out as she attempted to spew her words. "D-d-daaaaaddy…d-did…t-t-t-that."

Kyle reached out and touched the carving, running his fingers along its edges. Squeezing underneath his outstretched arm, Valentine turned the doorknob and swung the door open.

Relief washed over Kyle as he peered into the open doorway. It wasn't the dungeon-like room that he'd been expecting (based entirely on the dingy hallway). The room, like the downstairs, was full of nicely finished wood. Kyle thought it a relief that the gross corridor seemed to be an outlier in terms of grittiness. He looked down at the lone queen-size bed in the center of the room. "There's only one bed."

Before he could say anything else, Sage blurted out, "Dibs!"

Kyle leapt onto the mattress. "Hey! I'm older!"

"But…I'm a *girl!*"

"Barely," Kyle said as he reached for a pillow behind him and flung it at his sister.

Sage ducked under the flying pillow. "You're gonna get it now!" She picked the pillow up from the floor and held it over her head.

Kyle grabbed another pillow that leaned against the headboard and stood up on the bed. He wielded the pillow like a sword. "En garde!" Jumping off the bed and onto the floor below, he and Sage began walloping each other with their weapons, laughing hysterically.

After a minute, Sage was laughing so hard, she couldn't fight back and Kyle overwhelmed her. She dropped her pillow and threw her hands in the air. "I yield! I yield!"

Kyle reared back and smacked her one more time.

Thwap!

He hit her directly in the face, knocking her back onto her rear. Kyle's face dropped. "Oh, shit! Are you okay?!"

Sage's eyes spun in circles before she burst into laughter. "Oooo, you swore!"

Kyle chuckled, relieved he hadn't hurt his sister. "Oh, quiet." He looked over, and Valentine still stood in the doorway, just staring at them, wearing a blank expression.

Kyle stared back, his pulse quickening as he eyed the unblinking girl. *What's her deal?* he thought.

After a moment, he pulled his gaze away and back toward Sage, who also eyed the girl cradling her wrapped-up doll. Sage had picked her pillow back up and held it to her mouth, covering the lower half of her face. He knew his little sister was frightened. He walked his way to the doorway and put his hand on the knob. "Thanks for showing us the room."

Valentine continued glaring at him—not blinking—not moving.

Then Kyle heard Sage whimper from over his shoulder. "I think we got it from here," he said to Valentine, smiling uncomfortably.

It had been only a few seconds, but felt like a lifetime before Valentine finally turned and walked out of the door-way, leaving the Boyes siblings alone. Kyle shut the door, doing so as quietly as possible. He saw no reason to give the creepy girl an excuse to come back. Keeping his eyes on the back of the door, he let out a quick shiver, and felt his heart rate returning to normal. He then heard Sage's small voice pipe in from behind him. "Her eyes…"

Kyle straightened up at Sage's comment. He thought she'd been imagining things back at the inn—but what if she'd been telling the truth? What if there *was* something up with Valentine? With the other little girl back in town?

"Kyle…" Sage said, breaking her brother's concentration on the back of the door. He turned to face her as she sat on the bed, against the headboard, clutching the pillow. "I don't want that girl to come back."

"Don't worry. When we wake up in the morning and Mr. Abin fixes the boat, we'll be back in town and you won't have to see her ever again."

"But what if she follows us back to our room?"

Kyle moved to the bed and sat down at the end of the mattress. "What are you talking about?"

"Like she did before…when she was looking at me through the window."

Kyle chuckled. "I told you that you had too much sugar. Your brain was making it up."

"I didn't make it up!" Sage shouted.

"Okay, okay!" Kyle lowered his hands, telling her to quiet down. "You didn't make it up, but you said it was the little girl from town. The one that ran out in front of the car."

"It was *her!*"

"You heard them downstairs. They just look alike. And how do you think Valentine got to our room in town? She swam?"

Sage had no response.

"See? Sounds crazy, doesn't it?"

Sage nodded. "I guess so… But I saw *someone*. I didn't make it up."

"I believe you," Kyle said. He was really starting to believe that she'd seen someone outside their window. He was even beginning to jump on his dad's crazy theory that Valentine and the little girl in town were the same person. He'd never heard of two people who weren't related looking like identical twins. It sounded absolutely nuts, and he was well aware of that, but at the moment, his only concern was making sure Sage's mind was at ease—at least until they were off the island and preferably in Miami.

"Why don't we go to bed? The faster we do that, the faster we're out of here," he said.

Sage nodded in agreement, this time more confidently. "Will you sleep in the bed too?"

Kyle smiled. "Did you really think I was going to adhere to your dibs?"

"What's that mean?"

"Nothing. Of course I'll sleep in the bed too. I'll make sure you're safe."

Kyle went to the wall and shut off the light before laying on his side of the bed and getting under the covers. "Night, Sage," he said. She didn't answer, but her heavy breathing made him assume she'd already passed out. He pulled the blanket up to his chin and closed his eyes.

Kyle shot awake when he heard a sound—a sort of banging—coming from somewhere outside his room. He sat up in bed and whispered, "Sage…Sage…" She stayed quiet. *This she can sleep through.* He carefully stood up from the bed and looked around the darkened room, hoping to find the source of the noise. A light shone outside the room's window, and he walked over to investigate.

Peering out of the window, he saw a lighting rig set up on the grounds. Beneath the light, Abin's son, Ethan, carried large pieces of lumber on his shoulder. He was hauling them toward pieces that had already been arranged in a rectangle on the grass, like the base of a tiny house or shed.

Ethan dropped the lumber to the ground and lined a piece up with the already established rectangle. He then began hammering the pieces together with a thick wooden mallet.

It's the middle of the night, Kyle thought. *What the hell is he doing down there?*

He looked back at Sage to make sure she was still asleep, then walked over to the bedroom door and slipped on his shoes. He turned the knob, trying to be quiet. The door creaked as he pulled it open, and Valentine was standing in the doorway, staring at him with her unblinking eyes, and holding her wrapped-up doll in her arms.

Kyle jumped back and shouted, "Jesus!"

He knelt down and whispered, "What are you doing here?"

Valentine continued to look into Kyle's eyes, not even attempting to speak.

"You scared me." Kyle's eyes moved back and forth. "I, uh, have to go to the bathroom."

Valentine stared for a few more seconds, then turned and ran down the hall. Kyle listened for the thudding of her footsteps to fade away before he stood back up. He glanced back at Sage one more time to make sure his shout didn't wake her. She was still sound asleep in the bed, so he left through the bedroom door, closing it behind him.

Kyle plodded through the darkened house and exited through the back screen door onto the deck that surrounded the home. He looked out over the railing, where Ethan continued manhandling large pieces of lumber as if they were only large sticks. Kyle glanced around to make sure nobody else was nearby and descended the stairs.

As he approached the large man, Kyle waved at him. "Hi," he said sheepishly. Ethan ignored him and kept working. Unsure if the man had heard him, Kyle tried again, this time louder. "Hey!"

Ethan halted and turned, swinging the massive piece of wood that sat on his beefy shoulder. Luckily for Kyle, Ethan was over a foot taller than him, so the piece of lumber swung right over his head.

"I'm Kyle…you brought me and my parents in when your dad's boat broke down."

Ethan eyed Kyle, not saying a word, emotionless behind the neck gaiter that still covered the lower half of his face. His heavy breathing bounced his hulking frame up and down slowly. Kyle wasn't sure if it was from lugging around the large pieces of wood or if it was out of anger.

"W-what are you building? It's so late."

Ethan turned away, the lumber swinging right over Kyle's head again, as he went back to work. Kyle scratched his head, dumbfounded, as he watched the man go back to hammering. Then a voice called out from behind him, causing him to jump. "Excuse me, son!"

Kyle spun around and saw Abin approaching him from a large wooden shack just off the water. "What are ya doin' out here? Shouldn't ya be sleepin'?"

Kyle looked around nervously. "I was, but I heard banging and it woke me up. I was coming to see what it was."

Abin threw an arm around Kyle's shoulder and chuckled. "Why's ya voice tremblin'? Ya ain't in trouble. Yer a grown man."

Kyle let out a nervous laugh. "I…I don't know!"

"Don't worry. I ain't yer daddy. I ain't here to give ya no guff."

"What do you mean by that?"

"I mean, I ain't here to give ya a hard time."

"No. I mean, about my dad."

"Oh!" Abin said, removing his arm from Kyle's shoulders. "I didn't mean nothin' by it. Seems like he's on yer case an awful lot, is all."

"He's not all that bad. Sometimes I deserve it."

"Well, he should feel lucky to have ya… I know I would."

"No offense, Mr. Abin, but you don't even know me."

"Ahh, but I can tell. Yer a good kid…creative, strong-willed."

Kyle took a step back, feeling uneasy. "I-if you say so."

"I'm sure yer not used to hearin' 'em, but don't be afraid to take a compliment, son."

Kyle looked down, unsure what to make of what Abin was saying to him. He thought the words coming from him were nice, but not entirely accurate. Sure, his dad could be rough on him, but he chalked it up to tough love… although, he thought Abin may also have a bit of a point. *I'm really not as appreciated as I should be, am I? Doesn't like me going to film school…called me a 'wuss' for doing theater instead of playing sports in high school…picks on my weight…*

Kyle looked back up to see Abin staring at him, wearing a sly smile, almost as if he could *hear* what Kyle was thinking. "Why don't ya go on back to bed? Should be an early mornin' tomorrow."

"Is the boat fixed?"

"Nah, not yet. I'm close, though." Abin pointed over his shoulder with his thumb, toward the wooden shack. "I still got 'er in the boathouse, but she'll be ready after church."

"You have a church here?"

"Absolutely," Abin said, smiling. "Our mass is very important to Snake Bight. Ethan over there is buildin' the stage." He once again threw an arm over Kyle's shoulder. "Come on, I'll tell ya all 'bout it on the way back to the house."

Kyle smiled ear-to-ear and began walking back with Abin.

Abin continued walking with his arm around Kyle's shoulder. "What do ya wanna be, Kyle?"

Kyle raised an eyebrow. "I'm not sure what you mean."

"Like, as a job. Fer a career."

"Well, I'm currently in film school in New York."

Abin shuddered, and Kyle chuckled. "What was that for?"

"Ah, nothin'. Don't necessarily care fer their…*politics*."

"Oh…well, I'm just going there to get my degree, then I'll be going to Los Angeles."

"Yuck! Even *worse!*" Abin said with a hearty laugh. Kyle laughed along, unsure of whether or not the older man was messing with him. "The good thing 'bout Snake Bight is, here, ya can be *anythin'* ya want!"

"I-I can't really be a director here. Everything is made in LA or New York or Georgia."

"Well, shoot! Georgia is just above us! I don't mean to *make* movies here. Don't be silly. I meant ya could *live* in Snake Bight. Free from rules an' regulations…an' doubters. People who may tell ya that ya can't be what ya want to be. People who make fun of ya. Then ya could travel fer work."

Kyle began to think about his dad again.

As the two approached the house, Abin removed his arm from around Kyle's shoulder. "We're here. Think 'bout what I said, an' you'll find out more at Mass tomorrow."

Kyle grabbed the railing and took one step up the deck stairs before coming to a stop and turning around. "Thanks for walking me back…and for the chat."

Abin smiled at him. "Get a good night's sleep, son. It's gon' be an early one."

"Yeah. Right," Kyle said as he turned and walked up the stairs and into the house.

Chapter Twenty-Two

GREG FELT THE WARMTH OF THE SUN COMING THROUGH the guest room window onto his closed eyelids as he stretched his limbs as far as they would allow. He rolled over to drape his arm over Lisa, and his eyes fluttered halfway open when his arm fell to the mattress. "Lisa?" he called out. He rubbed his eyes with his palms before opening them all the way. He then sat up on the bed and glanced around the room, looking for his wife. "Lisa?"

Finally, he heard the bathroom door open and, not too long after, Lisa emerged, wearing only her bra and panties.

"Well, hello," he said seductively, pumping his eyebrows up and down.

Lisa rolled her eyes. "Not now, Greg."

He noticed the slight worry in her voice. *What on earth could have gone wrong now?* he thought. *Let me guess, someone fell in the water…or an alligator made its way onto shore and is wreaking havoc.*

He patted the spot next to him on the bed, telling her to sit down. "What's wrong? You have that *look*."

"'What's wrong?'" Lisa repeated as she stomped back

into the bathroom. "They invited us to their church service…" She emerged from the bathroom again, holding pieces of clothing in both of her hands. "…and all I have to wear is a tank top and fucking *booty shorts!*"

"Oh, come on. It's not *that* bad."

"Have you ever heard 'sweating like a whore in church?' I'm going to be doing that while literally *looking like* a whore in church."

Greg stood up from the bed. "Nobody is going to judge you. They obviously know the boat broke down. It's not like they'd expect you to bring a change of clothes for a few hours long tour. We're not going to be staying long anyway. As soon as there's a break or something, I'm telling Abin to have his son take us back, and I'm not taking no for an answer."

"Ugh. That's not the point!" Lisa said, throwing her head back as she turned and re-entered the bathroom, slamming the door behind her.

Greg sighed, lowered his head, and mumbled, "…Jesus Christ."

He turned his head toward the window when he heard someone shouting from somewhere outside. Approaching the window, he peered out below. Brent was walking up to Candy, who stood next to a large cardboard box. Brent gave her a hug. Then she reached into the box and pulled out what appeared to be a white sheet. Her mouth seemed to move a mile a minute. *Shocker*, Greg thought. She handed the white cloth over to Brent, and he simply walked away.

"Hey, honey," Greg shouted. "Brent's here."

Lisa's muffled voice came from behind the bathroom door. "Who?"

"Brent! He works at the general store in town. You

know the little girl who ran in front of the car? He's her dad."

Lisa exited the bathroom, fully dressed in her tank top and shorts. "Oh, the guy who didn't teach his kid to look both ways before jetting out into the street?"

Greg chuckled and shook his head. "It was an honest mistake." He pulled his attention away from the window and turned to his wife. "You almost ready? They're probably going to be starting soon."

Lisa held out her arms to her sides and looked down at her body. "I feel ridiculous."

"What? You look hot!"

"Exactly," she said, dropping her arms back down to her sides. "I guess I'm as ready as I'll ever be."

"Alright," Greg said. "Let's wrangle up the kids."

"Want to bet they're still sleeping?" Greg asked, smiling as he and Lisa approached Kyle and Sage's door.

"No way! It's going on ten o'clock. I guarantee Sage has been awake for at *least* three hours."

Greg laughed as he knocked on the door. "You think she can stay quiet for *that* long?"

After a few beats with no response, he knocked again.

Still nothing.

"Sage!" he shouted. "Kyle!"

Greg and Lisa glanced at each other, and Greg raised his eyebrows. "Told you. Pay up."

Lisa playfully punched his shoulder. "We didn't even bet anything!"

Greg laughed as he turned the doorknob. "Nice excuse." He pushed the door ajar, poking his head through the crack. "Sage? Kyle?" he whispered. "It's time to get up."

When he didn't hear any movement on the other side of the door, he opened it the rest of the way and entered, with Lisa right behind him.

At first glance, the room appeared bare. "Where are they?" Greg asked. Lisa tapped him on the shoulder, then pointed toward the bed, where the blankets bundled up into a small heap. Greg smiled at her and tiptoed toward the bed. As he approached it, he reached down and clutched a fistful of blankets. Turning back to Lisa, he mouthed, "One…two…three." He *ripped* the blankets off and threw them to the floor, then shouted, "Wake up!"

Sage was curled in the fetal position, using the back of her arm to shield her eyes.

"Come on, kid! It's time to get up!" Greg said cheerfully. He loved nothing more than to wake his sleeping kids with his cheery dad's voice. He knew it irritated them to no end.

Sage groaned and rolled onto her back, peering through her half-opened eyelids. "Nooo. I'm *tired*."

Lisa sat down on the edge of the mattress and brushed Sage's hair with her hand. "You never sleep *this* late."

"Kyle kept me up," Sage grumbled.

Greg looked around the room. "Speaking of…where *is* Kyle?"

Sage shrugged her shoulders.

"What do you mean?" Greg asked as he mimicked Sage's shrug.

Sage finally sat up. "I mean, I *don't know*. I woke up at night and he wasn't here."

"He wasn't?"

Sage shook her head. "He came back after a little

while. He lay down and kept rolling around on the bed. He said he couldn't sleep…then he left again."

Greg crossed his arms, his voice turning stern. "Did he say anything?"

"He said he was going to see Mr. Abin."

"And he never came back?"

Sage shook her head again.

What the hell would he be doing with Abin in the middle of the night? Maybe he went to help him with the boat? No, no. Kyle doesn't know shit about boat motors. Get your head out of your ass, Greg.

Greg turned to Lisa to see that she was already looking at him. She had worry in her eyes. *No point in freaking out and upsetting Lisa anymore.* "He must be downstairs waiting for us for Mass then," Greg said, forcing a smile. "Why don't we head down there and meet up with him?"

Lisa's eyes seemed to relax a little—at least, they didn't appear to be on the verge of tears anymore. "Yeah, I think that's a good idea."

Greg walked toward the door. "Great! Get Sage ready, and I'll be just in the hallway."

Chapter Twenty-Three

GREG EMERGED THROUGH THE BACK SCREEN DOOR OF THE house and onto the raised deck. "Save the fancy glass for the front of the house where everyone sees it. Smart," he joked. He held the door open for Lisa and Sage as they followed him out. He was looking at Lisa as she looked off the deck, speechless. Sage ran between them and scampered up to the railing and stuck her head between two wooden pickets to look out onto the island.

"Wow!" Sage said in amazement.

Greg spun around, the screen door slamming behind him, to see what his family was so taken aback by. He approached the guardrail and leaned on it as he peered out. "What in the *Jonestown* is *this*?"

Overnight, someone had constructed a wooden stage on the island's grounds. About twenty feet in length, the stage had tall posts on either side of it that were draped with large white cloths that gave the appearance of boat sails, while a podium with a microphone stood in the middle. Rows of plastic folding chairs filled the front of the stage, interspersed with the residents of Snake Bight, all wearing ankle-length white robes that were cinched at the waist with corded belts.

"Or *Caligula*," Lisa added.

"What's that mean?" Sage asked.

Greg put his hand down on Sage's head and ruffled her hair. "Nothing, Sage. But if anyone offers you Kool-Aid, don't take it."

"But I like Kool-Aid!"

Lisa put her hand over her mouth to stifle her laughter.

"I guess we should head down there," Greg said as he started down the deck stairs.

Lisa held her hand out to Sage. "Give me your hand, honey." Sage grabbed hold of it, and they followed Greg down the steps to the ground level.

Jeez. It looks even bigger up close, Greg thought as he stepped off the bottom stair and onto the grass, getting a better look at the stage.

Sage jumped from the last step, landing with both feet at the same time. She had a look of awe on her face as she admired the sage. "Are we here for a wedding?!"

"No." Lisa laughed. "At least I don't *think* so."

Then a voice came from beside them. "I'm glad you finally made it!"

Greg turned, and Candy was walking over to them, smiling and holding a stack of white cloth in her hands.

Greg thumbed toward Sage. "Someone slept in this morning."

"It's not my fault!" Sage said. Her voice sounded irritated, as if she were tired of defending herself.

"Hey, Candy, have you seen Kyle by chance?" Lisa asked.

With her hands full, Candy nodded her head forward. "He's right over there, helping Abin out."

Greg and Lisa both looked to where Candy was

gesturing and saw Kyle standing at the front of the stage, donning a white robe and handing out pamphlets to the Snake Bight residents as they passed by him.

"Such a splendid boy you have there," Candy said, with admiration in her eyes.

"Sage said he left their room last night and didn't come back. We were concerned," Greg said.

"Don't worry. There's no trouble he can get into here. In fact, quite the opposite. He saw Ethan building our stage last night, and he came down and helped him."

"Really?" Greg asked, shocked. *I've never known Kyle to even look at a tool, let alone use one to build something.*

"Oh, yeah. Abin even tried seeing him back to the room, but he insisted on helping. Great kid, that one is." Candy stared at Greg, almost glaring at him as her face went flat. It seemed as if she was really trying to drive her point home.

Yeah. You said that. I got it. Greg felt awkward that this couple seemed to be speaking so highly of his son so often —in fact—it began to bother him.

Suddenly, Betty's shrill voice sounded off in the distance as she and Norm walked up. "You weren't lying when you said the whole town comes, huh?"

Candy's smile returned. "No, ma'am. I never lie. Everyone looks forward to it!"

The Hillards approached the group, and Norm stood next to Greg.

"Norm," Greg said.

Norm looked at him and only nodded.

Candy held out the white robes in her arms. "Now that all of our special guests are here, why don't you put these on?"

Greg shook his head. "No, thanks."

"Pass," Norm added.

From seemingly out of nowhere, Abin swiftly slid in between Greg and Norm. "Now, I can't have y'all attendin' the service not wearin' the proper attire!" He grabbed a robe from the top of the pile and held it out to Greg. Greg once again shook his head. Abin pushed the robe into Greg's chest. "Please...I *insist*."

"No...*I* insist..." Greg forcefully pushed the robe back into Abin's chest. "...I'm not wearing your *fucking dress*."

Steam practically shot out from Abin's ears as his cheeks turned deep red and his jaw clenched—as much as he tried to mask it. Seemingly in the blink of an eye, he wiped the anger from his face and forced a smile. "Well, then...see y'all at the service." With that, Abin left toward the stage, saying nothing more.

Lisa looked at Candy. Greg could tell he'd embarrassed her. "I'm sorry," Lisa breathed.

Candy watched Abin's back as he walked away. "Don't worry about it," she said flatly. "Abin is a sucker for tradition." She held the robes out to Lisa. "Service will be starting soon." Lisa took the stack from her, and then Candy left, following behind Abin.

Lisa took a robe from the top of the stack and handed it to Sage. "Here, Sage. Put this on over your clothes."

Sage held the robe up, examining it. "I don't like this dress."

"Mr. Abin and Miss Candy were nice enough to bring them to us. Let's be polite guests and put them on with no fuss, okay? We only have to wear them for...whatever *this* is."

Sage continued to look sideways at the robe. "Okay, I guess."

"Thank you, honey."

Lisa glanced over at Greg. "No," he said matter-of-factly. She turned away from him dismissively and then toward Betty.

"You guys grab us some seats," Greg said with a determined look on his face. "I'm going to talk to Kyle."

———

Greg waded through the rows of folding chairs, the residents of Snake Bight greeted him, but he focused only on one person. "Kyle!" he shouted, trying to get his son's attention. He was either too far away to hear his dad or was blissfully ignoring him—Greg thought either option was viable.

Just as Greg was about to reach him, an eye with a scar over it appeared right in his line of sight.

Brent.

"Greg! It's Greg, right?!" Brent said excitedly.

Greg moved his head around, trying to get a good look at his son, but Brent was moving right along with him, blocking his view.

"It's great you stayed for Mass! I thought you and your family would have been *out* of here by now." When he said this, Greg noticed his eyes were darting around frantically —as if he were trying to tell him something.

"I didn't really have a choice."

Brent continued, clearly ignoring Greg. "You're going to *love* it. Abin has this way of speaking where…even on an island full of people, he makes you feel you're the only one there. He makes you feel…well, I don't know how to explain it."

Greg stopped bobbing his head around and grabbed Brent by the shoulders, looking him in the eyes. "Listen, Brent. That's great, but I'm in the middle of something."

Brent straightened up, and his eyebrows furrowed. "Oh. It's like that?"

"I don't mean anything by it. It's good to see you, but I need to talk to my..." Greg stepped around Brent to see that Kyle was no longer handing out pamphlets at the front of the stage. "...son."

"Wow! I still can't believe you guys stayed. I *really* thought you would've gone back to town after that gator almost capsized Abin's boat," Brent said, his eyes still wild.

How did he know...whatever. Greg figured word gets around in a small town and continued toward the stage. "Excuse me," he said dismissively as he wormed around Brent.

It was impossible to see through the sea of people making their way to their seats, but Greg continued frantically looking around for his son when, suddenly, he arrived at the front of the stage.

Lisa's voice appeared behind him. "Greg!"

He spun around and was pleasantly surprised: his family, including Kyle, sat in chairs in the front row. Norm and Betty sat next to them. His joy quickly diminished when he saw everyone except Norm wore Abin's white robes. *Oh, God. They look like they're in a cult,* he thought.

"What are you doing wearing those?" he asked. Before they could even think about answering, he realized the robes were the least of his worries and he turned to Kyle. "Where the *hell* have you *been*?"

Kyle stared at him blankly.

"Answer me! You left your sister alone in the middle of the night in a *stranger's* home! What could've been so important?"

"She was safe. Abin isn't a stranger."

Greg's voice was getting louder. "That isn't what I asked!"

"Greg…" Lisa said quietly, trying to get his attention.

He ignored her and bent down, getting closer to Kyle's face. "So? Tell me! Where *were* you?"

"Greg!" Lisa spat.

He snapped his head over to her. "What?!"

Her eyes were wide, and her lips barely parted when she spoke, like a parent reprimanding their child. "Maybe this isn't the time." Her fiery eyes shifted from side to side.

Greg stood up straight and glanced around at his surroundings. The residents of Snake Bight were all seated, their eyes on him. A burning sensation of embarrassment filled his chest as he felt the color disappear from his face.

"Just *sit*. We can deal with this later," Lisa said under her breath.

Kyle blankly eyed Greg the entire time as he swallowed his pride and occupied the empty seat next to his wife. He thought something seemed off about his son—his gaze caused a sharp tingle at the nape of his neck. Greg looked away, but could still feel Kyle staring at him. His skeleton felt like it wanted to crawl out of his body. *Why do I feel this way? What, am I scared of my son?* After a moment, he turned his gaze to Kyle and mouthed, "What?"

Kyle coldly moved his eyes back to the stage and calmly said, "The service should start soon."

Chapter Twenty-Four

Greg had hoped that his wife would've picked a spot other than the front fucking row, but it was too late now. He craned his neck back to look at the townsfolk behind him. It was quite a sight to behold. Thirty-ish people, all wearing long white robes with mud covering their bare feet, all doing the same thing—staring ahead at the stage, wearing soft smiles with a hopeful gleam in their eyes. Nobody was moving; nobody was talking.

Lisa leaned over and whispered in Greg's ear. "There sure are a *lot* of people here."

Greg continued observing the crowd. "Look at them; how they're just...*staring*. It's like they're in a *trance* or something."

His eyes narrowed as he honed in on Brent in the crowd, just a few rows back. His daughter, Ashley, sat next to him; Valentine next to her. Now that he'd seen them both at the same time, his theory of them being the same girl was out the window, but they definitely looked like twins.

What the hell is all this? he wondered.

Suddenly, the crowd erupted into applause, causing Greg to jump in his seat. He twisted back around to look toward the stage. He glanced over at Kyle, who was also clapping. He watched on as Kyle took to his feet, the rest of the crowd joining him as their applause grew louder.

Then, finally, the reason behind their ovation made itself clear as Abin walked out onto the stage from behind one of the white drapes hanging from a side post. He smiled ear-to-ear as he waved to his adoring crowd. *Odd,* Greg thought, examining Abin's dress. He wasn't wearing the ceremonial robes like the rest of the residents—he still wore his usual floral print button-down, white chino pants, and straw fedora. *I guess he didn't need to dress for the occasion.*

Abin sauntered up behind the podium in the middle of the stage as the crowd continued their uproarious applause. Feedback hissed as he tapped his forefinger on the microphone perched on a stand on the podium. He put a fist up to his mouth and cleared his throat before bending into the microphone. "Alright, alright. Settle down, y'all," he said, smiling like a pig in shit. He loved every minute of the adoration and had no problem showing it.

"I'd like to start today's service as I normally do, by thankin' y'all fer comin'. Thank y'all." He extended an arm out toward the front row. "We got some *special guests* here this evenin'. Some of y'all may've seen 'em when they showed up in our little town, but just in case ya haven't, I'd like to formally introduce y'all to the Boyes family an' the Hillard family!"

The surrounding crowd began clapping again, and Greg awkwardly raised his hand in a half-wave.

"Come on now!" Abin said, excited, as he took the microphone from its stand. "Give 'em a *real* Snake Bight welcome!" And the applause grew louder.

God, make it stop.

"That's more like it," Abin said, the applause dwindling underneath his voice. He closed his eyes, bringing the microphone close to his lips. "Let's get started." He began pacing back and forth along the front of the stage, his eyes closed. "I'd like y'all to take a little time at the beginnin' of this service to thank our great *creator*. Thank 'em fer givin' y'all the good fortune of livin' in this little community we built together."

Abin stopped pacing and snapped his body toward the crowd and pointed out at them, his voice raised as if he were talking down to children. "Y'all heard me right, I said '*we*.' Reason I say that is, I realized with our guests here, that y'all give me too much credit. 'Abin built the town. Abin did this. Abin did that.' I say that's a bunch of *bull sugar*." His posture relaxed, and his voice lowered to normal volume. "Without each an' every one of y'all, there would be no community where we *love* an' *care* 'bout each other so much. There'd be no Snake Bight."

Abin turned away from the crowd and moved back behind the podium before facing them again. "So, next time yer thinkin' 'bout thankin' me…remember to thank yerself, too." A switch flipped, and his face turned grim. "I'm sure y'all have been keepin' up with what's been happenin' in the world… So I come bearin' good news, as it seems *the prophecy* is comin' to fruition right before our very eyes. Sooner than we thought! An' those of y'all that take the time fer the creator…take the time to speak with 'em every day, yer salvation will soon be upon us."

Greg glanced over at Norm, who had already been staring at him, and they shared an uncomfortable look. It had been the most emotion he'd seen Norm show since he'd met him. Was he looking to Greg for some sort of comfort?

Lisa whispered into Greg's ear, "Prophecy?"

"I-I don't know…but I don't like the way it sounds," Greg said, still locking eyes with Norm.

Abin placed the microphone back onto its stand and leaned on the podium. "That's right. Increasin' wars, leaders that only seem interested in perpetuatin' 'em…and how do the citizens of the United States handle it? By only fightin' with each other. Political parties, races, religions… fightin' like school children because *they're* the one that's right and everyone else is wrong. Now, let me ask ya this… do y'all think that's a coincidence?" He stared into the crowd, his mouth closed as though he were actually waiting for an answer.

Greg once again looked around, observing the townspeople surrounding him. He couldn't believe they were still gazing up at the stage, fully engaged in whatever bullshit Abin was spewing.

Abin's voice was calm as he continued. "The United States of America. Folks once called 'em the world's peacekeepers. Maybe that was true once…maybe. But nowadays, it would seem they spend their time creatin' these *proxy wars*. Only problem is, these other countries are catchin' on, an' they've had enough! It's only a matter of time 'fore the *pigs* in Washington, D.C. light the final fuse to ignite the third world war…a matter of time 'til the United States an' these other countries start chuckin' nuclear bombs at each other, *destroyin'* mankind as we know it!"

Greg heard a gasp next to him and looked past his wife and daughter to see Kyle engrossed in Abin's words; his eyes open wide and covering his mouth with one hand. *Don't tell me he's actually listening to this shit,* Greg thought.

Greg snapped back to the speech when Abin's words turned from somber to menacing. "Who's gon' be there when that happens, huh? Who's gon' be there to pick up the pieces?"

The voice of a female resident rang out from the back of the crowd. "Us!"

Greg turned and saw Murial standing up in the middle of the seated crowd, one fist raised in the air, before taking her seat again.

"That's right! *Us*, that's who!" Abin said, nodding aggressively. "*We* will be there to drag the government *scum* from the safety of their shelters! *We* will be the ones to *cut* their *throats* an' watch 'em *bleed out* all over the land they *claim* to love an' protect!"

The crowd erupted in applause and cheers.

Abin again took the microphone off its stand. "Settle, settle." He approached the edge of the stage. "I'm afraid our uprising may happen sooner than we previously planned. Our numbers ain't *quite* where I'd like 'em to be, but it is what it is." He then squatted down on the edge of the stage, right in front of Norm.

Greg couldn't be certain, but it appeared as though Abin was looking Norm directly in the eyes; like he was trying to burn a hole in him as he continued. "I have a feelin' the government is onto our community an' may send spies to gather intelligence on us…or maybe even to *kill* us."

Greg sat stunned, trying to comprehend what was happening around him. Since arriving in Snake Bight, a lot of weird things had happened, but nothing beyond reasonable explanation. But *this*—this was the first time he'd felt isolated—like there was something much bigger happening.

At least I have my family, he thought.

He focused his eyes on Kyle, who was still entranced—and now seemed to be on the verge of smiling.

...For now.

Chapter Twenty-Five

Lisa's voice was flat and quiet. "I want to leave." Greg noticed she was looking straight ahead, her eyes glassy. "This isn't church."

"No. No, it's not," Greg said. "It's some sort of…anti-government *rally*."

"Was he talking to Norm? Calling him a spy?" Lisa's frantic voice didn't match her stoic face.

"I don't know, but it sure *looked* like it." Turning his head slightly, Greg scanned the crowd behind him; they still seemed focused on the stage.

He faced back forward, and Abin had gotten up from the edge of the stage and had his back turned as he walked back to the podium. He was still speaking, but Greg couldn't focus on his words. They sounded far away… muffled. He leaned over, looking past his family, and hissed, "Norm…Norm!"

The old man was seemingly stuck staring at the stage where Abin once squatted. He had a look on his face that Greg hadn't thought possible—fear.

Betty nudged Norm, knocking him out of his trance.

He looked over at her, and she slyly pointed in Greg's direction.

The chords in Greg's neck popped as he tried to keep from shouting. "We need to get *out* of here!" Norm just stared at him, his expression nearly frozen in shock. "Snap the fuck out of it! We have to go *now*!" Norm blinked a few times in quick succession, then nodded his head in agreement.

Greg, Lisa, Sage, and the Hillards all rose from their chairs—everyone except Kyle—staying hunched over to not cause a distraction. Using his hands, Greg ushered the group forward.

Lisa turned back to her husband, her eyes full of worry. "What about Kyle?"

"I'll take care of him. Just go!"

The group kept moving until they were out in the center aisle and ducked out toward the back of the crowd. *Four down, one to go.*

Kyle stared straight ahead as Greg kneeled next to him. "Let's go; we're leaving." Kyle didn't even blink. "Kyle… *come on.*"

"I'm not leaving."

"What?"

Kyle twitched his head to face his dad. "The service isn't over. It would be *rude* to leave." His voice was calm, almost robotic.

"Son, *please*. Something isn't right here."

Kyle's eyes met Greg's for only a moment before they moved back forward.

"*Fine*," Greg said. "When you're done here, we'll be at the house."

Greg glanced back at the stage, and Abin still had his back turned. He was talking with someone on the side of the stage. *It's now or never. It'll be easier to grab Kyle and knock some sense into him when we have our shit together and we have a way out of here.*

Greg mimicked the actions of his group and ducked into the center aisle of the crowd, making his way toward the back. He tried to keep his head down when he noticed Ashley sitting at the end of a row right in front of him. As he got closer to passing her by, he saw Valentine cradling her wrapped-up doll. He thought they looked like the *Grady Sisters,* the way they looked like a mirror image of each other and eyed him down, unblinking. He held up a finger to his lips as he snuck by them—then Valentine blinked. A thin set of translucent eyelids met in the middle of her eyes a split second before the normal set.

Greg wasn't positive about what he'd just seen. While his body continued to move forward, his face was stuck on the little girl. Not paying attention to where he was going, he walked right into a man seated a couple of rows behind the girls, knocking him over in his chair.

"What are you doing?!" the man asked.

"Shit! Sorry!" Greg helped the man to his feet.

"Shouldn't you be in your seat? The service isn't over."

Greg raised an eyebrow and thought, *You're welcome?*

Suddenly, Greg got a feeling that he was being watched. He slowly craned his neck and saw that everyone in the crowd was now looking right at him. *So much for sneaking.* Greg turned and ran, not waiting to see what the townspeople had planned for him.

Greg made it back to Abin's house, where Lisa, Sage, Norm, and Betty were standing outside at the base of the deck. "What are you doing out here?" he asked. "Were you able to find a phone? Get ahold of anybody? Grab our stuff?"

"No! Someone locked all the doors up there!" Lisa said frantically.

A familiar Southern voice then wormed its way into Greg's ear as he felt his stomach move up to his throat. "Hey there!"

Greg closed his eyes and took a deep breath before turning around to face Abin. The man stood there smiling, his hands in his pants pockets, looking as harmless as a fly. "Where y'all goin'? The service ain't over yet."

Greg glanced at Norm next to him, then back at Abin. "No offense, Abin. I don't think this service is for us. Like I said earlier, we're not really church people."

For a moment, Abin stood still, his gaze fixed without moving or blinking, as if time had stopped. "Why are ya *really* leavin'?" The corners of his mouth slowly lowered as his face went flat, and he lifted a single finger to point at Norm. "Did I make the government *rat* uncomfortable?"

Norm, showing his true colors, stepped up toward Abin. "Now, you listen here—"

Before he could get too close, Greg stepped in front of Norm, placing his hands on his chest. "I'll take care of this, Norm," he breathed. Greg spun back around to face Abin. "Listen, Abin. I appreciate you letting us stay—" He stopped when he noticed Abin was looking through him.

Then he heard Lisa shriek from behind him. "Greg!"

He turned back around, and there was Ethan—all almost-seven-feet of him—standing behind Norm.

Greg pointed over Norm's shoulder and shouted, "Shit!"

As Norm turned around, Ethan brought his large wooden mallet across the older man's face; the force sent him reeling to the grass. Greg watched, frozen, as Norm's body hit the ground with a *thud*. His limbs straightened out, his jaw clenched tight, and he began shaking uncontrollably as a single streak of blood dripped from his ear and down his cheek.

Betty's face went pale at the sight of her husband. Her eyes fluttered, and she let out a groan as she also fell to the earth.

Greg snapped out of it, and his instincts kicked in as he charged toward the massive man. Just before Greg reached him, Ethan reared the mallet back—and that was the last thing Greg had seen before his vision went black.

He couldn't explain it, but he still *felt* his body hit the ground. His thoughts swirled around, but the voice in his head had slurred speech. *I'm still alive.* He could hear Lisa's screams of terror, although they sounded far away. And then, just like his vision, her screams faded away to nothing.

Chapter Twenty-Six

FUCK. MY HEAD. GREG'S VISION WAS A SLATE OF BLACK—A void. *I…can't move. Am I in my body? Am I dead?* Slowly, the sound of someone's voice came into his head. The voice began muffled, but became clearer rather quickly. Soon enough, he made out the voice to be Abin Moses— although he still couldn't make out what he was saying. *Great. Either I'm still alive…or I'm in Hell.*

One by one, the surrounding sounds began coming to him. Abin…the sound of the cicadas coming from the nearby trees…the low chatter of the surrounding towns-people…then someone weeping softly.

Lisa, he thought.

He didn't know if it was only time bringing him back to consciousness or if the sound of his wife's cries gave him some sort of extra strength—like a mom lifting a car off a baby—but Greg began to feel the different parts of his body come back to life. He could wiggle his fingers and toes, but couldn't move his arms and legs…they felt *bound.* Horizontal slits appeared before him as he struggled to separate his eyelids. It was still black, but a different kind of black. *Nighttime.*

He finally forced his eyes open and, when his vision unblurred, he was looking down at his legs. A faint wet spot stained the front of his pants. *Jesus. Did I piss myself?* Moving his eyes to his torso, he saw that he'd been tied to a plastic folding chair with nylon rope.

His head felt like it was the size of a boulder as he lifted it up and turned toward the source of the cries. Lisa was looking down, her face barely illuminated by a nearby torch. Someone had also tied her to her chair.

Greg struggled to speak through his parched throat. "L-Lisa…"

Lisa sniffled, sucking up the snot running from her nostrils as she turned her head to face her husband, and her eyes opened up wide. She had a gash above her eyebrow, dripping blood into her eye. "Greg…you're alive."

"What h-happened?"

"These people are fucking *crazy*! That thing hit you with a hammer. I tried to attack it, but it just swatted me away like I was *nothing*."

"It? Ethan? That big man?"

Lisa's face turned grim. "I saw its face… That's *no man.*"

"Wha—that makes no sense. Where are Kyle and Sage? Are they safe?"

Lisa leaned back to show Sage seated next to her, also tied to her chair. "Sage is right here. She's fine. Nobody hurt her."

"And Kyle?"

Lisa stared with her mouth open, as if she were trying to find the words to say. After a moment, she finally muttered, "I don't *know*." The volume of her voice began to rise. "T-They brought us back here and tied us to these chairs a-and Kyle was gone. He was *gone!*"

"Shhh, shh! Okay, keep your voice down!" Greg hissed. "What about Betty? Norm? Are they…okay?" He feared the worst for the older couple, figuring at least Norm hadn't made it. The old man looked tough, but he really got *walloped* with that hammer. Greg at least had the advantage of *seeing* his blow coming.

"Betty is still out cold."

"And Norm?"

Lisa moved her eyes to the side of her head, using them to point toward the stage. Greg followed her eyes and, up on the stage, Norm sat tied to a chair where the podium once stood. A spotlight at the top of the stage shone down on him. His head was hanging down. Greg started to ask, "Is he—"

"I don't know," Lisa quickly interjected, not letting Greg finish his question. He figured she didn't want to put it into the universe that Norm might be *dead*.

Feedback hissed from the speakers on the stage; the terrible sound intensified Greg's already pounding headache.

Once the popping and hissing settled, Abin's smooth Southern accent came through the speakers. "Welcome back, y'all. Sorry we had to take a quick *unexpected* recess." He stood a couple of feet behind Norm, barely illuminated by the outermost part of the spotlight, with one arm behind his back. He took a few steps forward until he was next to Norm and pulled his arm from behind his back. He looked down at a small piece of paper in his hand that appeared to be laminated. "Do y'all know what this is?" he asked as he held it up to the crowd.

They remained silent, waiting on his every word like highly trained dogs waiting for a treat.

Moving the paper in front of his face, he read from it. "United States Air Force. Master Sergeant. Heh. Sounds pretty important, doesn't it?" He turned the paper back to the crowd again. "What this is…is *proof*! Proof of what I was *just* tellin' y'all earlier! The government knows what we got down here, an' they're gon' send their agents to try an' *stop* us!"

Greg couldn't take it anymore. "That's bullshit!" He was so parched, so dehydrated, his vocal cords felt like they were going to tear with each word. "He's…just an *old man* trying to take his wife on vacation! He wants nothing to do with you, you…*psychopaths*!"

Abin chuckled. "Psychopaths, eh?" He turned his full attention to Greg in the front row. "I'm glad ya woke up to join us, Greg! I didn't want ya to miss *this*." Abin placed the military ID in his back pocket and moved to the side of the stage, leaving Norm alone in the spotlight. "Tell me… how well do ya *really* know this man ya met what, two days ago?"

Greg stayed silent.

"Cat got yer tongue all the sudden?" Abin asked as he walked back into the light, carrying a plastic five-gallon pail.

"Daddy, what's Mr. Abin doing?" Sage asked. Greg could barely hear her tiny voice through the sound of his own heartbeat.

Luckily, Lisa was there to answer for him. "He and Mr. Norm are just playing a game, sweetie."

"Can I play?"

"No, no. It's a game for grown-ups. Why don't you close your eyes and hum one of your songs? I'll let you know when we're done playing."

"Okay," Sage said with no resistance as she did as her mom had instructed her.

Abin held the plastic pail with both hands as he swung it toward Norm, splashing its contents all over him. Greg felt relieved to see that the liquid was clear. *Just water…hopefully,* he thought.

Norm's head bobbed up and down as he coughed and groaned. Abin approached him and gave his cheek a few tiny slaps. Norm slowly picked his head up as his eyelids fluttered. He turned to look at Abin, and his eyes shot open wide. His shoulders moved back and forth as he attempted to get out of his restraints. Greg figured he hadn't woken up enough to realize that he'd been tied down yet.

"W-what the *hell* is this?! What's going on here?!" Norm shouted, his voice sounding like he had a mouthful of marbles.

"Sleepin' beauty!" Abin said, dropping the pail to the stage floor.

Norm continued to fight the rope that held him down. "The hell am I tied up for?! That giant…*freak* son of yours hit me with a goddamn *hammer!*"

Abin knelt next to him. "He only did what he had to do fer the *safety* of the community."

"*Safety*?! I was just minding my own damn business! Now, untie me!"

"I know who you are!" Abin pulled the military ID back out of his pocket and held it up to Norm's face.

"So what?! I was in the Air Force! I'm *retired!*"

"Yer full of it! I know they sent ya here to stop us…to kill us!" Abin shoved the ID card into Norm's mouth, and he spit it back out immediately.

Norm began to laugh—probably out of nervousness, Greg thought. "I have no *idea* what you're talking about, son."

"Really?" Abin stood back up and reached behind his back. "Then do ya mind explainin' *this?*" He then pulled a snub-nosed revolver out from his back waistband and held it in the air.

Norm quickly stopped laughing. "I-I don't know what that is… I-It's not mine! It's not *mine!*"

Abin turned to the crowd, holding the revolver in the air. "I saw him with *this* in his pocket! He left the service an' when I went to tend to him, to see if I could help him with anythin', he *reached* fer it!" He lowered the firearm and glared at it in his hand. "He knew someone had discovered him. Revealed him as a spy." Abin closed his eyes and tilted his head back. "But luckily, by the grace of our creator, my son Ethan was there to subdue this man before he could hurt me or any of y'all."

"Oh, that's a load of horseshit, and you *know* it!" Norm's face was beet red and spit flew from his mouth like a rabid dog. "Now let me the *fuck* out of this chair!"

Abin glared at Greg as if he were the only other person on the island. "Ya still think he's just some sweet old man on vacation, Greg?"

Someone next to Greg let out a groan, then Lisa said, "Betty…"

Greg looked over to see Betty waking up. She shook her head, then realized someone had tied her to her chair. "What's going on?" Her breath began to quicken into short bursts.

Lisa spoke to her in a calming voice. "Betty…Betty, listen to me. We've had a bit of a misunderstanding, but we're getting it all sorted out now. What I need you to do is breathe slowly. Focus on your breath going in…and out."

"W-where's Norm?" Betty frantically moved her eyes around—until they landed on her husband. She let out an ear-piercing shriek at the sight of him tied to a chair and bleeding from his head.

Abin ignored her and continued addressing Greg,

shouting over Betty's cries. "Well?! Do ya see now?! Do ya see him fer the government *pig* he really is?!"

Greg only stared at Abin, unsure of what to do. What *could* he do? He'd been tightly bound to a chair, surrounded by apparent maniacs whose leader had no intention of listening to reason.

Abin's voice lowered once more. "Since yer not gon' answer that, maybe ya can answer *this*. It's quite simple." He took a step back from Norm. "Do ya know what we do to dirty little pigs? Huh?"

Greg continued to glare up at him. He felt his jaw clench. "Abin…"

"We send 'em to *slaughter*." Abin raised the revolver, aimed it at Norm's head, and pulled the trigger.

Bang!

Blood and brain matter spewed from Norm's temple and sprayed all over the white drape hanging next to him as his head slumped over against his shoulder.

Chapter Twenty-Seven

KYLE TRAVELLED DOWN A DIM HALLWAY, LED BY ABIN'S SON, Ethan, still holding the blood-drenched mallet. The man's frame was so wide and muscular, his shoulders almost touched the walls on either side of him. "Where are we going?" Kyle asked.

Ethan remained silent.

They soon approached a wooden door at the end of the hall. Deep scratches covered the door, making it look like a lion or bear had attacked it. Kyle felt his stomach twist into knots. He wasn't sure why he'd been ushered away from the service. Was Ethan taking him back to his parents? Was he going to hurt him? The latter seemed unlikely since Kyle had done nothing wrong. Shit, he even helped build the stage for Mass—but something about the massive, quiet man made him uncomfortable. Kyle wanted only to stay and listen to what else Abin had to say. Ethan had to have known that.

Ethan opened the door, and inside was only darkness. He turned to the side and held out his arm, gesturing for Kyle to enter.

"M-me?" Kyle asked, and Ethan nodded. Kyle took a few steps forward, and then halted. "Why don't you go first? I'll be right behind you."

Ethan lunged at Kyle and grabbed him by the back of his neck, squeezing tightly. "Ow, ow! That hurts!" He began dragging the boy toward the open door. Kyle fought back, thrashing his limbs around. "Hey! Let me go! Let me gooo!"

The big man thrust him forward, into the black abyss, and Kyle shouted, "What the fuck, man?!"

Ethan stomped ahead, following Kyle into the room, and slammed the door shut behind them.

Inside the room was not only dark but also humid. Kyle began sweating immediately, and every movement he made felt as if it were in slow motion because of the thick air. "What are we doing in here? Where are we?"

There was no response from Ethan—only the sound of his heavy breathing. Then, the *click* of a light switch flicking as the room illuminated in a bright red. Kyle shielded his eyes from the sudden burst of light. When his eyes adjusted, he saw the source of illumination. Large cone-shaped lamp heads were affixed to the corners of the walls. The insides appeared mirrored, and large red bulbs sitting in their centers. Turning on the lights made the room even hotter. "What are these? Like heating lamps?" Kyle asked, wiping the sweat from his brow.

Ethan, standing in the middle of the room, threw his head back and dropped his mallet to the floor, as if he were basking in the red light. Kyle scanned the room, noting the small amount of furniture. A dirty mattress on the floor, a desk with a pair of chairs, and a large wooden crate against a wall. Kyle inched around the room, keeping one eye on the large man. "Is this your room? Cozy." Ethan brought his head back upright and moved over to the desk.

He pulled out one chair and nodded down at it, grunting. "You want me to sit?" Kyle asked, taking a cautious step forward. Ethan grunted again.

Kyle approached the chair and sat down. As soon as his ass hit the wood, he almost got whiplash as Ethan forcibly turned the chair around and pushed Kyle up to the desk. "Whoa, easy!" Kyle said.

Ethan turned away and walked over to the wooden chest. He opened the lid and reached inside, pulling out a burlap sack. Kyle's brow lowered. "I'm not really sure what we're doin here, but—"

Ethan returned to the desk and turned the sack over, spilling its contents onto the desk—action figures. "Toys?" Kyle asked. Ethan sat in the chair next to him and grabbed two figures. Kyle watched on as the man began clashing the figures together as if they were fighting. After a moment, he stopped and looked over at Kyle. He pointed at the pile of action figures and grunted. "You want me to play?" Kyle slowly reached for the pile and grabbed a couple of figures. He began softly banging them together, pretending to play, and Ethan went back to his own toys.

Kyle stopped playing and looked over at the big man, who barely fit in his chair. "So, why do you wear that mask?" Ethan grunted loudly and angrily looked at the toys in Kyle's hands. "Right, sorry." Kyle started hitting the figures together again. "So? The mask? Your dad said it's allergies, but we're inside. Doesn't it get *hot* wearing it all the time?"

Ethan stopped colliding his figures together and placed them on the desk. He turned to Kyle and sighed. He moved his hand to the top of his gaiter, where it covered his nose. He grabbed hold of it and began slowly peeling it down when a gunshot rang out from outside. He quickly pulled the gaiter all the way back up and craned his neck toward the door. The chair screeched against the floor as Ethan pushed it back and stood up. He stomped over to the door, picking his mallet up off the floor on his way. He opened the door, and Kyle said, "Wait! Where are you going? What *was* that?" Ethan looked back at him for a moment, then turned out of the door, slamming it behind him.

Chapter Twenty-Eight

GREG SAT LOOKING AT THE STAGE, UNABLE TO EVEN THINK as he watched the blood pour from Norm's head to the wooden floor at his feet. Betty opened her mouth to scream again, but only vomited.

Lisa leaned over as far as she could toward Sage in an attempt to keep her from opening her eyes and seeing the violence. Greg could hear her talking to their daughter, although her words were too quiet to hear. "Keep your eyes shut, sweetie."

The surrounding crowd was going wild with cheers and applause. Greg's eyes moved over to the blood-drenched drape hanging off the side of the stage; pieces of Norm's skull and brain fell to the floor, making an awful slopping sound. Abin walked directly into his line of sight as he moved along the front edge of the stage with his arms held high in the air, celebrating victory and pumping up the crowd even more. Greg glanced back at the civilians. Saul, Murial—even little Valentine—all screamed their heads off like blood-thirsty maniacs. *These people are fucking crazy*, he thought.

"Do ya see *now*, Greg?" Abin asked, bringing Greg's attention off the crowd and back to the stage. Abin was standing back in the middle of it, his arms crossed, wearing a shit-eating grin.

Greg swallowed the bit of saliva left in his mouth to lubricate his throat. "See *what*? All you did was murder a man in cold blood!"

Abin dropped down to sit on the stage, his legs dangling off the edge. "See that I was tellin' the truth…'bout the government tryin' to take us down…'bout sendin' Norm to do their dirty work."

"You didn't prove *anything*! You spewed a whole lot of bullshit and shot him!"

Abin held the snub-nosed revolver out. "What's this if not proof? They sent him to assassinate me."

Uncharacteristically, Betty shouted out, "That's not my Norman's! He would never take his gun with him anywhere!"

"Exactly," Greg said. "That gun could have been yours for all I know."

"Well, that just hurts," Abin said, holding his free hand up to his heart. He made his way back onto his feet. "I'd be lyin' if I said I wasn't disappointed, Greg. Y'know, Snake Bight doesn't have any sort of *police* force. I was kinda hopin' you'd be it."

"What, you're bummed I'm not so easily *brainwashed* like all these sickos?"

"Brainwashed?!" Abin appeared legitimately offended. "They're all here of their own free will; nobody brainwashed 'em. Any of 'em could leave at any time, but they believe in the *message*. They know they're the superior organisms…an' y'all will too in due time…just like *Kyle*."

"You son of a bitch! If you hurt my son—"

Abin's calm voice quickly went away. "Don't pretend

like ya care fer that boy now! I seen the way ya talk to him! He made his choice, just as all the people behind ya did!"

"What choice? What are you talking about?"

Abin picked his head up high, looking over the front row. "Ah, Ethan, my boy! I assume ya heard the ruckus. We took care of that dirty *spy*, but unfortunately, Mr. Boyes here seems to be hesitant in believin' in the *cause*. Why don't ya take him an' the rest of his group away until they come to their senses?" He held his arm out toward Norm's slumped over corpse. "The gators need to *feed*."

Greg looked back, and Ethan was lumbering through the crowd, toward him and his family. Behind the large man, he noticed Kyle standing near the back row. Greg shouted, "Kyle!" *Thank God he's okay.* "Kyle, what are you doing back there?" Greg made brief eye contact with his son before Kyle looked away.

Ethan approached Greg from behind. "Don't touch me!" Greg shouted as the large man grabbed the back of his chair. "Don't touch me, you *bastard!*" Ethan pushed down on the back of the chair, tilting Greg backward, and then began dragging the chair behind him, toward the back of the crowd. Greg frantically moved his head from side to side. "Stop! Let me go! Stop!"

Ethan dragged Greg past the last row of chairs, and right by Kyle. "Kyle! What's going on? Tell him to stop!" Kyle looked ahead like he didn't hear his dad's cries for help. His eyes appeared glassy—Greg knew he wasn't completely ignoring him. *Why is he doing this? This isn't him,* Greg thought. "Kyle, *please*! Tell them to stop…whatever *this* is!"

Abin's voice came over the speaker once more. "Kyle! Nice of ya to join us. Could ya do me a favor? Grab yer sister there an' follow Ethan. Make it a little easier for 'im. One less trip an' all."

"What?! No!" Greg shouted as Ethan began dragging him away again. "Kyle! Don't let them touch Sage!" Ethan continued to drag him until they made it to the back door of Abin's home. The large man opened the door and pulled Greg in with him. Greg shouted one last time, "Don't let them touch her!" before Ethan slammed the door closed.

Chapter Twenty-Nine

Greg bounced after each step as Ethan dragged his chair down the stairs leading to Abin's basement. He'd stopped trying to escape his restraints once they entered the house, realizing it was useless—he wasn't going anywhere. *I'd better save my energy. On the off chance he unties me, even for a second, I'm gonna need my strength to attack this big fucker.*

After the last step, Greg felt relieved, knowing his tailbone would finally get a break from slamming into the hard plastic seat. Ethan spun the chair around, revealing the basement to Greg.

Greg scanned the room. *There's got to be something to fight with in here.* Unfortunately for him, the room was barren except for a tool bench against one wall, a heavy-duty-looking metal door, and the support beams scattered about. He observed Ethan as he moved to the tool bench, noticing the large man still held the mallet used to attack him and Norm. *Poor Norm,* he thought, staring at the bloodstain on the mallet's head.

With his back turned, Ethan placed the mallet down and rummaged through something on the bench. Maybe a drawer? A toolbox? Greg couldn't be certain since he couldn't see past the man's wide back. Ethan spun around, holding something metallic in his hands. *Handcuffs.* He plodded over to Greg and held the cuffs up. He pointed at the cuffs, grunted, and then pointed at one of the support beams.

"You want to handcuff me to the beam?"

Ethan grunted.

Greg looked down at the rope tied around his waist. "I'm already tied up."

Ethan tilted his head to the side, seemingly confused.

"You can't handcuff me if I'm already stuck to this chair." Greg spoke loudly, as if that was going to help the man understand any better. *Christ. All brawn, no brains.* He shook his body up and down quickly, looking back and forth between the rope around his waist and Ethan. "You. Have. To. Untie. Me. First."

Ethan's head propped back up straight in what looked like a moment of realization. He walked behind Greg and crouched down. *Now's my chance.* Once he felt the rope loosen enough, Greg lunged forward and made a beeline for the tool bench.

Ethan roared and tossed the folding chair to the side as he gave chase. Greg reached for the bench and grasped the mallet. Without thinking, he spun around, swinging the hammer with all his might, cracking Ethan directly in the side of his face. For the first time since he had arrived in Florida, Greg felt like luck was on his side. Ethan stood there, bent over, his hands on his knees, as his back heaved up and down with each heavy breath. With the monster of a man composing himself, Greg readjusted his grip on the mallet, preparing to strike again at a moment's notice.

The mallet shook in Greg's hand as he aimed it at the

man. "I-I didn't want to do that, but I had no choice. Now…you're going to let me go back to my family."

Greg watched on in horror as the man stood back upright. The blow from the mallet had knocked the gaiter down off his face, revealing a horrific sight. A row of long, sharp pointed teeth lined the top half of his jaw, and he was missing his entire lower jawbone. Out of his exposed throat hole, a wide, pink tongue slithered around, down near his collarbone.

Greg gawked at him, shocked. "What…the…*fuck*."

Ethan hissed from the black hole behind his tongue and charged at Greg, who, in a panic, threw the mallet at the man and made a break for the heavy-duty door. He wrenched at the handle, but the door was locked. Ethan shouldered him through the door, then grabbed hold of his head with his massive hand. He slammed Greg's face straight into the door, and the sound of his nose breaking reverberated off the walls. The massive man then threw Greg to the floor with ease, as if he were a doll, and pounced, laying on top of him; his grotesque tongue slopped against Greg's cheek, covering it in thick saliva.

Greg groaned through the pain of his shattered nose as he winced, looking at his assailant through one open eye. *What is that?* He looked closer at the disgusting throat hole in Ethan's neck and noticed the skin directly around it had a faint green hue and appeared as though it would be rough to the touch. *It looks like…scales.*

Suddenly, he heard a clicking sound and felt something tightly squeeze around his wrist. Ethan rose from the ground, and as he did, one of Greg's arms went with him. He looked down to see Ethan had slapped one end of the handcuffs on him and held the other end in his hand. He dragged Greg by the cuffs across the floor to one of the support beams and sat him up against it. Wrenching Greg's arms behind his back and around the beam, he connected the other cuff to his open wrist.

"What *are* you?!" Greg shouted.

Ethan pulled his gaiter back up over his nose and walked toward the stairs.

Greg's whole body shook as he used all of his strength to scream. "Answer me! What is this?!"

The monstrous man paused at the foot of the stairs. He stood with his back to Greg for a moment before turning around. Greg quickly lost all confidence, cowering as the man stomped toward him. "Shit, shit, shit, shit!"

Ethan stopped short of Greg and bent down to pick up his mallet. He then turned and went up the stairs, exiting the basement. Greg's muscles relaxed, thinking he was safe—for now.

After a few minutes had passed, his eyelids began getting heavy. He figured the adrenaline rush had zapped any energy he had left. Soon, it became too hard to resist, and his eyes shut. "Lisa…Sage…" he mumbled, trailing off as he fell asleep.

Greg felt his eyelids twitch. *Ugh. Please tell me that was a dream.* The metallic taste that filled his mouth as the blood from his broken nose dripped down the back of his throat told him it wasn't.

A muffled voice entered his ear. At first, he couldn't make it out, but as it repeated, it became more and more clear. "Greg…Greg?"

He forced his eyes open, and his vision was blurry. Three misshapen blobs sat before him.

"Greg? What happened?" said the voice Greg now recognized as Lisa's.

His vision unblurred, the amorphous figures in front of him shaped into Lisa, Sage, and Betty—all handcuffed to support beams—just as he'd been.

He looked them all up and down, eyeing them for any cuts or bruises—or, God help him—anything worse. *Thank goodness nobody hurt them,* he thought.

Lisa continued, "Greg, your face is all busted."

"I saw him," Greg said.

"Who?"

"Ethan. The son...I *saw* him." Greg's eyes narrowed, his voice calm. He wasn't sure why he was speaking so softly. Was he unbothered by everything and giving up, or were his cop instincts making him lock in? Nothing made sense. "I saw what you meant back there...at that rally. He...*it* did this to me. Bashed my fucking face against that door over there." He noticed Lisa was the only one who seemed aware of what was happening. Sage looked around, innocently examining the basement while Betty kept her head down, only eyeing her crossed legs. "What about you? Are you all okay?"

Lisa turned her gaze to Sage. "We're okay. They were gentle."

"Betty? Betty, look at me," Greg said, trying to get her attention.

"She hasn't looked up from the ground since you were taken away."

"And Kyle?"

Lisa looked back at Greg, and tears began to fill her eyes. "He walked Sage down here. I-I tried to talk to him, and he wouldn't even *look* at me."

Greg's eyes shot over to the stairs as the basement door opening echoed throughout the cellar-like room—then—the sound of tiny footsteps. He continued eyeing the stairwell as he saw Valentine skip down the steps, looking as if she didn't have a care in the world, holding her wrapped-up doll. "Valentine," he said. "Valentine! Over here!"

The little girl jumped down the last step, not even looking in his direction as she walked over to Sage.

Greg pleaded, "Valentine, help us!"

She continued to ignore him as she sat down next to Sage. "Y-your h-hair is p-p-pretty." She reached into her doll's blanket and pulled out a hairbrush. "C-can I b-brush it?"

Greg felt kind of bad watching her struggle to speak. "Please, help us, and you can brush her hair."

Sage recoiled at the doll. "That stinks!"

Valentine put the hairbrush against Sage's skull and began brushing her hair gently, wearing a sweet smile. "S-so p-p-pretty." As she continued brushing Sage's hair, she appeared to be pushing down harder.

"Ow," Sage said. "That's starting to hurt."

Valentine's smile suddenly turned from soft to more *wicked* as she started to show her teeth, and Sage's expression turned to pain.

"Ow! It really hurts!" Sage cried.

Greg shouted, "Stop that! You're hurting her!" He did the only thing he could think of and gripped one thumb with his other hand behind his back. He wrenched on the thumb, dislocating it. He did everything in his power to not scream as he thought of what he had to do next. He began pulling his mangled hand through its handcuff, blood running down his palm. As he looked at his daughter being abused by this little girl, he realized he was taking too long. In one very painful motion, he pulled his dislocated hand through the handcuff, taking half of the hand's skin with it. He let out a roar and stood up from the support beam, making his way toward Valentine.

The fear in Valentine's eyes was indescribable as Greg

scooped her up with one arm, causing her to drop her hairbrush and doll. When the doll hit the floor, the blanket that wrapped it became unraveled, revealing something Greg thought he'd never see. It wasn't a doll—but the corpse of a newborn baby that had sharp, monster-like teeth, and a quarter-sized hole in the top of its cranium.

Lisa saw the baby and screamed in terror. "What the *fuck* is that?!"

Lisa's shriek finally caused Betty to look up from her own legs, but she only looked back down, seemingly unfazed—like she didn't care about anything anymore.

Greg struggled to hold Valentine as she flailed her arms and legs.

He moved the single strand piece of his open handcuff to Valentine's throat and then—she stopped kicking.

Lisa looked horrified. "Greg… What are you doing?"

"Hang tight. We're going to see Abin."

Chapter Thirty

G REG *BURST* THROUGH THE BASEMENT DOOR, HOLDING THE small child. He meant her no *actual* harm, but knew she was the way to the man he needed to see.

He screamed, "Abin!"

No answer as he looked down a dim corridor.

"Abin!"

Again, no answer.

Fuck. This isn't much better, he thought as he looked around, not sure of how to find his target. He continued, hoping for the best, keeping his wits about him. Valentine struggled, but stopped again with a little pressure from the cuff. *She took the bait.*

They finally came upon a swinging door.

Has to be the kitchen.

Greg kicked the swinging door open and entered.

Candy was bent over, tending her oven.

Greg's adrenaline surged as he began to breathe heavily, knowing he had little Valentine by the throat. "Candy..."

Candy slowly stood upright.

He repeated with more vehemence, "*Candy!*"

The older woman turned around with a flat face, even at the sight of her daughter with a makeshift weapon at her neck. "Hm. Please, let my daughter go," she said calmly.

She said it so *flatly*, Greg didn't know how to take it.

Is Valentine in trouble too? Should I take her with me? He loosened the cuff from against the little girl's throat, and she immediately tried biting him, causing him to push it back again.

Christ! Those teeth didn't sound…human, he thought as he continued. "G-give me Abin, Candy." His voice began to shake.

Candy laughed. "Do you want me to be more convincing?" She scoffed. "Noooo! Let her gooo!" Holding her fists to her eyes, she said, "Should I try crying instead?"

Dumbfounded, Greg's jaw nearly dropped.

Candy winked. "You want Abin? Fine." She turned—Greg's eyes following her head—and she shouted, "Abin! We have a visitor!"

A familiar Southern drawl came from another room. "What?"

"We have a *visitor*!" she repeated.

"Gimme a minute!"

Greg became uncomfortable, his pulse racing even higher. "Tell him to hurry the *fuck* up!"

"He's coming. You *just* heard him," Candy responded with a wicked smile.

Then—Greg heard footsteps—just before the door next to Candy swung open.

Abin came through the door, his eyes wide. "What… what is this?"

"Someone has taken our baby," Candy said nonchalantly.

"Well. That's unfortunate. How'd ya get out?" His eyes moved down to the arm that wrapped around Valentine. "I see your hand is in a bad way there."

Agreeing with Abin, Greg didn't have many words. "I don't care what you've done here. Let my family and me go."

"Let ya go?" Abin laughed. "Why would I do that? I want y'all to *stay*. I think y'all would be *perfect* additions to our little community."

"I'll give you *one* minute," Greg said, his voice hoarse.

Abin took a step forward, reaching a hand out. "A minute fer what? Why don't ya let me take a look at that *nasty* hand?"

Greg pushed the cuff harder into Valentine's neck; this time drawing a small amount of blood.

Abin took a step back, retracting his hand, and his eyes narrowed to slivers. He placed both of his hands behind his back, as if relaxed, and his face turned sinister. "If yer gon' do it, then *do* it."

Then, Abin pulled a hand from behind his back, wielding the snub-nosed revolver, and fired.

Bang!

The bullet passed through Valentine's forehead, then through Greg's shoulder. Greg dropped the girl into a pool of her own blood as he fell to his knees.

Greg felt nothing. No pain. No anger. No sorrow. "How could you...*how*...*could* you—"

Abin moved his revolver up toward Greg. "Oh, shut up! Ya think I was gon' let *you* kill 'er?! Cut the *shit*, Greg!" Abin moved closer. "I assume ya saw the doll, seeing as how she don't have it…so, tell *me*…what do ya think is goin' on here?"

Greg's knees felt warm—and wet. He peered down to see his lower legs soaked in the little girl's blood. "I don't know!" he screamed, veins protruding from his forehead. Then the pain came all at once. He felt as if boiling cooking oil covered his skinned hand. His shoulder felt like a hundred bald-faced hornets stung him all at once.

He lowered his head, his voice low and defeated. "Just…let us go. We'll take a boat. One the townspeople used to get here. It'll still be back at Snake Bight when you get back there." Greg's eyes welled up. "We won't *steal* it, I *swear*." He picked his head back up to look his would-be shooter in the eyes. "We just want to go *home*."

Abin shouted, "Home?!" then craned his neck back toward Candy. "Hear that? He just wants to go home!"

Candy's eyes seemed to fill with flames. "Just *kill* him, Abin! Kill him and get this over with!"

"Oh, shut it, woman!" Abin said, turning back to Greg, his voice notably calmer. "*This* coulda been yer home. Don't ya *get* that? But nah…ya had to go an' kill my daughter."

He's crazier than I thought…he's a monster. "You don't understand. You're making a *mistake*, Abin. I'm a *police officer*!"

Abin's wide grin filled his face. "Now, how exactly do ya think sayin' that is gon' make this *any* easier on ya, son?" He then turned his head and shouted throughout the house. "Ethan! Didn't ya hear the gunshot? Get yer big ass out here! Got another *pig* needin' takin' to slaughter!"

Tears streamed down Greg's cheeks, his voice remaining calm. "Please, Abin… *Please*. You don't have to do this. You have the choice to let us go."

Abin took the revolver off Greg. "Why, *sure* I do! But I *won't!*"

"M-my family then! Let *them* go!" Greg's voice picked up pace as he pleaded. "I-I'm the cop. *I'm* the government pig! They haven't done *anything*! M-my wife, Lisa, is a schoolteacher! Sage is just a little girl in school, and my son—"

Abin cut him off. "Yer *son*! Hmph. Wasn't it *obvious* back at Mass...y'all have *lost* yer son? When y'all tried to leave, an' he wouldn't even so much as *look* at ya. I'm no expert, but...I don't think he'd piss on y'all if ya'll was on fire."

"Shut the *fuck* up! You don't know anything about my family!"

Abin topped the tiny barrel of his revolver on his chin. "Hm. Have ya *noticed* the only member of yer family that's *not* currently handcuffed in the basement? An' *who* do ya think could get yer daughter down there safely without her causin' a fuss or gettin' hurt?"

"Because you're *so* against violence."

"Comin' from the man that *murdered* a child today. We don't hurt children 'round here."

Greg gritted his teeth so hard, it felt as if they were going to crack. *There's no getting through to him.*

Chapter Thirty-One

WITH THE RED HEAT LAMPS OFF, THE LIGHT FROM THE TV
illuminated Kyle's face. He looked down at his feet, tired of
the bright light burning in his retinas—not that averting his
eyes helped much in the darkened room. He at least felt
more comfortable now that he was out of those itchy
robes.

The sound of Abin's cheery voice came through the
TV speakers. "Hello, new viewer! If yer seein' this, it
means that ya been chosen…chosen to be *saved*, that is!"

Kyle turned his head to the side and saw Ethan with
his back to him, sitting at his table. *Stop playing with your
fucking toys*, Kyle thought. The sound of the colliding action
figures was almost inaudible over the excessively loud TV.

"Then an' *only* then will ya be able to help salvage the
world when it's in *ruins*!"

Kyle finally had enough. "Shut this *off*! Ethan!" He
began stomping his feet on the floor, trying to get the large
man's attention. "Come *on*! I *get* it! I'm already in!"

Ethan quickly spun around, glaring at Kyle over his
gaiter.

Kyle planted his feet back on the floor. "I'm not getting up!" *Trust me, I'm not getting my ass kicked for that again.*

Ethan pointed at the TV before turning back to his action figures.

Kyle looked back up at the TV.

Abin's grin made him shake in anger as he continued to speak. Whatever Kyle was feeling before—about his dad, about staying in Snake Bight—this propaganda video seemed to have the opposite effect on him. "And *that* is when the creator deems ya worthy."

Suddenly, Abin's voice—a second voice—came from somewhere else. "Ethan! Didn't ya hear the gunshot? Get yer big ass out here! Got another *pig* needin' takin' to slaughter!"

Kyle glanced over at Ethan just in time to see him slam his fists on his table. Ethan abruptly slid his chair back and stood up. Staying still for a moment, his shoulders heaved up and down as if he were taking deep breaths before finally turning around.

"What was that?" Kyle asked.

Ethan lumbered by the TV, pressing the power button as he did so. He approached his bedroom door and stopped. Turning his head, he waved Kyle toward him.

"Y-you want me to come?"

Ethan grunted, and Kyle quickly stood up from the chair and followed the big man out of the room and into the dimly lit hallway.

Kyle attempted to get around Ethan to look him in the face, but his shoulders were too wide. "I think they only called *you*. Maybe I should stay back…it sounded like trouble."

Ethan remained silent, seemingly ignoring Kyle.

They turned the corner into the kitchen. Kyle could finally get around his large companion, and when he did, his mouth hung open. "Dad?!" The sight of Abin pointing a gun at Greg, who was kneeling in a puddle of blood next to what appeared to be a dead little girl, turned his stomach sour as he bent over and vomited all over the floor.

Candy glanced over to see the contents of Kyle's stomach splashing on the tile. "Oh, *great*! All over my floor!"

Abin kept his aim on Greg. "About time, boy! This *bastard* killed yer sister!"

Wiping the vomit from his mouth, Kyle asked, "Dad? Is that true?"

Greg looked up at Kyle. "No! Of *course* I didn't! Y-you gotta believe me, son!"

Kyle didn't *want* to believe him. He thought he'd finally found a place where he was accepted—where he was *liked*—but his father's eyes told him he was telling the *truth*.

Abin turned back to look at Ethan. "What're ya waitin' fer, boy?! Get him outta here!" He turned back to Greg and said, "It's *feedin' time*!"

Kyle recoiled at Abin's words. *Feeding time? They're going to kill him!* Ethan began stomping over to Greg, and Kyle grabbed his shoulder. "Ethan, wait!" The large man stopped and turned back. "It's my *dad*…" Ethan pulled his shoulder away and continued toward Greg.

Greg stood up, blood dripping from his knees, and held his hands out defensively. "Come on, Ethan. I didn't do this. Abin did," he spoke calmly. Kyle figured it was probably not to anger the beast of a man. As Ethan got closer and grabbed Greg, the volume of his voice rose. "No, no, no! I didn't do this!" Greg tried punching Ethan, but it didn't matter. It looked like he was hitting a brick wall. Ethan picked Greg up with ease—as if he were a toddler—and threw him over his shoulder.

I have to do something. I can't let them kill him! Kyle thought.

Abin waved his revolver toward the door. "Take him outside. I'll be out in a minute…after I grab the *others*."

Shit. Mom and Sage. Kyle felt defeated as he watched Ethan carry his father out of the house, most likely to his certain death. Abin turned to Candy. "Take Kyle an' go outside with Ethan."

"Abin, I-I'll wrangle up the ones downstairs," Kyle said, eagerly stepping forward.

"Ya will?" Abin's eyes squinted a bit.

"Yeah. I mean, if I'm gonna be part of the family, I have to pull my weight, right? Plus, Sage pretty much only listens to me."

Abin stared at him a little too long for comfort before cracking a smile and slapping Kyle on the back. "Boy, ya really *are* smart." He nonchalantly pointed his revolver at Valentine's corpse. "All…*this* goin' on. I didn't even think 'bout you gettin' yer sister up here." Abin sighed. "Alright. Change of plans. Me an' Candy'll go outside an' prepare then." Abin tucked his snub-nose into one pocket and pulled a set of keys out of the other and tossed them at Kyle. He then placed his hand on Candy's back and led her outside. "Come on, hon."

Kyle listened for the sound of the door closing. He ran over to the sink and began frantically opening and closing drawers. After a few drawers, he finally found the one he was looking for. He reached in and pulled out a chef's knife. He slid it into his belt and then sprinted toward the basement door. He whipped it open and ran down the steps so fast, he felt as if he were floating.

The dank basement was dark, and the little bit of light that *was* down there came from the doorway upstairs. "Mom? Sage?"

He heard a cough before Lisa spoke up in a harsh,

raspy voice. "K-Kyle? There's a…pull string here…on the ceiling."

Kyle carefully moved into the darkness, waving a hand above his head. "I can't see shit."

"L-Language…"

Even when she's in danger…

Kyle felt his hand brush against a thin rope as the darkness enveloped him. "Got it!" He grabbed hold of the rope and pulled, illuminating the room with a long fluorescent tube on the ceiling. His gut lurched into his throat when he saw his mom and sister, their lips chapped and faces ghastly pale.

He stood staring for a moment. *Oh, my God…I did this…*

Lisa's faint voice barely wormed its way out of her lips. "Kyle…Kyle, what are you doing?"

Finally, the sound of Sage's voice snapped him out of his stare. "Kyle!"

He fumbled with the keyring and kneeled behind Lisa, unlocking her handcuffs. "Mom, I'm *so* sorry."

Lisa pulled her arms in front of her body and rubbed her wrists vigorously. "Don't worry about that now. Go unlock your sister. Where's your dad?"

Kyle moved behind Sage and unlocked her cuffs as well, staying silent.

"Kyle! Where's your dad?"

He looked at her grimly. "Abin…took him back outside."

"What?! We have to get outside! Help Betty!"

Kyle looked down at Betty, whose head was down. "Is she okay?"

Lisa stood up and stretched her legs. "She's fine. She's just not talking. Get her off that damn beam! We have to go get your dad!"

Kyle unlocked Betty's handcuffs. Her head stayed

down as she let her arms fall to her sides. "Betty?" He grabbed her shoulder and shook her a few times. "Betty, can you hear me?" She didn't budge.

"Just help her up," Lisa said.

Kyle squatted down in front of Betty and hooked his arms under her armpits. He strained, but was able to pick her up onto her feet. *I'm lucky she's light,* he thought. He leaned her against the support beam, keeping a hand on her shoulder so she didn't fall over. She picked her head up, and her mouth appeared to be moving slightly, as if she were trying to speak. "What?" Kyle asked. He turned his head and leaned his ear close to her mouth, trying to hear what she was saying.

"Norm…Norm…" Her words started soft, but soon enough, she was screaming in Kyle's ear. "Norm! Norm! Norm!"

He recoiled and covered his ear with his hand. "Jesus! My eardrum!"

Lisa rushed over to Betty and grabbed her by her shoulders. "Betty. Look at me. Look at me in the eyes."

Betty continued screaming. "Norm! Norm! Norm!"

Lisa hauled back and slapped the old woman across the cheek, shutting her up instantly. She looked straight at Lisa, her eyes welling up with tears. "Betty, snap out of it. I know what happened to Norm was terrible, and I'm *sorry*, but you've got to hold it together until we get off this island."

Kyle felt a tug on his T-shirt. He turned and looked down, and Sage was looking up at him. "Why did Mom slap Miss Betty?"

"It's okay," Kyle said. "It's adult stuff."

Betty moved her head back down to the floor. "Listen to me," Lisa said. "Greg is in trouble. I'm sorry about Norm. I *really* am. But *both* of us don't have to lose our husbands today, and I will not leave you behind." Betty moved her gaze back up to Lisa. "So, I need you to be strong. Please. If not for me, if not for Greg, for our *children*."

"O-okay…" Betty breathed.

"Thank you."

Kyle approached his mom from behind and placed a hand on her shoulder. "Mom, I'm running out of time. You three should stay down here. Everyone went outside, so you should be safe for now. If you hear anyone come down that isn't me or Dad, grab something from that tool bench and defend yourselves."

"Go. We'll be fine," Lisa said. "Get your dad and let's get the *fuck* off this island."

Chapter Thirty-Two

THEY SHOULD'VE JUST SHOT ME IN THE KITCHEN, GREG thought as he bounced up and down on Ethan's massive shoulder. *This guy…this thing smells like fucking swamp water.* The sun was rising, and the only things Greg could see were Ethan's large, smelly back or the ground. He felt like he was going to be sick from being upside down for so long. *I could've walked*, he thought. The ground soon turned to wooden steps as Ethan walked up what Greg assumed to be the stairs leading up to the stage. The steps turned into flat boards, meaning they were on the stage now, and Greg heard Abin's voice from behind him. "Just throw him there."

Greg felt Ethan's massive hands grab him on either side of his waist, then with a grunt, the large man tossed him off his shoulder as he landed hard on the wooden planks. A stinging pain shot throughout his body as if he were being tased. He rolled over to his side, and Abin was standing behind his podium with his elbows resting on it. He looked annoyed. "I meant the chair…"

"What's going on?" Greg asked through the pain.

"Why didn't you just shoot me before?" He gestured toward the empty rows of seats in front of the stage. "You don't have your *audience* here to watch!"

Ethan approached and stood over Greg. He reached down to grab hold of him, and Greg knocked his arm away. "Don't fucking touch me!" Ethan eyed him for a moment, then pulled down his neck gaiter, revealing his top row of teeth and disgusting, slimy tongue. He let out a sinister hiss. The breath that came from his throat hole smelled putrid and caused Greg to gag. The large man took the opportunity to scoop Greg up off the stage floor and sat him in the chair near the podium. It was still stained with Norm's blood. Ethan used a rope to tie Greg to the chair.

Greg screamed, "Just kill me and get it over with!" Ethan reared his giant arm back and smacked Greg across the face, almost knocking him out of the chair. Greg's head dropped, and a mouthful of blood dripped down to the front of his shirt. He heard an amplified popping sound behind him and picked his head up to look. Abin was topping the microphone on his podium.

Abin leaned over to Ethan, covering the microphone with his hand. "Why don't ya go check on the boy? See where he is with the others?"

Ethan grunted and headed back toward the house.

Feedback hissed over the stage speakers as Abin cleared his throat into the microphone. "Ahem. I'm sorry to do this to y'all, but I'm afraid it's time fer an *emergency service.*"

Greg looked out at the empty seats in front of him, then back at Abin. *I thought he was crazy before. Now he's seeing people?!*

"Please. Y'all come forward an' take yer seats!"

"Are you out of your mind?!" Greg asked.

"Don't be shy! I promise this won't take long!"

Greg gawked at Abin, unable to comprehend what was happening. Was he watching him fall deeper into insanity?

"Ah. There we are."

Greg looked back out toward the empty seats, but still saw nothing. Then, behind the rows of chairs, past five hundred feet of grass, he saw the swamp water—and it appeared that it had been disturbed. Suddenly, he saw something rising out of the murky water. It was far away, but he thought it looked to be a human head. A few seconds later, he realized his eyes weren't fooling him when the rest of a human body came out of the water and walked onto the shore. A bald man wearing a white robe— he was meandering toward the stage. Behind him, more heads began popping up out of the water, and trudging to shore; all of them adorned in white robes. There were *dozens* of them.

Greg craned his neck to look back at Abin. "Abin, what the hell is this?!" He blissfully ignored Greg as he watched the people emerge from the swamp. "Answer me, dammit!"

Abin gently moved his gaze down to Greg. "Didn't ya hear me? I said it was an emergency service. I said it into the microphone an' everythin'."

Soon enough, the swamp people made it to the front of the stage. Saul, Murial…the whole town. They filled the rows of empty chairs and calmly took their seats in their soaking wet robes.

"I'm truly sorry to call y'all back here on such short notice," Abin said, leaning into his microphone.

Saul stood up from his chair. "As our only vessel to our great creator, we would do *anything* for you, Abin!"

The surrounding crowd all mumbled in agreement as Saul looked around, smiling and nodding his head.

"Thank ya, Saul. I'm *touched*."

Saul sat back down in his chair, still grinning.

Abin put on a smile to match that of Saul. "Y'all are gon' be happy when I tell ya what I got here!" He pulled the microphone out of its stand and moved to the front of the podium. "I have gathered y'all here tod—"

"How can you all just *sit* there and *watch* this?!" Greg screamed, interrupting Abin. "You're all *sick!*" He looked around the crowd, eyeing all the townspeople. There was something about their eyes—they were really enjoying this. "And you're going to regret sitting idly by when I *kill* every last one of you on my way out of this shit hole!" Greg could feel his heartbeat pumping in the bullet wound in his shoulder; the pain getting more intense. He figured they had to know his threat was an empty one—they could see the shape he was in, after all.

With Ethan gone, Abin walked over to Greg and smacked him himself, shutting him up. Greg moved his tongue over his teeth to make sure they were all there; the taste of blood once again filled his mouth. He could *feel* Abin glaring at him.

"Better," Abin said as he turned his attention back to the crowd of residents. "As I was sayin'…I gathered y'all here today to give y'all another *message*. It would appear the ol' United States government *refuses* to give up! Turns out not one, but *two* of our special guests were sent here to *spy* on us!" There was an audible gasp from someone in the crowd. "That's right! Our friend, Mr. Greg Boyes, was in *cahoots* with that other filthy pig we sent to slaughter! I gotta hand it to him, though…he *almost* had me. He's a sneaky one, alright." Abin gripped the microphone with both hands and lowered his head; his voice turned somber. "This man…just *killed* my sweet little Valentine in cold blood not thirty minutes ago…"

The crowd began booing loudly when someone shouted, "Kill him!"

Abin held one hand in the air, and the crowd slowly silenced itself. He raised his head to look at them, a tear running down his cheek.

Jesus. He's fake crying. I can't believe they're buying this.

"Now, now…I ain't gon' kill him."

The crowd started booing loudly again.

Abin turned to look at Greg and smiled. "Hold yer horses, y'all. I ain't gon' kill him *yet*… I have somethin' a little more *special* in mind."

A voice came from behind Greg. "Let *me* do it." Greg looked back, and Kyle, wearing the white robes, walked out from behind the stage and approached him. He stood next to his dad, raised Abin's snub-nosed revolver, and aimed it at Greg's head. With a flat voice, he said, "Hello, Father. It's *feeding time*."

PART THREE: FALSE PROPHET

Chapter Thirty-Three

Abin raised his arms in victory. "Well, *hot damn*! This is even better than what I had planned!"

Greg lowered his eyes to the stage floor, blood continuing to drip from his mouth. He took a few deep breaths. "Kyle…what are you doing?"

Kyle said nothing.

Greg turned his head up to look at his son, the barrel of the revolver now pressed against his forehead. "Answer me! What are you *doing*?! What's *wrong* with you?!" The boy's eyes were wild. For the first time ever, Greg was actually scared of his own son.

He looked back at the floor, his heart about to burst through his chest. His voice lowered. "You don't *have* to do this, Kyle. *Please* don't do this…"

Kyle pulled the revolver back and swung it at Greg, smacking him on the back of the head with its butt. "Shut up!" He aimed the gun at his dad's head again. "You have always kept me down. Even when I accomplished things most parents would be *proud* of, you still found a reason to *crap* on it."

"Kyle…"

"Even when I was at my *lowest* point, not sure what I wanted to do with my life, you continued to *kick* me when I was down…made fun of my weight, called me a pussy… and have you ever *once* told me you were *proud* of me? For *anything*?! No!" Using his other hand, Kyle wiped a tear from his face. "Thank *God* I met Abin. He saw something in me that, apparently, you never did. He saw something *special*." He pulled back the hammer of the revolver. "And now…I know what I want to do with my life."

Greg squeezed his eyes tight, causing tears to stream down his cheeks as he prepared to die. "Kyle…"

He heard footsteps getting closer to him. Then he heard Abin shout, "Just do it!"

Greg opened his eyes and turned his head to see his son one last time.

Suddenly, Kyle turned, lowered the revolver to Abin's knee, and fired.

Bang!

Abin screamed as he fell to the stage floor. "Argh!"

Kyle pulled apart his robe and grabbed the chef's knife out of his belt. He moved behind Greg and sawed the rope that bound him to the chair.

Greg got to his feet and pressed his disfigured hand against the bullet wound in his shoulder. He was hoping a little pressure on it would relieve the pain, but it didn't— not that he could apply much pressure with his broken, half-skinned hand anyway.

Greg looked down at Abin. He was sitting on the stage floor, leaning back on one hand. His other hand was covering the bullet wound in his knee as blood leaked between his fingers. Oddly enough, he was smiling.

Greg approached him, snatching the revolver out of Kyle's hand as he passed by. He gripped the gun by the barrel and pulled it back. "You *motherfucker!*" He brought the butt of the gun down on the bridge of Abin's nose, knocking him all the way down to the stage floor.

Abin got back up, once again leaning back on one hand. Blood leaked from a crack in the bridge of his nose, down into his mouth, coating his teeth light red. He was still smiling somehow.

"You think you can hold my family *hostage*?!" Greg whacked him in the face again; and again, Abin got back up. "You think you can just *kill* innocent people?!" He hit him with the gun butt a fourth time. This time blood sprayed out of his nose and misted Greg's face. *This* time, he didn't get back up. "You think you can turn my own *son* against me?!"

Abin lay motionless on the floor. "Speak!" Greg shouted, his voice cracking. Then he heard something— laughter. Greg grabbed a fistful of Abin's shirt collar and pulled him up.

His laughter only got louder as he smiled in Greg's face. "Ha…Ha…Hahahaha!"

Greg bent down and pulled Abin closer to him. Their faces were almost touching. "What's so *funny*?!"

Abin concealed his laughter just long enough to speak. "Ya… Ya think yer gettin' outta here, don't ya?" His laughter suddenly ceased, and his face turned flat. "Feed!"

Greg looked out into the crowd when he heard what sounded like retching. He saw Saul, the innkeeper, bent over in the front row, holding his stomach. It sounded like he was throwing up his insides. After a moment, Saul shot up, arching his back with his arms out to his sides as they bent backward; the sound of his bones cracking echoed throughout the open sky. His mouth was wide open, his lower jaw elongated as Greg watched his teeth begin to fall out—no—they were being *pushed* out. Pushed out and replaced with larger, pointed teeth. Soon, his mouth was full of them.

A woman screamed in agony, drawing Greg's attention over a few rows. Murial was holding her shaking hands in front of her face as her fingernails turned space black and grew an extra two inches out of her fingertips. Greg turned his gaze back to Saul, who gripped the collar of his robe and ripped it apart, tearing it down the middle and exposing his upper body. Green patches began forming all over his face and body. He was too far to tell for sure, but Greg thought the green patches appeared to be bumpy—almost like *scales*.

Greg corrected his grip on the revolver to hold it properly and aimed down at Abin. "What the *fuck* is going on here?!"

Abin only let out a sinister laugh through his bloody smile while holding the bullet wound in his knee.

"Uh, Dad…" Kyle said, his voice uneasy.

Greg looked up at his son to see him pointing out toward the front of the stage. Greg's eyes followed the boy's hand while keeping the gun aimed at Abin. Out in the crowd, all the townsfolk had green, scaly patches. They had pointed teeth, long sharp nails, and their eyes had turned a light shade of green speckled with black, and their pupils had changed shape into thin vertical slits.

Greg couldn't believe what he was witnessing.

The creatures started plodding toward the stage.

"Dad, they're coming for us!"

"Where are your mom and sister?"

"They're back at the house! I told them to stay put while I got you."

Greg turned his attention back to Abin as he continued aiming the revolver at him. Kyle grabbed Greg's shirt and pulled on it as he began to walk away. "They're getting closer! Let's go!"

I can't believe I'm about to let this man live, Greg thought. He groaned, decocked the revolver, and followed Kyle. As they jumped off the side of the stage, Greg heard Abin shout, "Yer not gettin' outta here alive!"

Greg followed Kyle down one side of the chairs as they headed toward Abin's house. Suddenly, Greg felt like he'd been hit by a truck as one creature tackled him to the ground, landing on his wounded shoulder as the revolver flew out of his hand. He rolled over onto his back as the creature straddled him. He put his hands up to push the creature off him; the pain in his broken hand was excruciating as he fought off the monstrosity. From behind him, he heard Kyle shout, "Dad!"

Then—*Bang!*

Green liquid sprayed all over Greg's face, and the creature went limp on top of him. He pushed it off of him and onto the grass, then quickly rolled over onto his belly. Looking up, he saw Kyle standing behind him, holding the smoking revolver. The boy's eyes were wide, as if he were shocked at what he'd done. Kyle dropped the revolver and took a step back from it, eyeing it the whole time. Guttural roars sounded behind Greg—he knew they were closing in on them.

Greg got to his feet and rushed over to Kyle, picking the revolver up off the ground on the way. He spun around and saw the mass of creatures chasing after them. He fired two shots, popping two creatures in the head, and they went down quickly, causing the creatures behind them to stumble. *Now's our chance!* He grabbed Kyle by the arm and started running. "Come on, son!" Greg shouted, and they both continued toward the house.

Kyle, out of breath, said, "Dad…I…have something…to tell…you."

"What is it?" Greg asked.

"The…airboat…there's…nothing…wrong with it."

"*What?!*"

"Abin…he was lying!"

"That son of a—where are your mom and sister hiding out?"

"They…should still be in the basement."

Greg made it to the back door and turned around, aiming the revolver. "Get inside now!"

He kept his aim on the creatures as he heard the door behind him open and close. *At least the boy is safe,* he thought. He fired carefully three times, taking down three more creatures, and then—

Click.

Click.

Click.

He looked down at the weapon in his hand. *Shit!* He spun around, entered the house, and slammed the screen door behind him.

Chapter Thirty-Four

Once inside, Greg slammed the heavy interior door and cranked on the thumb turn, locking the deadbolt. Something *slammed* into the other side of the door, causing him to jump back. *It sounds like they're throwing their bodies at it,* he thought. He took a quick breath, relieved, if only for a moment. As he turned around, he ran into Kyle's back. "Oof! Sorry, son."

Kyle was standing still, as if he didn't even notice his dad running into him. "Dad…" he breathed.

Greg walked around Kyle to see what he was looking at. "Everything okay?"

Greg stopped dead in his tracks when he saw Candy leaning over the kitchen sink, cleaning dishes, and placing them on a drying rack on the counter next to her.

"What do we do? I-I thought she went outside with everyone else," Kyle said.

"She must've come back. Let's just be quiet and try to sneak into the basement," Greg whispered.

Greg tiptoed into the kitchen with Kyle right behind him, and when they were about halfway through, Candy spoke up. "You're still here?" She had her back to them as she continued working at the sink.

Keeping quiet, Greg and Kyle looked at each other.

"Yes, I'm speaking to you," Candy said.

Greg spoke up, and his chest puffed out like a wild turkey in a face-off. He didn't mean to do it; it seemed to be some sort of instinct. "We're here to get our family. Just…stay out of our way." His voice beamed with confidence, although that confidence seemed to be misplaced as his words had no effect on Candy.

A plate clanked against another as Candy set it on the drying rack. "I'm sorry. I think you misunderstood me." She calmly spun around to face Greg and Kyle. Her eyes, like the others outside, were green with black speckles and thin vertical pupils, and she had patches of green scales on her face and arms. "I meant 'you're still here' as in, 'you're still alive!'" She opened her mouth wide, revealing a gross, slimy tongue, and let out a shrill roar. Her long, pointy teeth pushed her old teeth out, shooting them across the room, and her fingernails grew long and black.

Greg shouted, "You too?!"

She lunged at Kyle, taking him to the tile floor. Greg approached her from behind and wrapped his arms around her in an attempt to lift her off his son. Candy dug her sharp nails into his half-skinned hand, and he loosened his grip as he screamed in agony. Candy, still straddling Kyle, turned her upper body and swiped at Greg with her claws, causing him to stumble backward. He tripped over his own feet and fell on his ass and hit the back of his head against the counter. She turned her attention back to Kyle, who was swinging his arms wildly. She grabbed his wrists and pinned them down to the floor, then leaned forward and took a massive *bite* out of his biceps. Kyle screamed, but the bite seemed to awaken something in him as he found the strength to push his hands up off the floor.

Greg shouted, "Kyle!"

Kyle continued fighting with Candy. "Go! Get Mom and Sage! I'll be fine!"

Still dazed from hitting his head, Greg began to rise to his feet. "I'm not leaving you!"

Kyle rose his hips off the floor and rolled Candy over, switching positions with her, and now he had the upper hand.

Candy lifted her head a few times, snapping her jaws at Kyle. The sound of her pointed teeth colliding sent a chill down Greg's spine as he finally stood upright.

Kyle looked around and saw a power cord hanging off the dining table next to him. He quickly took a hand off Candy and yanked on the cord, pulling down a metal toaster.

Seeing that Kyle seemed to be handling himself, Greg leaned on the counter to try to regain his composure.

Kyle punched Candy square in the face, causing her to cover her nose with her free hand. He reached over and grabbed the toaster off the floor, and raised it high above his head. He waited for Candy to move her hand before he came down with the toaster—full force—onto her head. He picked the toaster back up and brought it down again. And again. And again. Finally, when Candy's limbs had stopped moving, Greg approached Kyle and grabbed the toaster from his hands when he brought it up for the last time.

"That's enough, son. You *got* her." Greg looked down and felt his stomach turn when he saw the pulpy mess of green blood and mush that had once been Candy's head.

Kyle leaned backward and scooted off of the woman;

his eyes staying trained on her lifeless body. "Oh, God… Oh, Jesus!"

Greg's eyes followed his son. "It's alright, Kyle. Calm down."

Kyle wiped his face with both hands, then looked down at them, and he gagged when he saw the green blood smeared on his palms.

Greg bent over and hooked his arm around Kyle's elbow and helped him to his feet. "Up you go." He grabbed his son's chin with his good hand. The boy's eyes were darting around wildly. "Kyle. Look at me." His eyes settled, and Greg could feel he had his attention now. "Listen. And I mean *really* listen. You did what you *had* to do. It's understandable that you're freaked out, but I need you to be *cool* right now. Your mom, your sister, and Betty are *counting* on us…okay?"

Kyle nodded erratically, and Greg gave him a couple of small slaps on the cheek. "Say it."

"S-say what?"

"You did what you *had* to do."

"I did what I *had* to do…"

"Say it like you mean it!"

Kyle shouted, "I did what I *had* to do!"

Greg could tell by the look in his son's eyes that he meant it and that he was fully there and ready to get to work. "Good! *That's* what I like to hear! Now, let's get a move on. Those things are going to get in here any minute." Greg moved to the basement door, with Kyle following right behind him.

The steps creaked as Greg and Kyle slowly descended the stairwell to the basement. Luckily, the fluorescent lightbulb still barely lit the room. Greg called out, "Lisa?" He reached the bottom step and scanned the room. In the corner, he saw Lisa standing in front of Sage and Betty, wielding a flathead screwdriver with both hands. "Lisa!"

His wife's eyes opened wide. "Greg?!" She put the screwdriver in the back pocket of her shorts and ran over to her husband and wrapped her arms around him. Sage wasn't too far behind, and she skipped up to Kyle, who bent down and hugged her with his good arm.

"What happened?!" Sage asked.

Kyle looked down at the chunk missing in his arm and winced at the sight. "A bad person hurt me. I'm okay now, though."

Lisa glanced over at Kyle and did a double-take. Greg felt her push him off of her and watched as she rushed over to tend to her son. "Oh, my God! My baby!"

"I'm okay, Mom."

"Hold on one second. Stay right there!" Lisa scurried over to the tool bench and opened a drawer and pulled out a handful of white rags, then walked back to Kyle. "I found some clean—well, clean-*ish* rags when I was looking for a weapon. Give me your arm." Kyle held his arm out, and Lisa tightly wrapped a rag around his wound and tied a knot in it.

Kyle squeezed his eyes shut. "Shit!"

"Language," Lisa said, smiling.

She walked over to Greg, holding another rag between her hands. "Your turn. Hand."

Greg rolled his eyes. "Lisa…"

"Hand!"

Greg held his battered hand out, and Lisa wrapped it in the rag. "There," she said. "We don't want you two getting some weird swamp infection."

"Lisa…"

"Wouldn't that be *strange?* We go through all *this* and you guys end up with some exotic disease?"

Greg shouted, "Lisa!" and she snapped to attention. "We're in *big* trouble here."

"What do you mean?"

"The people...in the crowd. The people that live in Snake Bight. They...they..."

Kyle jumped in. "They're alligator people!"

Lisa moved her gaze back and forth between Greg and Kyle, and a small smirk came upon her face. "What?"

"It's true," Greg said. "I-I don't know how to explain it. Kyle *saved* me from Abin and the people, like, transformed. Their skin turned green and scaly, and their teeth *popped* out of their mouths and were replaced with sharp ones, a-and their fingernails grew into, like, claws!"

Lisa's smirk vanished. "If this is some practical joke, it's *not* funny."

Kyle put his hand on his mom's shoulder. "Mom. It's not a joke. They chased after us, but we made it into the house and locked the door." His face turned grim as he looked down at his wounded arm. "That's what did this to me. Candy...she was one of them. We took care of her, but the others...we don't know how long until they find their way in."

Lisa's jaw hung practically on the floor. "What are we going to do? I have a fucking *screwdriver!*"

Greg pulled the snub-nosed revolver from his pocket and held it up. "I have Abin's gun, but used all the bullets getting us to the house."

"I saw a door," Sage added in her tiny voice.

Greg put the firearm back in his pocket and approached Sage, toking a knee in front of her. "What door?"

"When Kyle left me alone at night, I saw a door next to

my room and I opened it, and there was a *big* gun in there."

Greg glanced at Kyle, then back at Sage. "Can you take us to the room?"

"Sure!"

Greg stood back up and noticed Betty still standing in the corner, just staring ahead blankly. He pulled Lisa to the side and whispered, "What's up with Betty? Is she going to be okay?"

"She'll be fine. She's in shock, but I got her mostly snapped out of it."

"Shit. I guess she *did* have a front-row seat to her husband's execution."

"She'll be able to keep up with us. Just don't expect any conversation out of her."

"Noted." Greg stepped away from Lisa and toward the rest of the group. "Okay, guys. Sage will take us to this room and let's *pray* there's actually a big gun up there. We have to move quickly. Like Kyle said, those things could be in here any minute, so keep your head on a swivel." He turned his attention to his son. "Kyle, cover your sister's eyes through the kitchen so she doesn't see Candy."

"Got it," Kyle said. He pulled the handcuff keys out of his pocket. "Let me get that for you." Greg held his hand out, and Kyle unlocked the cuff still attached to his dad's good hand and let it fall to the floor.

Lisa put her arm around Betty and walked her up to everyone else. "Come on, Betty. We're going to get out of here." Then the group led by Greg walked up the stairs and out of the basement door.

Chapter Thirty-Five

GREG HELD HIS HAND OUT, SIGNALING FOR LISA, KYLE, Sage, and Betty to stay put in the hallway. He took a few steps forward and peered over the swinging door that led to the kitchen. He saw no creatures, but couldn't see the entire room. There was no noise, and he figured if they'd made their way into the house, they would cause a ruckus, so the coast had to be clear, right? He looked back at the group and nodded. Turning back to the swinging door, he cautiously pushed it open and stepped into the kitchen.

Shit! Greg thought as he saw Ethan kneeling over Candy's corpse on the floor. His head was down, and the straps of muscle on his back flexed as his shoulders moved up and down quickly.

Is he…crying? He stepped softly backward, back through the swinging door and into the hallway.

Lisa looked concerned. "What's wrong?"

"Ethan, that big bastard, is out there. He found Candy."

"How…how are we going to get by him?"

Greg put his forefinger on his chin, thinking. "I don't know. He'd surely tear us all apart. *Easily*, at that."

After a few seconds, Kyle spoke up. "I'll go."

Greg recoiled in surprise. "What?!"

"I'll go out there and try to comfort him, and you guys can sneak by."

"I don't know if that's a good idea, son."

"Ethan wasn't out there when I shot Abin; he was sent in here to check on me. He *must* think I'm still with them!"

Greg sat on it for a moment, trying to think of another way—one that wouldn't put his son in immediate danger—but nothing came to mind.

"Come on, Dad. It's our only chance of getting out of this."

Lisa put a hand on Kyle's shoulder. "Honey…"

"He's right," Greg said. "I don't like it, but he's right. It's probably our only shot." He then nodded to Kyle.

Kyle stripped off the cult-like white robe and adjusted the chef's knife in his belt and, with a look of determination, he passed by Greg and headed for the kitchen. He put his hand on the swinging door and paused. "Dad…" He sat for a moment before halfway looking back. "That stuff I said…back on the stage…"

"Kyle, don't," Greg said.

"…I didn't *mean* it." Kyle moved his head back forward and looked toward the floor. "I suppose I did before, but after all this that's been happening…I realized you were only trying to make me a better man."

"No, son. I was trying to make you a better man than *me*. I'm not a good cop. I've done some *bad* things. I guess I pushed you into joining the force so you could erase my mistakes…give Boyes a good name. That was *wrong* of me, and trying to get my way by bullying you into it was even *worse*. I'm sorry."

"Thanks, Dad." Kyle took a deep breath and walked into the kitchen. Greg rushed up to the swinging door and held it open a bit, bending down to peer through the crack as he watched his son.

Kyle approached Ethan as he seemingly wept over his mother's body. Kyle's hand trembled as he placed it on the large man's shoulder. Ethan stood up and turned to face Kyle, towering over him. Greg saw his son's arms waving and figured he must've been saying something, but he wasn't speaking loud enough for him to hear.

Every muscle in Greg's body tensed up as he watched on nervously. *Come on, Kyle. You got this.*

Then something seemed off. Ethan's eyes narrowed, and he bent his upper body forward, moving his face closer to Kyle's, as if he were *inspecting* him. Kyle took a step back, almost defensively, and Ethan moved a hand up to the boy's face and wiped his forefinger against his cheek.

What the fuck is he doing? Greg thought.

Ethan brought his fingertip close to his face and examined it, moving his head from side to side.

Suddenly, Greg's heart sank as the realization hit him like a Mack truck. *Candy's blood!*

He gasped out loud, drawing the attention of Lisa. "What's wrong, Greg? What do you see?"

Greg turned his head back. "Kyle might be in trouble."

He looked back through the crack and saw Ethan put his hands on Kyle's shoulders before he crept them up to either side of his head. It appeared he was just…staring into Kyle's eyes. As far as Greg knew, the large man couldn't talk; the fucker didn't even have a bottom jaw.

Greg felt like he was going to be ill when Kyle finally spoke up loud enough for him to hear. "Ethan! Dude! You're *hurting* me!"

Ethan's fingertips *dug* into the back of Kyle's head—

like he was squeezing it. "Stop! That hurts!" Then, in one fluid motion, Ethan twisted his massive hands in opposite directions, and—*crack*—he spun Kyle's head all the way around, so he was looking directly at Greg. The boy's eyes had turned blood red and were bulging from their sockets. A small gurgling sound made its way out of his mouth before his body collapsed to the tile floor in a heap.

Greg screamed, "Nooo!" and burst through the swinging door, charging toward Ethan. As Greg approached, the man swung one of his gigantic arms and swatted him away like an annoying bug. Greg flew across the room horizontally and hit the cabinets under the sink before crashing to the floor.

As Ethan stomped toward him, Greg saw the swinging door open once more, and Lisa was crouched down with her screwdriver in hand. *Lisa, don't. Please,* Greg thought.

Lisa stood up from her crouched position and charged into the kitchen like a lineman exploding out of a three-point-stance with the screwdriver held high above her head. She leaped onto Ethan's back and drove the screwdriver into the side of his neck, sending green blood spurting out.

Ethan swung his torso violently and sent Lisa reeling to the floor. He grabbed hold of the screwdriver handle and yanked it from his neck, letting out a monstrous roar, and then fell to a knee.

Greg's eyes moved down to the chef's knife tucked in his son's belt. He glanced back at Ethan and saw that he was still holding his neck, still recovering. Greg crawled over to Kyle's body as smoothly and quietly as he could and slid the knife out, keeping an eye on the large man the entire time.

Ethan's head suddenly *snapped* over. *Shit! I'm caught!* Greg rolled onto his ass, then crab-walked until he was once again butted up against the cabinets under the sink. Ethan wobbled to his feet, still holding his neck, and lumbered over to Greg. He pulled down his neck gaiter, revealing his devilish maw. A throaty hiss expelled from Ethan's black abyss of a throat hole, and his long, slimy tongue wormed around in front of Greg's face, taunting him.

Ignoring the rancid odor, Greg brought a hand up and snatched the bottom of Ethan's tongue and pulled it back, stretching it out to its full length. Then, with the other hand, Greg brought the knife up and stuck it through the bottom of the tongue. Ethan's eyes opened wide as he gazed upon the top half of the knife sticking up through the meaty muscle. He threw his hands in the air and froze. Greg was certain the man didn't want to lose his tongue.

Lisa cried out, "Greg!"

Greg looked over at her, standing by the dining table with her hand in a box that read: ".38 AMMUNITION."

Abin must've left the box earlier!

Lisa pulled a handful of bullets from the box and threw them in Greg's direction. Any enthusiasm he'd gained instantly vanished when the bullets spread throughout the kitchen. Looking around, he saw a single bullet a few feet away. He looked back at Ethan, who appeared worried as he continued to eye the blade sticking up through his tongue. Greg pulled the knife straight back, slicing and splitting Ethan's tongue down the middle. The beast roared and threw his hands over his mouth, and Greg crawled away from him, toward the nearby bullet.

Greg pulled the revolver from his pocket and opened the cylinder with one hand while he grabbed the bullet with the other, skinned hand. With his hands trembling, he attempted to load the bullet into the cylinder, when it slipped out of his fingers and clanked against the floor. He lifted his gaze and saw Ethan standing up straight, his tongue split in two, dangling down to his collarbone. Ethan turned to look at Greg and once again began stomping over to him.

Greg managed to pick the bullet back up and slide it into the cylinder. He snapped the cylinder shut and, as Ethan lunged at him, he pulled the hammer back, aimed in the large man's general direction, and pulled the trigger.

Bang!

The bullet entered right into Ethan's throat hole, stopping his advance as he bent over and let out an awful gurgling sound, struggling for breath.

Now's my shot! Greg thought, scrambling to his feet. He rushed to the dining table and stuck his hand into the ammunition box, pulling out another handful of bullets. He loaded them into the revolver carefully, trying not to fumble them this time. Once the bullets were in, he took a deep breath and walked up to Ethan with authority. He turned his body sideways and lifted the revolver, aiming it at Ethan's head. Ethan turned his face up to look at him. When their eyes met, Greg unloaded.

Bang!

Bang!

Bang!

Bang!

Bang!

Bang!

Click.

Click.

Click.

Ethan stood hunched over, and his face resembled one giant hole, as if someone had shot him with a cannonball. Greg continued to aim at him for a moment, panting, and then the massive man finally collapsed. Greg lowered the revolver, then fell to his hands and knees and vomited before rolling over onto his ass, leaning back on his one good hand.

Lisa ran out from behind the swinging door with Sage right behind her. They both kneeled on either side of Greg and hugged him. Sage put her face into Greg's chest as she wept uncontrollably.

Lisa had tears in her eyes. "Greg, are you okay?!"

"I-I shouldn't have let Kyle do it…"

"Don't. Don't blame yourself."

"I could've *stopped* him. Instead, I encouraged him."

"When has he ever listened to you before? He'd already made up his mind."

Greg was looking at Kyle's corpse; he couldn't take his eyes off him.

"Greg. Look at me."

He ignored his wife, but she grabbed his chin and forced his head to face hers. "Kyle would want us to get out of here. Don't let his sacrifice be for nothing."

Suddenly, the banging at the back door resumed, causing Greg and Lisa both to look. Then a green, scaly arm with long black nails burst through the interior door, sending wooden shards across the kitchen.

Lisa looked back at Greg. "We have to get to that room!" She stood up and grabbed Greg's arm, helping him to his feet. "Betty! Come on!"

Greg walked back to the dining table, grabbed the rest of the bullets from the ammunition box, and loaded six into his revolver before shoving the remaining bullet into his pocket. He turned to the swinging door. "Betty!"

The swinging door opened slowly, and Betty meandered her way out of the hallway, still wearing a blank face.

Lisa rushed past Greg and grabbed Betty's hand. "Come on, I'll help you. We have to pick it up!"

Greg stood at the opening of the opposite hallway. "Come on, Sage! Show us where the room is!"

Lisa, with Betty in tow, picked up the screwdriver on her way to the hall. She picked up Sage and took the lead. They kept Betty in the middle, making sure she kept up pace, and Greg brought up the rear, keeping the revolver aimed at the back door as the green arm withdrew from the hole in the middle—but the banging continued. They had made a hole, and now Greg definitely knew it wouldn't be long until the group was in immediate danger again.

Chapter Thirty-Six

THE BANGING ON THE BACK DOOR CONTINUED AS GREG, Lisa, Sage, and Betty walked upstairs to the hallway that held the bedrooms. Betty's shoulders jumped up with each bang. "It's alright, Betty. We're almost out of this mess," Greg said reassuringly. Were they, though? For all he knew, he was lying right to her face—to *everyone's* face.

At the top of the steps, Lisa set Sage down to the floor. She gripped Lisa's tank top with both hands; it seemed like she didn't want to be let go. She was obviously terrified, and Greg wanted nothing more than to hug her…squeeze her tight and never let go. He was always close to Sage, but now with what happened to Kyle…Sage would be lucky if Greg ever let her out of his sight again.

Lisa grabbed her daughter's hands, pried them off her shirt, and held them in her own hands as she stared into her eyes. "Sage, I know you're scared, but I need you to be brave right now… We *all* do, okay?" Sage barely nodded. "Can you show us where the door is?"

Sage tapped her cheek with her forefinger. "Ummm…I

think it's *that* one." She removed her finger from her cheek and pointed at a black, nondescript door. It resembled a closet that one would overlook unless someone pointed it out.

Lisa placed her hand on the doorknob and Greg said, "Wait! Let me go first."

He squeezed past Betty and Sage and walked up to the door with Lisa. He held up his bandaged hand. "Can you grab the door?" Lisa put her hand on the knob. "Open it quickly and get back," Greg said. Lisa nodded, turned the handle, then yanked the door open and immediately retreated to stand in front of Sage and Betty, hoping to shield them from any threat.

Greg breached the room, and when he made eye contact with a green eyeball with black speckles and a thin vertical pupil, he fired two shots from the snub-nosed revolver.

Bang!

Bang!

The green, scaly figure in front of him didn't move, didn't fall to the floor. It just…*stayed put*. When his eyes adjusted to the lighting in the room, he saw he had shot a taxidermied alligator that stood on a raised platform. After a brief moment of relief, he realized there wasn't just one taxidermied alligator, but a whole swath of them filling the room. Goosebumps covered his arms as the stuffed reptiles seemed to glare at him with their glassy green eyes. He then heard a noise coming from somewhere deeper in the room and had to wonder—were they *all* stuffed?

Greg turned back at the open door leading to the hall-way. He made eye contact with Lisa and held his hand out, signaling for her to stay put with Sage and Betty. He turned back toward the room and began walking cautiously further in. He passed by the stuffed alligators, keeping an eye on them, looking for any sort of movement. Every once in a while, he'd nudge one with his elbow to see if it would react, but nothing. He felt paranoid—maybe even a little crazy—but he *knew* he'd heard something.

Jesus. This room is enormous. A little further down, the museum-like display of stuffed alligators came to an end. Sick of being surrounded by the beasts, Greg picked up his pace, but continued to monitor them, just in case. When he reached the end, he turned the corner and quickly raised his revolver, aiming it at the back wall. "What the hell are *you* doing in here?"

"Why don't you put the gun down, Greg?" Brent asked, aiming a pump-action shotgun back at him.

Brent stood with his back to the wall. A reclining chair sat next to him, and a framed photo hung on the wall behind it. The photo was of Brent, Ashley, and a woman Greg hadn't seen before. He figured she was probably Brent's wife. On the other side of Brent, opposite the recliner, was a half-wall that appeared to lead to another room.

Greg's thoughts whirled like a hurricane as he kept the revolver trained on Brent. "I-I don't understand. You were out there in the crowd."

"What's so hard to understand?" Brent asked. "I simply left."

"But *why*?"

"I'm not one of *them*. I'm a monster, sure, but not *that* kind of monster. So, like I asked before, why don't you put the gun down, Greg?"

Greg took a step forward, his brow lowering in anger.

"Not until you tell me what the hell is going on here. What are those…things?"

"Here. I'll go first." Brent lowered the barrel of his shotgun and waited in silence for a moment. "Come on. Your turn."

Not again, Greg thought. He'd fallen for this trap before…and had the scar to prove it.

Back when he and Jake Coleman still had their detective badges, they were present at a hostage situation—a small bank branch in Flint, Michigan. The perpetrator had entered the bank wearing a long coat, and witnesses would later tell the police he'd been sweating quite a bit and was fidgeting—at least enough for them to make a note of it. The elderly teller apparently noticed his odd behavior as well and, as a precaution, pressed the silent alarm under her counter once the man stood in line. As the perp reached the counter and slipped a note to the teller demanding money, the police arrived outside.

Already on edge, the perp freaked out and pulled a gun from an inside pocket of his coat. He then reached over the counter, gripped the collar of the elderly teller's sweater, and pulled her over the counter. When the police approached the doors to the bank, the perp held the teller in front of his body and held the gun to her head, threatening to shoot her if anyone entered the building. After talking with the police over the phone, the perp agreed to let an officer come in to negotiate.

Greg and Jake stood before a cluster of police cars as they strapped on Kevlar vests, eagerly anticipating their negotiation. "When we get this guy, it has to be some kind of record, right?" Greg asked.

Jake smiled. "*Has* to be. What are we on? Ten hostage situations?"

"Nine. Soon to be ten." Greg winked.

"You two are a little too excited," the sergeant said as he approached them.

Jake chuckled. "It's okay to be jealous, Sarge."

The sergeant rolled his eyes. "Whatever. You know the deal by now. Keep him talking, keep him busy. Be the girl who says she doesn't put out on the first date. Play hard to get, but relent and give him what he wants. Get as many people out as you can and get a clear shot for the sniper."

Greg ejected the magazine of his handgun, checked the ammunition, and slapped it back in place. "Awe. What fun is that?"

"I don't want any of your John McClane shit! Just get in there and do your jobs *properly*!"

"Don't worry, I'm just messing around!" Greg rubbed the top of the sergeant's bald head, and the sergeant slapped his hand away.

"Just get in there and help those hostages!"

Greg approached the bank with Jake right behind him, their guns drawn. As soon as they entered the door, they were met with the perp holding the teller at gunpoint. Greg and Jake both raised their weapons and aimed at the perp.

The perp pressed the barrel of his gun against the teller's temple. "Whoa! What the fuck is this?! I thought this was a negotiation!"

"Take it easy, buddy," Greg said. "I don't intend to use this. Nobody needs to get hurt here."

"Then why don't you put it down?"

"You know I can't do that."

"Here. I'll go first." The perp removed the gun from the teller's head and tucked it back into his inside coat pocket. He still held onto the teller, but held his now-free hand out toward the detectives. "See? I'm a reasonable guy."

Greg sat for a moment, considering holstering his weapon.

Jake called out from behind him, "Don't even think about it, Boyes." The two detectives spent so much time together, they could practically read each other's minds.

"Come on," the perp said. "It's your turn."

Greg exhaled heavily. "Okay…" And he put his weapon in its holster. As soon as he did, a man posing as a hostage stood up from behind a chair and pulled a gun from his waistband.

Bang!

He fired, shooting Greg in the arm and causing him to fall on his ass on the floor. Jake turned and fired at the man.

Bang!

A direct hit to the head.

The perp quickly pulled his weapon back out from his jacket and shot the elderly teller in the head, spraying her brains all over the cubicle wall next to them before her life-less body collapsed. Jake turned to the perp and continued firing.

Bang!

Bang!

Bang!

The three shots hit the perp in his torso and sent him to the ground alongside the teller.

"You alright?" Jake asked, looking down at Greg.

Greg held the bullet wound in his arm. "Yeah, I'm fine."

"Good. You're a fucking *idiot*." Jake approached the perp lying on the ground—he was still breathing; although his breaths seemed labored. Jake aimed his gun at the perp.

Bang!

The perp's breathing stopped when the bullet entered the front of his skull.

Brent sounded impatient. "Hello? I said it's your turn."

Greg squeezed the grip on the revolver. "You know I can't do that. Just talk."

Chapter Thirty-Seven

Brent shook his head and smirked. "Where shall I begin?" He placed the shotgun on the recliner next to him. "Abin is a certified *maniac*."

"Yeah. I got that," Greg said.

"Years ago, he worked for the government at some sort of...*black site*. A military facility that's off the books. Almost nobody knows about it except for the people who work there and *very* few higher-ups. Like the top of the top. If you get contracted to work there and they find out that you even *mention* it to anyone—your significant other, your kids, your priest..." Brent slashed his thumb across his throat. "...You disappeared."

Brent picked the shotgun up off the recliner, and Greg pulled back the hammer on his revolver. "What are you doing?" Greg asked.

Brent looked at him flatly and leaned the shotgun against the wall behind him. "Point your gun at me all you want, but I'm sitting down. My legs are tired." He took a seat in the recliner.

Greg decocked his weapon, but kept his aim on Brent. "So, what did Abin do at this black site?"

"Biochemistry. He was scarce on detail, but it had something to do with seeing the effects of biochemical weapons on animals."

"But chemical weapons are illegal. War crimes."

"No shit. That's why nobody knew about this place. Anyway, he got caught doing his own experiments that he claimed were for the greater good, and he was about to get the axe. He caught wind of it, and when they came to scoop him up, he took whatever he could carry and split... disappeared down here to the Everglades and founded Snake Bight, starting with this island."

"What, they were going to kill him?"

"I can't say for sure. I wasn't there. He seemed to think so, though...enough to shed a little blood of his own on the way out."

Greg was so entranced by the story, he didn't notice he'd been subconsciously lowering the gun. Brent moved in his chair to readjust himself, and Greg snapped back to reality, picking the revolver back up to aim it properly. "What experiments was he doing that would cause them to fire him?"

Brent threw his head back and smirked. "Do I really need to *spell* it out for you? He was extracting DNA from alligators in order to splice it with human DNA. And as you've seen firsthand, he succeeded. He took his potential firing as a personal attack; as the government using its power to control him and infringe upon his rights."

"If you're not one of them, why are you here? In Snake Bight?"

Brent lowered his eyes, looking down at his lap. "I was the first successful experiment." Greg's eyes widened, and Brent raised his head back up to look at him. "I was on a sight-seeing trip with my wife and daughter. We'd gotten turned around somewhere in the Everglades and, luckily, we stumbled upon Abin…at least we *thought* we were lucky. We'd been wandering for hours longer than we'd planned and were out of food and running low on water. Abin invited us back to his house for lunch and to rest. Who wouldn't take that offer? Especially from such an innocent-looking, charismatic man?" Brent stood back up from the recliner and turned to face the wall, pulling the picture frame down. He held it in his hands at waist level and stared at it. "After a few hours, he changed. He wanted us to 'volunteer' for his experiments and threatened us with violence if we didn't…said he'd kill Ashley in front of us, so what were we supposed to do?"

Greg looked at the revolver in his hand, and his stomach lurched. What was he doing? This man was clearly in pain; he had no intention of hurting him. He thought for a second before lowering the weapon to his side.

Brent looked up at him and nodded, then looked back down at the photo. "He didn't let us pick. I would've volunteered for it. I *tried*, but he wouldn't have it. He wanted Vanessa. My wife." Brent wiped a tear from his eye. "Abin hadn't refined the process because he was so eager to get started. No test runs once he got down here with his own equipment. He went straight into human trials. Vanessa's body rejected the gator plasmids, and she had an acute hemolytic reaction. As soon as she woke from her anesthesia, she was pale as a ghost, sweating profusely, almost as if she had the flu. And her back. She had an indescribable pain in her back. Said it was so bad she wanted to *die*. I-I tried to care for her… Abin said it was normal…that it would pass, but it didn't."

Brent hung the photo back on the wall and ran his

finger over his wife's picture. "Eighteen hours." He turned to face Greg. "Eighteen hours of pure torture until she finally went into shock. Then cardiac arrest. Her heart stopped beating right in front of me. I did CPR until my arms gave in and I literally couldn't anymore. Meanwhile, Abin just left her to die; only referred to her as a 'failed experiment.'"

Greg felt his eyes brim with tears. "Jesus. I'm sorry. I… didn't know."

"Abin ditched her body, fed it to the gators, and started back to work. He'd realized his hubris was the reason for his failure and took his time to better his process. He held me and Ashley captive for a few months until he was ready to try again." Brent held his arms out as if he were presenting himself. "And although he didn't *perfect* the process the way he'd hoped, you're looking at the first successful human-gator hybrid."

Greg was in disbelief. "You're shitting me. What makes you so different?"

"You've seen me before. In the swamp." Brent pointed to the scar over his eye, and then Greg remembered.

"That scar…the alligator that attacked the boat. That was *you*?"

Brent nodded. "I wasn't *attacking* the boat necessarily. I was trying to scare you, hoping you'd get Abin to turn the boat around and head back. I was trying to *help* you. I didn't choose this. I don't want to be here, and I was going to do anything I could to prevent it from happening to others."

"But…*you* were the one that recommended the tour to us, Brent."

"I did. But I had a change of heart. I saw you and your loving family, and I just…couldn't let you suffer the same fate as me and my family."

"Weren't you afraid of what Abin would do to you? I mean, he had to have known what you were doing when you 'attacked' the boat."

"What, like kill me?" Brent laughed. "No, not at all. He would be destroying his first breakthrough. I'm his trophy, his muse."

"The others. Are they here of their own volition? Did they volunteer for this?"

"Not at first. After my transformation, I was stuck here. Because my DNA is spliced with gator plasmids, I need the tropical sun, humid air, and water. I couldn't live in a normal society, so I helped Abin build and establish Snake Bight on the mainland. A few people were stragglers, looking for a fresh start in a new place, but most were like you. Stumbled upon our town while on vacation and took the swamp tour. But to answer your question, nobody volunteered. They, like me, were forced into it. The thing is, Abin found a new way to perform the procedure…he'd basically perfected it, and when he did, he made the creatures you saw outside. He was able to splice the DNA so perfectly that when they're in their human form, they're just normal, run-of-the-mill people. But when they transform, the gator becomes the dominant gene. Sort of like a…Dr. Jekyll and Mr. Hyde situation. However, the gator gene's takeover slowly rots their brains, greatly reducing their lifespan. When they're humans, they may seem and act normal, but the suppressed gator gene is still strong enough to control their thoughts. They're evil and will do whatever Abin says. Ethics aside, what he was able to accomplish in a relatively short amount of time is really an amazing scientific feat."

"Reduces their lifespans?"

"Yes. And thank God for that. If they didn't die off,

Abin would have an army by now. He's working on a fix for that now, and he needs to be stopped."

"How exactly does he plan on doing that? With us?"

Brent's eyes turned grim. "No. You and your family were just to replace a few that recently passed. He already has what he needs to accomplish a longer lifespan. He just hasn't figured out *how* yet."

"Well, what is it?" Greg asked sternly. "Point me in the right direction and I'll take care of it."

Brent turned his head toward the half-wall. "Come on, honey. It's okay."

Ashley came out from behind the half-wall and stood next to Brent, and he put his arm around her. "My daughter, Ashley, is the key."

Chapter Thirty-Eight

BRENT POINTED AT HIS WIFE IN THE PHOTO ON THE WALL. "The beginning." Then to the photo of himself. "The past." Then, finally, to Ashley's. "The future."

Ashley waved at Greg, and he hesitantly waved back. Greg asked, "Is she—"

"One of them?" Brent asked, finishing Greg's question. "No. She's Abin's golden goose. He'd found out that she has a rare genetic disorder associated with her connective tissue. Her skin stretches like elastic, and her joints are hyperflexible. So much so that it's physically impossible for her to dislocate any bones. Abin found that if he extracted her DNA and spliced it with gator DNA, he could essentially make a *super* strand of DNA, which he could then splice with his subject. He sees Ashley as a divine force that came to him to help him wage his war on the government that wronged him and took over the country, then the world. She's the *creator* he speaks of in his sermons."

Greg couldn't believe what Brent was telling him. It sounded like an 80s sci-fi B-movie. "He's a fucking mad scientist."

"Indeed. And I'm afraid he's close to achieving his goal of a longer lifespan. He began his newest process by experimenting with Ethan. Guy was a pro wrestler who lived in Orlando. He came to the tour for research on a new gimmick where he was an alligator hunter or something. I don't know if you saw that fucker without his neck gaiter on, but he doesn't have a lower jaw. That's one of the side effects. I think Abin would be fine with them losing a few pieces of their body for now, but he's not sure about the lifespan yet. He has to wait for signs of further deterioration of the brain."

"Ethan isn't Abin's son?"

Brent's eyelids closed partly; he was looking at Greg as if he were a moron. "Are you serious?"

Greg shrugged.

"No, Ethan is not his son. And Valentine isn't his daughter either. Abin doesn't have the *time* to wait to see whether or not Ethan has an extended lifespan. As you heard, he thinks the government is coming to get him any day now. So, he took it a step further."

"How so?"

"You noticed Ashley and Valentine are identical, right?"

"Don't tell me he kidnapped your other daughter and made her his own…"

Brent shook his head solemnly.

"No," Greg said, his eyes growing wide. "Don't…don't tell me he *cloned* Ashley!"

Brent nodded. "He splices the gator plasmids into the cloned embryos, so they're 'born' as hybrids."

Greg's mouth hung open. "You're fucking with me now. This is absolutely *insane*."

"I promise you I'm not. When you get to the boathouse, take a peek behind the big metal door. That's his lab. I wouldn't blame you if you wanted to take your family and just get the hell out of here, but if you really want to help stop Abin, you have to destroy it."

"I don't know. I just want to get my family out of here alive at this point. I've already lost my son."

"Oh, I'm sorry," Brent said, lowering his eyes. "He seemed like a good kid."

"He was. He died trying to save us. Listen, I'll consider it, but if it comes down to destroying the lab or losing someone else…"

"I totally understand. And I wouldn't blame you. It may prove difficult to get in anyway. It needs a retinal scan to unlock the door."

"Abin's retinal scan," Greg said matter-of-factly.

"Bingo." Brent stepped toward Greg, causing him to raise the revolver once more. Brent lifted his hands in surrender.

"What are you doing?"

"Take it easy. I have a favor to ask you." Brent approached Greg. "I need you to take Ashley with you."

Greg lowered his weapon to his side. "What?"

Brent's eyes looked full of sorrow. He didn't want to give up his daughter, and Greg could tell just by looking at him. "Please. If you destroy the lab, you'll slow Abin down, but if you were to take away his primary subject, the one person he *needs* to continue his atrocious campaign, you'll stop it all. He won't find another person with her disorder. It's so rare, he'd die ten times over before he even came *close*." Brent lowered his eyes to the floor. "She doesn't deserve to be a lab rat for the rest of her life. She deserves better. Something *normal*. I'm not asking you to adopt her and care for her. I'm only asking you to get her out of this place."

Greg hesitated for a moment before putting his hand on Brent's shoulder. "Okay. I'll get her off this island."

Brent raised his gaze, tears streaming down his cheeks. "I don't know what to say…*thank you.*"

"What about you? What are you going to do?"

"I told you. I'm stuck here. I deserve it, I suppose."

"What do you mean?"

"I helped Abin build this place; helped him gather people for years, only for him to turn them into monsters and ruin their lives."

"Come on, that's not fair. You yourself said that you and your family were threatened!"

Brent scoffed. "That may be true, but I could've fought harder. You can always fight harder. I've made my bed, and I'm okay with it…as long as my daughter is safe." He returned to Ashley and kneeled in front of her, putting his hands on her shoulders. "Ashley, sweetie, you're going to go with Mr. Greg and his family. They're going to take you somewhere safe, somewhere far from here, okay?"

Ashley looked confused, raising an eyebrow. "Where are *you* going?"

Brent appeared to be holding back more tears as he moved his arms around his daughter and squeezed her tight. "Daddy has to stay here and help Mr. Abin."

"Can't I just stay with you?"

Brent pulled himself back, gripping Ashley's shoulders again. "You can't, I'm sorry. It's getting too dangerous and scary here. I…won't be too far behind you. Wherever you go, I'll be there." He kissed her on the forehead and stood back up and patted her on the back. "Go on with Mr. Greg."

Ashley looked over at Greg and appeared hesitant. "Come on, Ashley," Greg said. "My daughter Sage is just outside the door. You guys can play together!"

She turned back to Brent. Greg understood why she was so apprehensive; he was a stranger, after all, and one of the first rules a child learns is don't talk to strangers. "It's okay," Brent said. "Mr. Greg will take care of you until I finish up here. He's my friend."

Ashley turned and walked toward Greg as he held his arm out, gesturing down to the back of the room filled with stuffed alligators. "Sage and my wife are right outside that door, waiting for you." He watched as Ashley waded through the taxidermy museum and out the door.

Greg turned back to Brent, who was approaching him with the shotgun in his hands. He extended his arms out toward Greg, handing over the firearm. "Here. You'll probably need this."

Greg placed his revolver in his pocket and took the shotgun from Brent's hands. *The big gun.*

"The shells loaded in there are all I could find, so make them count." Brent walked back to the half-wall, and Greg noticed he had a pistol tucked into his back waistband. As he reached the half-wall, Brent looked back and said, "Keep her safe, and thank you again." Greg nodded, and Brent disappeared into the side room.

Walking down the taxidermy room, Greg still felt uneasy as he passed by the stuffed alligators. He wiped his hand along the side of one, and a chill shot through his body. *These things are so fucking creepy.* At the end of the room, he grabbed hold of the doorknob and—*bang!*

A gunshot followed by a massive thumping sound from behind him caused Greg to jump. He squeezed his eyes shut and shook his head. *Jesus, Brent.* He took a deep breath, opened the door, and entered the hallway.

Chapter Thirty-Nine

GREG EXITED THE TAXIDERMY ROOM, AND TO HIS RELIEF, his group was still there and intact. Lisa's face looked as if she was ready to take on the devil himself as she stood in front of Sage, Ashley, and Betty, shielding them and wielding her screwdriver with both hands. When Greg made eye contact with her, her tensed-up body visibly relaxed, and her face turned to relief as she ran up to him and wrapped her arms around him. "Oh my God, Greg!"

"I'm alright," Greg said.

Lisa breathed into his ear. "I heard a gunshot."

"That…that was Brent."

"Did you—"

"No, he did it to himself."

After Greg explained to Lisa what Brent had told him, she looked back at Ashley for a moment before turning back to Greg. "So, she's *ours* now?"

"No, nothing like that. He just asked that we get her out of here safely." Lisa sat silently, staring at him. "What was I supposed to do? Say no? What if it was Sage being poked and prodded all day for this *sick* shit?"

"I didn't say you made the wrong decision," Lisa said. "It's…just a lot to process. We have a lot of people to keep safe."

"I know. And we'll all get out of this *together*. We'll worry about what we're going to do with Ashley once we're clear of Snake Bight."

Lisa smiled.

"What?" Greg asked.

"Always the hero."

I'm no hero, Greg thought. *How could she be so apathetic? Did she already forget I let our son march straight to his death? No, Greg. Don't do that. Not now. For all you know, she's doing her best not to break down.*

Greg extended his arm out, holding the shotgun out toward Lisa.

Her eyes moved down to the weapon, then back up to her husband. "What do you want me to do with that?"

"Do you remember how to shoot?" he asked.

Lisa's eyes moved around nervously. "Y-yeah, I remember."

Greg held up his bandaged hand. "Good. I'd only slow us down trying to use it."

Lisa took the shotgun and held it in front of her, admiring it. She then gripped it properly and aimed at the wall to check the iron sights. "Like riding a bi—"

Greg held his hand up again—cutting her off mid-sentence—this time to silence her. "Do you hear that?"

Lisa's eyes narrowed as if that would help her hear more clearly. "Hear what?"

Greg turned his head toward the steps that led downstairs. "The banging…it *stopped*."

"It stopped a while ago," Lisa said. "A few minutes after you went in that door."

"They know we're in here. Why would they stop trying to get in?"

Lisa shrugged her shoulders.

Greg pulled the revolver from his pocket and grasped the doorknob across the hall. "Stay here." He opened the door and entered, aiming the revolver, ready to shoot anyone or anything that got in his way. It was only an empty bedroom.

He walked to the lone window and peered out. It had started raining, so the view wasn't great, and all he could see was a couple hundred feet of grass, followed by swamp water. Luckily, the sky was lightening up as dawn was upon them. *Useless*, he thought.

He returned to the hallway, reuniting with the rest of the group. "Anything?" Lisa asked eagerly.

"No, I couldn't see shit. I don't know if that's a good thing or bad…only one way to find out."

Greg began the descent down the creaking steps as Sage, Ashley, and Betty followed, with Lisa bringing up the rear. They reached the bottom, and when he stepped into the kitchen, Greg halted in the doorway. The bodies, the blood, the gore—Greg suddenly felt dizzy. *I feel like I'm gonna be sick.*

Lisa's muffled voice entered his ear; he could barely understand her. "Greg…you…Greg…you okay…" He shook his head and her voice came through clearly. "Greg, are you okay?"

He looked down at his arms, and they were *drenched* in sweat. *Come on, man. Just breathe. They're counting on you.* He took a few breaths, and the dizziness went away, and he felt a cool rush over his body as he stopped sweating. He turned back to look at Lisa. "Yeah, I'm fine. Listen, I don't know if those monsters are still on the other side of that door or not, but wherever they are, they're still going to be coming for us, so we have to be ready. Lisa, I want you to take Sage, Ashley, and Betty and get to the boathouse as quickly as you can."

"What about you?"

"I'll be right behind you. I'll be providing cover to make sure you guys get there safe and sound."

"Isn't the boathouse a dead end? I don't know whether Ethan's boat can fit all of us."

"We're taking Abin's airboat."

"I thought it had broken down. Did he fix it?"

"There was never anything wrong with it. Kyle told me so. It was a lie so that *monster* could get us here." Greg bent down and peered through the hole that the creature had punched in the door, trying to scan the outside. "I don't see anything. Just the stage way back there." He looked over his shoulder at his wife. "I think now is our best shot to go." Lisa nodded, although Greg could tell she was about-to-piss-herself nervous. He turned back to the hole in the door and gave it one more look before standing up and gripping the doorknob. "On second thought…you guys stay back for a minute. I'll go out and make sure it's clear. *Don't* leave this house until I give the OK." He ripped open the door and raised his weapon, aiming as he exited the house.

He pointed his revolver on either side of him, clearing the immediate area. Turning back to the doorway, he opened his mouth to shout for the group to come out, but then he got an awful feeling in the pit of his stomach. Call it intuition, call it nerves, call it whatever you'd like—but *something* didn't feel right. He looked at Lisa in the doorway and gestured for her to close the door, which she did. *I should check a little further,* he thought.

Greg moved around the eastern corner of the house, the closest to the boathouse, and when he turned the corner, he heard a voice shout from behind him. "Well, well, well…now just *where* do ya think yer *goin'*?"

He stood up straight, stunned at the sound of the thick Southern drawl. *Shit.* Spinning around, he put the revolver behind his back. Abin stood before him with a bandage wrapped around his knee and using a cane to help himself balance. Greg carefully tucked his gun into his back waistband.

Behind Abin stood seven human-gator hybrids in their tattered white robes, their sickening, saliva-soaked tongues licking the tips of their pointed yellow teeth. The corners of Abin's mouth turned up, forming a sinister grin. "So, ya gon' answer me? Or are ya just gon' stand there with that stupid look on yer face?"

Chapter Forty

THAT'S NOT ALL OF THEM, GREG THOUGHT AS HE EYED THE creatures—watching their every movement—waiting for them to attack. *Where are the rest?*

Abin's eyebrow raised, his fingertips rhythmically tapping the handle of his cane. "Well, Mr. Boyes…I'm *waiting.*"

"What exactly are you planning here, Abin? What's your move?"

"What happens next depends wholly on you, Greg."

Greg felt his face drop subconsciously, as if someone else were controlling him. He wasn't sure if his brain thought he could trick Abin or if it just got tired of fighting, tired of running. For a brief moment, he thought maybe, just maybe, deep down, he wanted to *give up*. But he quickly pushed that terrible thought back down as an idea popped into his head. *Abin hasn't seen Lisa, or Sage, or anyone else*, he thought.

Greg lowered his head. "Just let me go. My wife, my kids…all of them…are *dead.*"

Abin's smile vanished, and his jaw muscles protruded

as he gritted his teeth. "I can't let ya go. Now, ya *know* that. Don't ya get tired of askin' the same damn thing over an' over again? I let Mr. Police Officer from bum-fucked Michigan go free, he tells his cop buddies about the resistance in lil' ol' Snake Bight, an' the government comes-a-knockin' even quicker. I didn't *kill* their spy so ya can go an' *blab* yer mouth an' ruin everything… No loose ends an' all that."

Greg raised his gaze toward Abin once again. "*Resistance*? What resistance?! You and your merry band of *circus freaks*?!"

One creature took a step forward. Abin picked up his cane and held it across the creature's chest, stopping it from advancing. "Ya should choose yer words more *wisely*, son. My children ain't got no problem *rippin'* the skin right off yer bones."

The creature hissed at Greg as its tongue slithered around its ghastly maw. Greg recoiled in disgust, watching its thick saliva drip down to the grass. "What's the point of this, Abin?" he asked. "The point of *all* this? Are you…" He looked from side to side and put a hand up to the side of his mouth, leaned forward, and whispered loudly, "… Are you *fucking* these gators?"

Abin slammed his cane back to the ground in front of him, placing both hands on its handle. Veins popped on his forehead, and he shouted, "Why, you—how *dare* you make a mockery of my *genius*! I single-handedly made scientific breakthroughs in genetic modification to birth these magnificent specimens!"

Greg chuckled to himself. *I knew that would get him riled up.*

Abin calmed himself and looked at the ground. He took a moment to pull a handkerchief from his shirt pocket and dab the sweat from his brow, then looked back up; his voice was calm again. "Y'know. Ya remind me of a much younger version of myself. So *naïve*." He placed the hand-kerchief back in his pocket. "Once the bombs fall——"

"You keep bringing up these nuclear bombs," Greg interrupted. "What do you think is going to happen to *you* when this supposed nuclear holocaust happens?"

"When I first spoke to the creator, an' they told me of the war an' devastation that was to come, I had the same question. What on earth would happen to me an' my chil-dren? After all, we've seen what nuclear bombs can do... the creator assured me that if I followed through with their plan, the way they intended, a *force field* powerful enough to absorb any number of bombs would be placed over this sanctuary."

Greg stared at him, dumbfounded. "You *cannot* be seri-ous. I mean, you're fucking with me now, right? The 'cre-ator' is a frightened seven-year-old girl you've used to perform experiments on!" Abin's face turned to one of apparent surprise. "That's right," Greg continued. "I know all about what really went on here. You may have brain-washed these freaks, but it won't work on *me*!"

Abin tapped the handle of his cane——either impatiently or angrily; Greg couldn't be sure, but it was quickly. He appeared to tongue the inside of his cheek, perhaps looking for the right words to say. And then he finally spoke up. "I wasn't lyin'...when I said I thought ya could help our society. I really thought ya had the potential to lead this race to *dominance*. But now..." Abin, his face full of disgust, spit on the ground toward Greg. "...Now, I see yer just like the rest of 'em. I see the way yer lookin' at me. Ya think I'm *mental*."

"*Think?!*"

"Ya think a man with my brainpower could be insane?" Abin asked, pointing a finger into his own chest as his voice got louder. "Ya think the creator woulda chose *me* to lead an army to take over the world if I was mad?!" Abin picked his cane up and pointed it at Greg. "In *my* world, there won't be no separate races to *hate* each other! There won't be no different religions to start wars 'cause they think they're right an' all the others are wrong! I finally will have created world peace…the way the creator intended.!"

Chapter Forty-One

Lisa crouched next to the door leading outside, huddled up with Sage and Ashley as Betty stood in the corner facing the wall. *Come on, Greg. Please tell us it's clear.*

Sage began to speak, "Mom, wher—" Lisa cut her off, placing her finger over her lips. Sage continued, whispering, "Where's Dad? Is he okay?"

"He's fine," Lisa breathed. "He's making sure the outside is safe." *God, I hope he's fine,* she thought. Crawling over toward the middle of the door, she got to her knees, and raised her head to peer through the hole made by the creatures. She scoffed as she still couldn't see anything, but she *did* hear Greg's voice. He was talking to someone.

She leaned the shotgun against the wall and grasped the doorknob and twisted it. *Nice…and easy. Ugh, this is a bad idea.* The knob stopped twisting as the latch bolt passed through the strike, freeing the door from its frame, and she cautiously pulled the door open just a crack; just enough to see. She put an eye up to the crack and looked outside. *Oh, shit!* She saw Greg standing across from Abin and several of the hybrid creatures. Quietly shutting the door, she collapsed onto her rear, leaning her back against the wall.

"What's wrong, Mom?" Sage asked.

Ashley crawled over to Lisa and kneeled in front of her, looking at her with unblinking eyes. "You saw them, didn't you? They're out there."

Lisa, her eyes brimming with tears, nodded at the little girl. Ashley grabbed Lisa's hand and pulled it. "Don't be sad. We can go the other way. It'll take us to the boathouse." She smiled at Lisa. "That's where Mr. Greg told us to go, right?"

Lisa chewed the inside of her cheek, unsure of whether or not they should leave without Greg—especially while he was in a standoff with a madman and those…*things*.

He's a big boy, Lisa thought. *He can stall long enough for us to get the boat ready.* "Okay, Ashley. Good idea." She rose to her feet and picked the shotgun up from the wall. *At least, I hope it is.* "Sage, honey, can you grab Betty's hand and bring her with us? I'm going to check the front door."

Ashley led Lisa through the living room to the foyer, where the front door lay. Lisa aimed the shotgun at the door. "Ashley, can you open the door, please? Slowly."

The little girl approached the door, placed her hand on the knob, and looked back at Lisa. Lisa nodded, and Ashley pulled the door open. Lisa stepped through the doorway, aiming the shotgun around the immediate area before lowering it. "Clear," she breathed, as a wave of relief washed over her. She glanced back at the doorway, where Ashley stood. "Did Sage and Betty make their way up here?"

Ashley shook her head.

Lisa re-entered the house and returned to the back door near the kitchen. Betty stood still, facing the wall, while Sage tried to pull her arm. "Come on, Betty! My mom said we have to go!"

Lisa walked up to them and put her hand on the small of Betty's back. "It's okay, Sage. Go with Ashley to the front door." She watched Sage run toward the living room, then turned to Betty. "Betty. Come on, hon. We're going to get the boat ready. We did it! We're finally getting out of here!"

Betty stayed silent.

Fed up, Lisa slung the shotgun over her shoulder before grabbing Betty's shoulders and forcefully spinning her around, staring into her eyes. "Listen to me! I've been nice and supportive up to this point, but now you're not the only person who's *lost* someone! So, I need you to grow a set of ovaries and follow me out to that goddamned boathouse so we can leave this fucking place!" Lisa's eyes were wild as she huffed, waiting for a response from the older woman.

Betty looked at her in silence. It looked like there was nothing behind her eyes—as if her soul had left. After a moment, she placed her hands on top of Lisa's and removed them from her shoulders. She then turned back around to face the wall.

Lisa threw her hands in the air. "Fine. Fine! I'll leave your ass here, then!" Lisa turned and stomped back toward the front door. *Maybe that'll get through to her,* Lisa thought. *We'll come back for her when we have the boat ready.*

Lisa entered the foyer, where Sage and Ashley waited by the partially opened front door. Lisa didn't stop as she walked past them and through the door. "Come on, girls."

With the two girls close behind her, Lisa walked across

the grass toward the large wooden boathouse that sat off the edge of the island, keeping her head on a swivel. *It looks even bigger up close*, she thought.

They entered through a small door on the side of the building. Inside, a dock was built along the edge of the swamp water and, just on the other side of the dock, Abin's airboat and Ethan's fishing boat floated in place, tied up to the dock posts. Lisa felt a tightness in her chest. It wasn't nerves or stress, but excitement…happiness. She felt as if she were about to explode with joy. "We did it, Sage! We *did it*! We're going *home*!"

Sage looked up at her mom. She appeared sad. "But… where's Dad?"

The overabundance of happiness that had surged through her suddenly vanished when she saw the look on her daughter's face. "He's going to meet us here. He's making sure there aren't any bad people out there to get in our way. He's going to meet us, don't worry." Lisa climbed onto the fan boat and set the shotgun on a bench seat. Turning around, she leaned over the side of the boat, holding her hand out to Sage. "Come on. I got you!" Sage grabbed hold of her hand and took a big step onto the boat, and Ashley followed right after.

Lisa moved to the back of the boat, near Abin's chair, and rummaged around the various crates that sat on the floor. "What are you looking for, Mom?" Sage asked.

"There's got to be a *manual* or something around here."

"You can't drive it?"

Lisa scratched the back of her head. "I don't know. I kind of watched Abin do it…it didn't look *that* hard." She scanned the boat floor one more time and spotted a small box next to Abin's chair. She opened it and found a folded-up booklet. "Bingo! There you are!"

Flipping through the booklet, she nodded along as she read. "Mhmm. Mhmm."

Sage's voice trembled. "M-mom?"

"Hold on, honey. Mom is reading," Lisa said, ignoring the fear in her daughter's voice. "Yeah, this is simple. I think I got it!"

"Mommy!"

Lisa looked up from the booklet toward Sage and Ashley. They had looks of absolute terror tattooed on their faces. Lisa felt her own face drop. "What's wrong, Sage?" She knelt in front of her daughter, looking into her eyes. In the reflection of Sage's pupils, she saw the silhouette of a figure. She couldn't tell who it was, but it was oddly shaped —as if it weren't human.

Lisa moved her eyes to Ashley, then back to Sage and mouthed, "Don't. Move." She then slowly reached toward the bench seat next to her. As her fingertips just barely touched the shotgun's stock, she heard footsteps thumping against the wooden dock. Gripping the firearm, she swung it in front of her as she spun around. She pulled back on the forestock, loading a shell into the chamber, but a creature was already leaping onto the fan boat. As she squeezed the trigger, the creature pushed the shotgun barrel toward the ceiling.

Boom!

Lisa looked up to see the shotgun blow a hole in the boathouse's ceiling as shards of splintered wood rained down upon her. She fell to the bench seat and moved her eyes back down, and the creature was lunging at her. Thinking fast, she grabbed the barrel with one hand and held the shotgun sideways, using it to fend off the sharp gator claws. Licking its teeth, the creature hissed as it dug its claws into the firearm's wooden stock.

Lisa hadn't seen the human-gator hybrids up-close.

The closest she got was seeing Ethan without his gaiter, but even *he* appeared more human. *These are different,* she thought as she took time during the struggle to observe the creature. She thought its eyes—olive green, filled with black speckles, with a reflective black vertical slit in the middle—looked oddly beautiful, almost like an abstract painting. But she didn't have time to admire the features of the thing that was trying to kill her and her family. She had to *act.* Putting her knees together, she brought them to her chest before jutting her legs out with as much force as she could muster, kicking the creature square in its torso. She managed to knock it back, but it took the shotgun with it.

Luckily, it's not focused on the girls, she thought, eyeing Sage and Ashley hiding among the crates at the back of the boat. *I have to keep it that way.* She pushed herself up from the bench, keeping her eyes on the creature as it examined the shotgun in its hands.

Lisa backed toward the front of the boat and shouted, "Come on! That all you got?!"

The creature's head shot up, and it roared, tossing the shotgun aside before taking off in a sprint toward Lisa.

Shit! Shit! Shit! Shit! Lisa panicked, looking around for anywhere to go, anything to grab to defend herself—but it was too late. With her mind and heart racing, the creature tackled her, sending them both tumbling over the front of the boat and into the swampy water.

Chapter Forty-Two

Boom!

The sound of an apparent gunshot caused Greg to turn his head behind him at breakneck speed. *Shit! I think Lisa may have found the rest of them*!

"Now, Greg...whatever could *that've* been?" Abin asked.

Greg turned back to face him. He could feel the distress *painted* all over his own face. "I-I don't know."

Abin smiled and took a step forward. "Maybe we should see what it was. Come on. We can go *together*."

Greg felt a vice-like tightness in his gut and pulled the revolver out from his waistband and aimed it at Abin. "No! Don't move another fucking step!"

Abin raised his hands in the air in surrender. As the creatures began to move toward Greg, Abin shouted, "Not *yet*! Stay!" And the creatures took a step back behind Abin once more.

The sweat from Greg's brow stung as it dripped into his eyes, and his breathing became quick and uncontrollable.

Abin looked at Greg, concerned. It was obviously a

put-on. "Yer lookin' awfully pale, son. I think ya might be havin' a panic attack. Just…put the gun down an' *breathe* 'fore ya pass out."

"Shut the *fuck* up!" Greg became lightheaded and stumbled a bit before regaining his composure. He turned his head back toward the boathouse. "Lisa?! LISA?!"

"Lisa?" Abin asked, and Greg turned back to face him. "Ain't that yer wife's name?" Abin wore a look of blissful bewilderment, but Greg knew damn well he was playing a game. "I thought ya said yer family was *dead?*"

Greg pulled back the hammer on the revolver. "Shut up!" He turned back again and shouted, "Lisa!" before turning back to Abin, who was no longer playing stupid. He looked angry.

"Yer *clearly* outnumbered here. So, yer either blind or stupid. An' I've been 'round ya enough now to know yer not stupid, which means ya must be blind. That it? Ya blind, son?" Abin moved his hands back down as the sinister smile returned to his face. "If I said it once, I said it a thousand times…ya ain't gettin' outta here alive."

The revolver trembled as Greg aimed it at Abin's head. *Pull the trigger. Just do it.*

Chapter Forty-Three

Lisa's nasal cavity burned as she descended into the depths, and the swamp water shot up her nose. The creature had caught her off guard when it tackled her into the swamp, and she didn't have time to hold her breath. Suddenly, she felt a tight squeeze around her sternum. She looked down, and the creature had wrapped its arms around her in a bear hug, pinning her arms to her sides. Lisa grunted, unable to scream without her lungs filling with water. She shook her shoulders, attempting to free herself from the clutches of the creature, but it was no use. The creature then wrapped its legs around Lisa's, binding them together, and they began falling fast toward the bottom of the swamp. *It's trying to drown me!*

Boom!

From above the water, Lisa heard what sounded like a muffled gunshot. She turned her head back and saw buckshot pellets break the surface of the water. She knew the creature had been hit when she felt it arch its back. She figured at least one pellet had struck it, and the small amount of green blood that snaked its way up through the water confirmed it. Lisa felt the creature's grip loosen a bit. She could tell it wanted to tend to its wound, but couldn't let her go—it had a job to do, after all. With the creature in pain, she had enough wiggle room to shimmy her body down until the creature's arms were now around her collarbone—within biting distance.

Fuck, this is gross, she thought as she opened her mouth wide and bit down, forcing her teeth into the creature's forearm. She felt the creature's blood fill her mouth as she tasted metal mixed with dirty swamp water. The creature let out a muffled underwater roar as it released its grip on Lisa.

Spinning around, Lisa kicked the creature in its face, drawing a small amount of blood from its mouth. She then turned and swam away, toward the rear of Ethan's boat. She looked back as the creature collected itself and began swimming after her.

As Lisa reached the boat's propeller, the creature caught up to her and latched onto her, once again gripping her in a bear hug. Before it could squeeze tightly, Lisa threw her head back, smacking the creature in its face. The headbutt caused it to recoil, allowing Lisa to escape its grasp again. The creature held its face, and Lisa swam around to the back of it, and spotted a hole in its robe, most likely made by the buckshot pellet. She grabbed the hole and stretched it out to make it bigger, then wrapped it around the boat's propeller a few times. She swam past the creature, toward the surface, when she suddenly halted. Looking back, she saw that the creature had grabbed hold of her foot.

It appeared to try to swim toward her, but was stuck in place. It turned its head back to see that its robe was holding it back, and that gave Lisa the window to pull her foot free from its clutches. The creature turned back to her, and she kicked it in the face one more time for good measure. With the creature recovering, Lisa swam toward the surface.

She breached the water and grabbed the side of Ethan's boat, pulling herself up onto the boat's floor. Exhausted, waterlogged, and soaking wet, she felt like she weighed an extra two hundred pounds, but she had to act fast—before the creature made its way out of her trap. Stumbling her way to the motor at the back of the boat, she grabbed the handle on the starter cord. She yanked on it, but the motor only let out a gurgling sound. After yanking it again, three times in a row, the motor still struggled to start. Lisa closed her eyes and squeezed them tight. *Please. Please. Please.* Opening her eyes, she pulled one more time, and the motor roared to life. She let out a squeal of joy, then grasped the throttle lever and cranked it up. The motor got louder as the swampy water behind the boat began to churn. A screech came from below the water's surface as the motor bogged down for a moment, then picked up momentum again, and the water behind the boat turned a dark green.

Lisa cut the motor and watched the water with bated breath. As the water became still, tattered pieces of white cloth floated to the surface, followed by flaps of scaly skin. Lisa fell back on her ass and put her face in her hands. Her shoulders bounced up and down as she wept, but then, oddly, her cries turned to soft chuckling, then into full-on laughter as she picked her head up from her hands. She found herself laughing like a madwoman, and didn't know why. Was it because she actually survived that creature's attack? Or was it the situation as a whole?

Hearing Sage call out, her laughter stopped abruptly. "Mom?!"

Lisa stood up on wobbly legs and looked back at Abin's

boat, where Sage and Ashley leaned against the front. "Sage! Ashley! Are you okay?"

"We're okay!"

"Are *you* okay?" Ashley added.

Lisa stopped for a second to compose herself. "Yeah. Yeah, I'm okay. I'll be right over." Turning toward the side of the fishing boat, she stopped when something on the floor caught her eye—something metal, mostly covered by a blanket. She bent down and tore the blanket off to reveal a hunting rifle. "Thanks, Ethan, you freak." Climbing over the side of the fishing boat, she planted her feet on the dock. As she walked to the airboat, she eyed the remains of the creature floating in the water. She snorted, hawked up a big loogie, and spat at it. "Fuck you," she muttered under her breath. As Lisa stepped onto the airboat, Sage ambushed her, wrapping her arms around her. As they embraced in a hug, Lisa saw Ashley meandering her way over. Lisa took one arm off of Sage and held it out. "Come on." Ashley came closer, and Lisa pulled her in, hugging both of them.

"Betty saved us!" Sage said with excitement.

Lisa pulled back from the two girls. "What?"

She heard a woman's voice. "I'm sorry I was a pain."

Lisa moved her eyes up and looked toward the middle of the boat where Betty stood, holding the shotgun. "Oh my God, Betty!" She stood up and ran over to Betty and hugged her tight.

Betty dropped the shotgun and returned the hug. "It was the least I could do."

Lisa released her embrace of Betty. "Let's get out of here." Then she heard a noise coming from outside the boathouse. It sounded like roaring. She snapped her head around and looked at the small door they'd come through. It was definitely roaring—and it was getting louder. "I think there's more of them coming!" She moved around Betty and sat in Abin's captain's chair. As she readied to start the boat, she noticed Betty moving toward the dock. Lisa called out, "Betty?"

The older woman kept her head down as she climbed over the edge of the boat and onto the dock. "Yes, dear?"

"Whatcha doing?"

Betty steadied herself on the dock, stood up straight, and pulled down on the front of her vest, straightening it out. She smiled softly at Lisa, and without a word, she turned around and approached the small door. She placed her hand on the handle, and Lisa shouted, "Seriously, what are you *doing*?! Those things are out there!"

Looking back, Betty said, "I'm going to be with Norm."

She pushed down on the handle, and Lisa cried, "Betty! Don't!"

"He's all alone. He needs me." This time, Betty didn't turn to look back. "Go on. I will keep them busy while you get the boat out." Betty continued pushing the handle the rest of the way, then pushed the door open. Beyond Betty, Lisa could just barely make out a swath of creatures. The older woman stepped through the threshold and walked toward the pack of blood-thirsty monsters.

Lisa's eyes were glued to the door as it crept to a close. Just as the crack in the door vanished, she saw the creatures pouncing on Betty. She lowered her head, and a tear fell from her eye onto the boat's floor.

Chapter Forty-Four

ABIN SWIVELED HIS HEAD TO EITHER SIDE OF HIM, LOOKING back at his beastly creations before turning back to face forward. Greg's elevated pulse made him feel like he was going to have a heart attack. *I thought I could talk my way out of this. I don't know what I'm going to do,* he thought.

Abin raised his cane, pointing it in Greg's direction, and shouted, "Feed!" through his sinister grin. The two creatures directly on either side of Abin took off, running toward Greg.

"Fuck!" Greg shouted as he fired the revolver twice—*Bang! Bang!*—Hitting both creatures in the head as green mist sprayed in the air.

Abin spun around to the remaining five creatures behind him. "What are y'all waitin' fer?! Get 'im!" The creatures broke into a sprint and rushed past Abin, gooey saliva flying from their open mouths.

As the creatures bum-rushed him—*Bang! Bang!*—Greg shot two more in the head, taking them down in an explosion of green blood. Unfortunately for him, Abin was right, and he would not win the numbers game. The remaining three creatures *pounced* on him, taking him to the ground.

One creature grabbed hold of Greg's legs, another moved to the top of his head and pinned his arms down, while the third creature straddled his torso, looking him in the face.

Greg turned his head to the side as the creature on top of him opened its mouth and let its long tongue flop out. It dragged its tongue along Greg's cheek, leaving a trail of bubbly saliva behind it. Greg gagged from the rotten smell of mud and fish guts, fighting to keep the vomit down.

The creature brought its head back and showed its teeth, almost as if it were *smiling*. Then its bottom jaw shot forward and dropped, increasing the size of its maw. As the creature began lowering its teeth down to his face, Greg squeezed his eyes shut. *I tried. Lisa…Sage…I'm sorry.* He sat waiting for the end—when—*bang!*

Greg heard the creatures hissing in unison, and Abin say, "The *hell* was that?!"

He waited a moment before opening his eyes, but when he did, Greg noticed the creature on top of him and the one holding his arms had moved their attention toward the water. *Wait. I can move my legs,* he thought. He picked his head up, and down by his feet, he saw the creature that once held his legs; a huge bullet hole in the side of its head spewed out copious amounts of green blood.

Bang!

Greg heard something whizz above his head and then a *thump*. Blood covered his face, then the lifeless corpse of the creature that held his arms hit the ground next to him; another one with a bullet in the head. Greg looked out toward the water, and Lisa was there, standing on Abin's airboat, aiming down the scope of a hunting rifle.

The creature on top of him was still looking in her

direction. *Now's my chance!* Greg grabbed the collar of the creature's robe with both hands—half skinned, half broken hand be damned—and shoved it upward, enough where he could bring his legs in, and place the bottom of his feet on the thighs of the creature. He pulled back with his arms and kicked upward, monkey-flipping the creature over his head. Greg scurried around on top of the now-supine creature and straddled it. He reached behind him, pulling the chef's knife from his belt, and ran it across the creature's throat. He watched as the slit in its neck flapped, gasping for air while it oozed green blood.

Bang!

Another shot knocked Greg out of his victorious trance, and he looked back over at Lisa, who was still aiming the rifle. *Abin!* Greg thought as he glanced around, looking for him. He looked toward the house, where he just caught Abin entering the back door. Keeping his eyes on the house, Greg rose to his feet. He walked over to the revolver, picked it up, and opened the cylinder—it was empty. He dug down into his pants pocket and pulled out a single bullet. He admired the bullet in his palm before loading it into the cylinder and snapping it shut. He turned and walked toward Abin's house.

From behind him, Greg heard Lisa yell from the airboat: "Greg! Where are you going?"

He stopped, took a deep breath, and turned to face his wife. "If I'm not back in ten minutes...*leave.*"

Chapter Forty-Five

GREG SLID INTO THE HOUSE, ENTERED THE FOYER, AND
closed the door behind him. *One bullet. Have to make it count.*
He scanned the room and noticed that picture frames had
been torn from the wall and that someone had knocked
over and shattered the antique, alligator-patterned vases.
*Looks like a tornado came through here. What's the matter, Abin?
Where's your cool Southern demeanor now?* He may have
watched Abin retreat in shame, but Greg had to wonder if
he should be so cocky as he wasn't out of the woods yet.
He tiptoed over the broken shards of ceramic, careful not
to step on them and cause any unwanted noise.

As he neared the kitchen, he heard an unusual noise.
Sounds like someone is…crying. Ducking his head through the
doorway, he peered into the kitchen. He didn't see anyone,
but the sound he'd heard was definitely louder. At a glance,
the kitchen appeared to look just how he'd left it, although
he wasn't entirely confident since it was such a mess the
last time he'd seen it.

Greg turned the corner, aiming the revolver toward the

source of the noise. Abin kneeled before Candy's corpse on the tile floor, a metal toaster where her head once was. Abin's face was buried in his hands, his shoulders shaking with sobs.

"Don't. Move," Greg said sternly.

Abin's shoulders ceased movement, and his weeping stopped. After a moment, he lifted his head. "What'd ya *do?*" he asked, not turning to face Greg.

"Hands up."

Abin's raised voice trembled as if he was trying to hold back more tears. "What'd ya do to my Candy?!"

"I said, put your hands up!"

Abin slowly raised his hands parallel to his shoulders. "Candy…she was my *everythin'*. She gave me a reason to *live*." His head dropped once more. "Do with me what ya will."

Greg felt the tension in his muscles vanish, and he felt a slight pain in his chest. *Oh, come on. I can't be feeling bad for this man…not this monster.* Shaking his head, he tried to wipe away any sympathy he'd started to feel. "You brought this on yourself. You know that, right?"

"I probably don't deserve it, but do me a favor?"

Greg remained silent.

"Don't kill me on my knees with my back turned. Please. Let me die with *some* dignity."

He's trying to pull something. He's got to be. Greg sat on Abin's request for a minute that seemed like a lifetime. "…Fine. Get up."

"Thank ya kindly." Abin grabbed his cane from the floor next to him and used it to balance as he rose to hit feet, keeping his free hand in the air, and groaning from the gunshot wound in his knee. He turned around, and it was apparent to Greg that it hadn't taken long for the stress to take a toll on him. His mouth hung open, and his soulless eyes drooped. He appeared as if he'd aged another twelve years in the last twenty minutes.

"I have to ask you, Abin. This whole…*thing*. You don't really believe it, right?"

Abin took a step back, clearly offended. "I mean every word I say, son." He limped forward, and Greg tightened his grip on the revolver. "What would I gain by makin' up a buncha bullshit? I created the *perfect* specimen to all live in harmony together." He took another step forward. His wounded knee almost buckled, but he'd caught himself with his cane. "My only regret is bringin' *y'all* here. I suppose I let my ego get the better of me. I thought I could *woo* ya into bein' sheriff of Snake Bight. We'd build ya yer own buildin' an' everythin'. Woulda been a simple job, seein' as everyone in town got along… but y'all had to go an' fuck *that* up. You an' that Air Force scum."

Greg chuckled in disbelief. "You still can't get it through your thick skull that me and Norm were just guys on vacation, taking our loved ones on a swamp tour. Unbelievable."

Abin stepped forward again. "I have a hard time believin' it was a coincidence that I went wide with the breakthrough I made a few years ago, an' all the sudden, a government employee pretty much shows up at my doorstep. Now, that just don't make sense, unless he was comin' to spy, an' ya ain't gon' change my mind no matter how many times ya claim he was some innocent old man."

"I don't believe you."

Abin raised an eyebrow. "What's that?"

"I think you made a bad judgement call, and now you don't want to admit that you *murdered* an innocent man in cold blood. You can't be *that* crazy." Greg knew the man *was* that crazy; he was just trying to push his buttons, and from the vein that protruded out of Abin's forehead, it seemed to work.

Abin looked as though he were about to explode when suddenly, Greg noticed his jaw unclench. "*Am* I crazy? All I wanted was world peace… I still want it—" Greg noticed just *how* close Abin had inched toward him while he distracted him with his nonsense, but it was too late, and Abin dropped his cane and lunged at him, tackling him to the floor.

Abin straddled Greg and stared down at him; his eyes were wild, like he had a fire burning behind them. "And I ain't lettin' anyone get in my way!"

Stupid, stupid, stupid! Greg thought as he tried to fight free of Abin's grasp. *How the fuck could you let him get the jump on you?!*

With his mouth foaming like a rabid dog, Abin hissed, "Any last words?!"

Greg's eyes shot open wide, and he felt a warming sensation in his abdomen, which quickly turned to stinging. He began getting lightheaded as he focused on Abin's wicked grin; the plaque buildup on the edges of his gums was vomit-inducing. The stinging in Greg's gut worsened to a sharp ache. He moved his eyes down and saw Abin had plunged a knife into his stomach. He looked back up at Abin and coughed. The corners of his mouth turned up, and blood leaked out of his mouth. "That…all…you got?"

A clicking sound echoed off the kitchen walls, and Abin's evil smile vanished. Greg freed an arm from under Abin and held the revolver under his chin, the hammer cocked.

Bang!

The back of Abin's skull exploded outward, coating the ceiling in red mist. Abin looked down at Greg. The force of the gunshot had knocked his teeth out and left his lower jaw hanging on by a few tendons. His eyes rolled up into the back of his head, and his body collapsed sideways onto the tile floor.

Greg let his head fall in relief, and he let out an exasperated sigh. He took a few breaths before picking his head back up to look at the knife sticking out of his stomach. "Fuck." He grasped the knife handle. "Come on. Just pull it out. One…two…" He slid the knife out of his gut, a bit of blood spurting out with it. "Argh, fuck!" The blade came out a lot easier than he thought it would. The knife clanged against the tile as he tossed it to the side and grabbed his wound, groaning in pain. He rolled onto his stomach and got up onto his hands and knees, and crawled to the dining table. Grabbing hold of the table's lip, he pulled himself up to his feet.

The weight of what'd just happened hit Greg all at once. Abin was gone, Lisa and Sage were safe—but Kyle. Suddenly, Greg's legs became weak and his knees buckled. He caught himself on the dining table before he fell, and then he burst into tears. "Kyle…my son…" He looked over at Abin's dead body and screamed, "You monsters killed my son! You took him away from me, you son of a bitch!"

Greg collected himself and headed for the foyer, using the wall to help him keep his balance. When he reached the front door and put his hand on the doorknob, he heard Brent's voice in his head. *Destroy the lab…*

He looked down at his stomach and moved his blood-soaked hand away from the wound, then he turned back toward the doorway to the kitchen and Brent's words entered his brain once more. *Retinal scan…*

Grunting, Greg placed his hand back over his wound and headed back for the kitchen. *I gotta do what I gotta do.*

He stumbled into the kitchen, still tracing the wall with

one hand, and approached Abin's body. Picking up one of its arms, he attempted to drag the lifeless corpse, but his strength was gone. He then grabbed Abin's shirt and tried dragging him that way—he still wouldn't budge. Then, as if a lightbulb went on above his head, he got an idea. His eyes moved toward the knife on the kitchen floor, then to Abin.

Chapter Forty-Six

GREG, WITH A BLOOD-SOAKED PAPER TOWEL IN HAND, limped into the foyer and exited through the front door. *She didn't leave,* he thought as he spotted the airboat still floating in the water just off the island. He glanced down at the paper towel and turned toward the boathouse.

He heard Lisa call out from the boat, "Greg?! Greg, honey! Where are you *going*?! This way!"

"I'll be right there," he breathed. He tried yelling, but didn't have the strength. Blood was leaking from his abdomen at an alarming rate, and he had to wonder if Abin had hit a vital organ. Approaching the boathouse door, he could still hear Lisa's faint shouts, but couldn't make out what she was saying anymore. He knew he had a job to do, so he ignored her for the time being. After all, Abin was gone, and she was safe. *She'll be fine.*

Greg entered the boathouse and looked around, admiring the extensive building. When he looked at the ceiling, his vision blurred, and he fell against the interior wall. *I'm running out of time.* He bent over, putting his hands on his knees, and took deep, slow breaths until his vision came back. At the back end of the building, he saw a metal door, which seemed very out of place in a building made entirely of wood. *That must be it.*

He pushed himself off the wall and staggered toward the back of the room. Passing by Ethan's boat, he noticed something floating in the water—slabs of scaly skin. *I hope you felt every bit of whatever happened to you.* He stared at it until it was out of sight.

Someone embedded a small screen with a camera above it into the wall next to the metal door. *Welp. Here goes nothing.* Greg unwrapped the paper towel, revealing Abin's eyeball, the optic nerve still hanging on like a bloody noodle. He gripped the eyeball between his thumb and forefinger and held it up to the camera. The lens emitted an array of thin red lights that drifted up and down, scanning the iris of the detached eye. Greg held his breath, waiting, until the screen lit up green and read:

ACCESS GRANTED.

A loud clicking noise reverberated throughout the barren boathouse, and then the metal door crept open. He exhaled, relieved, before entering.

On the other side of the metal door, the appearance of the lab surprised Greg. *Everything is so…clean,* he thought as he examined the room. For once on the island, a room wasn't completely composed of wood; almost everything was stainless steel—and sanitized. Greg felt like crying when the clean air passed through his nostrils. He'd gotten so used to the dank smell of everything else, he'd almost forgotten what cleanliness smelled like.

He walked along a steel table that held glass beakers, flasks, and vials, as well as a row of Bunsen burners. Someone had neatly organized various hand tools along the top edge, and next to them, a leather-bound notebook. The cover's design looked like scales. Greg ran his fingertips over the raised leather and opened the front cover. *A journal.* He leafed through the pages, stopping at a random entry. *Abin was keeping records of his experiments.* Flipping back to the beginning of the notebook, Greg read the first passage.

May 14th, 2010

I fear this may be my last time at the black site. While I've appreciated my time here, I believe they are on to me. There have been too many audits in my lab specifically for it to be called a coincidence. I thought I'd covered my tracks well, but I must have slipped up somewhere. I need to leave here before they come for me. I'll start over at the parcel of land I purchased in the Florida Everglades. Unfortunately, I'll have to destroy my embryos, as there is no way they'd make the trip. Such a waste. The good news is I'll be able to take my plasmids, so my research won't all be for naught. Maybe the climate in Florida will speed up the growth of the subjects? I will update after the move, when I'm set up in a new lab...unless I don't make it out of here alive.

June 16th, 2010

I said I would update when I was set up in a new place, but I couldn't resist. On my way to Florida, I ran into a lovely woman in a used bookstore. It was obvious that she was smitten with me immediately; very impressed with my knowledge of reptiles. We got to talking, and it turns out we share a lot of the same ideals. Her name is Candy, and she is going to join me on my new adventure in the Everglades. I think she'll make an excellent assistant.

. . .

Greg skimmed a large batch of pages that detailed Abin building his home and boathouse on the island, setting up the lab, and constructing the motel on the mainland, officially establishing Snake Bight proper.

September 8th, 2020

After a few test runs on local wildlife, I've concluded that the lab is fully functional and I'm ready to move on to human experimentation. I haven't yet thought of a plan to find test subjects. I've thought about making a trip to Miami to peruse the bars and clubs. I'm not sure how easy it'll be to convince someone to come out here with me. I have thought of other methods of persuasion... Although, I'm not positive how drugs would affect the experiments. Will update soon.

September 8th, 2020

Luck was on my side today as Candy and I ran into a couple touring the Everglades. They got lost, and I offered to help. I believe they would make perfect subjects for my initial human trials. They shouldn't take too much convincing to take part, as I have quite the bargaining chip. They brought their toddler daughter along.

September 12th, 2020

The first of the human trials didn't go as planned. The woman has passed on, but her death will not be in vain, as I know exactly where I made my mistake.

September 30th, 2020

Success! After a few weeks of reworking my technique, I was finally able to splice man's DNA with an alligator's successfully. They're going to be writing articles about me for ages. I can't celebrate too much yet, though. The man can transform, but it can be better. Much better. I just have to find out how.

September 30ᵗʰ, 2021

   I did it. I made bipedal, honest-to-God human-alligator hybrids. I'm so close to perfecting the process that I can taste it. A shorter life-span is the only thing holding it back now. The hybrids only live for nine months before their brains turn to mush and their bodies start to fall apart.

August 13ᵗʰ, 2022

   I think I've figured out my lifespan problem. I took in a profes-sional wrestler and tested on him. I learned that the girl who came with the tourists has a rare genetic mutation. I incorporated her DNA into the alligators, and then into the principal subject. That was eleven months ago, and he's still alive. His faculties all seem to be intact, but his lower jaw fell off after about a month. I recently brought Candy in for testing, and now I'm waiting to see if it's part of a bigger dete-rioration, or a lone anomaly. I did it after I dosed her tea and knocked her unconscious, so she isn't thrilled with me right now, but she'll get over it, I'm sure.

At least Brent wasn't full of shit, Greg thought, as he continued scanning the pages. He stopped when something in partic-ular caught his eye.

May 23ʳᵈ, 2024

   The girl spoke to me today in her sleep. At first, I thought she was sleep-talking through a dream, but then a light shone down on her; her voice was deep and vibrated throughout my whole body. Her eyes and mouth remained closed as she introduced herself as the divine being. The creator. And with that, she instructed me on how I could correct the mistakes in my experiments; how to perfect my perfect race. It is late now, and I'm having trouble keeping my eyes open, but I will start work first thing in the morning. I can't wait!

May 24*th*, 2024

After extracting oocytes from the girl's ovaries, I was able to genetically engineer embryos, essentially and effectively cloning her. In isolating her mutated gene, I made it possible for it to pass on to the embryos with one-hundred percent certainty. I can't believe I didn't think of this before. By creating the mutated embryos and splicing the alligator DNA into them, I take out the third variable, and the finished product will be more stable. No more deteriorating brains or body parts. And no more trying to find willing participants to join my cause. I'll be able to grow my army by myself, right here. I will have to add an incubator addition to the lab in order for this to work, though.

November 3*rd*, 2024

I can't explain it, but the first clone grew incredibly fast. It was as if the cells caught up with the cells of the host. Candy named the first one Valentine. I told her not to name it because she would get attached, but she insisted. As far as I can tell, the girl had only one major setback. Her tongue isn't developing as it should. We're trying to teach her how to speak, but she's having trouble. She understands, but her tongue doesn't seem to want to work. I don't need them to talk anyway. She wanted to play with one subject, but it was still a baby, still incubating. She snuck in while I was working and broke the baby out of its incubator. At that point, it was useless, contaminated, so I drilled a hole in its skull and ended it. Valentine took a liking to it, so I let her keep it. She won't leave the damned thing alone. She takes it everywhere with her.

Greg slammed the notebook shut and stared at the leather cover. *I've read enough. This is sick.* He glanced toward the back of the lab and spotted another metal door. He approached it and stood before a keypad with a small screen that read

ENTER PASSWORD

Greg scratched his head, thinking, and typed in

ALLIGATOR

The screen flashed red and the words

LOGIN ATTEMPT FAILED. TWO ATTEMPTS REMAINING.

appeared. He then tried

CREATOR

Failed again. *One more left. Come on, Greg. Think.* He typed in

CANDY

The screen flashed green, and then he heard a loud *clunk* as the door unlocked.

He opened the door; a sunlamp blinded him as humid air hit him like a truck. *This must be the incubator.* After his eyes adjusted to the light, he took a few steps into the room. Looking around the area, he noticed glass tanks filled with water lining the walls. Inside the water-filled tanks contained what appeared to be babies. He approached a tank for a better look and saw it wasn't a baby, but a small version of Ashley. It looked *exactly* like her, hair and everything; only the size of maybe a one-year-old baby. He moved to another tank, then another, then another—all of them the same. *He really got to work creating this army.*

A large red button was situated on the wall between two tanks. A sign above it read

EMERGENCY FLUSH

Greg didn't hesitate for even a second before he smacked the button. The sunlamp hummed as it shutdown, cooling Greg off instantly. Water began draining from the incubation tanks and pouring out of spouts at the bottom of them, and Abin's monstrosities floated to the bottom of the tanks, where they would lie and suffocate once the water had completely drained.

Greg limped out of the room, through the lab, and back out onto the dock. He scanned the interior of Ethan's boat until he found what he was looking for. He reached down and pulled out a red gas container.

His ears perked up when he heard Lisa's voice from behind him. "Greg! What are you doing?"

He spun around and faced Lisa, who was standing in the entry to the boathouse.

"Come on! We got the boat and the girls. Let's get the hell out of here!"

"Abin's dead," Greg said, looking down at the gas container. "We're *safe*."

Lisa's eyes moved down to the blood-soaked spot on the torso of Greg's shirt. "Oh, my God! Are you hurt?" She took a few steps toward him. "We have to get you—"

"I have to burn it down. There's more of those abominations in there. I'll be out there in a minute."

Greg noticed Lisa was looking at him with concern. He was sure he must've looked crazed. "Okay. I'll be on the boat," Lisa said and turned out of the doorway, back outside.

Greg walked through the lab and then to the incubation room. He held the gas container with his good hand as he splashed fuel all over the room. He then walked backward into the lab, pouring a trail of gasoline behind him. When the container was empty, he tossed it to the side. Turning to the lab table, he opened the propane tank underneath, then ignited a Bunsen burner, opening the air holes only partially, so the flame remained weaker. He moved the burner to the edge of the table and knocked it off; the flame landed next to the trail of gasoline. The trail ignited, and the flame made its way to the incubation room. Greg turned and left the lab, then limped out of the boathouse.

Once outside and at a safe distance, Greg turned to face the boathouse and watched as smoke billowed out, then the flames grew, then—*Boom*—there was an explosion as the boathouse became completely engulfed in flames. He watched the building burn for a moment and then heard something not too far away. Looking to the left of the boathouse, he saw a pack of creatures sprinting toward him. He then felt lightheaded. His eyes rolled into the back of his head as his vision went black. Sightless, he felt his body hit the ground, and heard the fading sound of his wife screaming his name as he lost consciousness. "Greeeeg!"

Chapter Forty-Seven

GREG SAW ONLY DARKNESS, BUT FELT THE SENSATION OF HIS eyeballs moving around in his head. The muffled sound of Lisa's voice appeared and slowly became clearer. "I think he's waking up. Greg? Greg?!" A tingling feeling ran down his arms, to his hands, as he touched each fingertip to his thumb. Then the tingling shot down his legs until he was wiggling his toes. Lisa's voice appeared again. "He's moving!" Slivers of light appeared in front of Greg as his eyelids slowly began to pry open and, after a moment, he opened them all the way. Lisa and Sage leaned over him, staring into his eyes.

"Dad!" Sage shouted, her eyes wide and blooming with excitement.

Greg groaned as he tried to sit up. Lisa gripped his arm and placed a hand on his back. "Easy, Greg. Take it easy. Go slow." She guided him as he sat up and saw they were at the front end of the airboat. Relieved, he scooted backward with Lisa's help and leaned his back against a bench. Greg glanced down at his stomach and noticed he was shirtless; a fresh bandage wrapped around his torso. He looked up at a smiling Lisa, who said, "First-aid kit on the boat." Greg smiled back at her. She handed him a water bottle and held out a fist. "Open your hand." Greg held out his hand, and Lisa moved her fist over it and opened it, dropping two white pills into his palm. "I found some painkillers there too. Hopefully, they'll hold you over until we can get you to a hospital."

Greg popped the pills into his mouth and mumbled, "Thanks." He uncapped the water bottle, took a swig, and gulped the pills down.

"Why don't you get some *actual* sleep, and I'll wake you when we get back to the mainland?" Lisa started to stand up, but Greg reached his hand out and grabbed her arm.

"Lisa, wait. There's something I have to get off my chest. It's been eating me alive."

Lisa's face turned to concern as she furrowed her brow. "What is it, Greg?"

Greg adjusted himself on the floor and grabbed his wound in pain. "Argh!"

"Easy, easy."

"Remember before we came here? When I said I wanted one more family vacation before Kyle was gone for good?"

Lisa smiled. "Yeah. I thought you were having a midlife crisis, seeing your boy being a successful college student."

"Well, that wasn't entirely true."

Lisa's smile vanished.

"I…I got suspended from work again."

"What?! Why didn't you tell me?"

"Jake and I—"

Lisa put her face in her hands. "Of *course* it was that fucking Jake."

"No, listen." Greg's eyes moved down to the boat floor. "We went on a drug bust…one we had no authority to execute. No warrant, our superiors didn't know…" Greg's eyes moved back to Lisa, and he felt them brimming with tears. "It didn't go as planned, and when shit went south, I found out that Jake was working with the dealers. Skimming money off them to let them keep dealing. He killed one; I saw him do it. And I don't know why, but I fucking covered for him! Argh!" Greg hunched over and cradled his gut.

Lisa wasn't as quick to comfort him this time as she looked at him in disbelief.

Greg sat back upright. "In the end, it turned out he blamed me for the shooting. I got suspended pending an investigation."

After a moment of silence, Lisa finally spoke up. "You didn't do it, did you?"

"No! Of course not!"

"Then the evidence will clear you, right?"

"It will, but I don't think they will look too kindly on me covering for that piece of shit. I…I could lose my job."

Lisa moved next to Greg and put her arms around him, hugging him. "We'll worry about that when the time comes. Lie down, get some sleep."

Greg lowered his head onto Lisa's lap and began sobbing into her thigh. "Am I a bad person?"

"No, honey. You've made bad decisions, but you're not a bad person. You were protecting someone you thought was your friend." Lisa's voice, although flat, comforted Greg as the painkillers took hold of him and lulled him to sleep. *She's just being nice. She won't look at me the same ever again,* Greg thought. And that was the last thing that went through his mind before he drifted off.

Greg's eyes opened once again as his vision filled with the night sky. *How long was I out?* He was no longer resting on Lisa's lap, but lying on his back on the floor of the boat. He figured the painkillers were still working because his stab wound now only throbbed faintly, unlike its previous sharp pain. And his skinned hand and the hole in his shoulder were numb. When he really thought about it, he smirked at how fucked up his body was. Oddly enough, he couldn't hear any chatter from the girls. *Is everyone asleep?* He thought it wouldn't be like Lisa to go to sleep, not knowing if he was okay. She was very much a worrywart.

Using the bench seat, he pulled himself up onto his ass and looked around the boat—nobody in sight. "Lisa? Sage? Ashley?" He pulled himself up onto his feet as he continued to examine his surroundings. *This is weird. Am I dreaming?*

He moved toward the middle of the boat when, in between two bench seats, he saw Lisa curled up in a ball on the floor. As he approached her, he let out an enormous breath of relief. *Whew. She must've been exhausted.* Approaching his wife, he noticed that the floor surrounding her was darker than the rest of the floor. *What the hell?* He bent down, grabbed her shoulder, and shook it. "Lisa…Lisa, wake up!" He pushed her over and recoiled when she rolled onto her back. Someone had gouged her eyes out of their sockets and ripped open her throat so deeply that her cervical spine was visible.

He covered his mouth, but the vomit found its way through his fingers. "Jesus, fuck!" He bent over, putting his hands on his knees.

Suddenly, he heard a trembling whisper from his side. "Daddy…"

Greg's head shot over to look, and Sage was sitting with her back against the side of the boat with her knees pulled up to her chest between two bench seats. She moved her finger to her mouth and put it over her lips as to say, "Be quiet." Then she moved the finger and pointed toward the back of the boat. Greg followed her finger, but couldn't see anything except darkness. He whispered, "Stay there." And stood back upright.

He began walking toward the back of the boat, and as he got closer, the darkness became more clear, and he saw the back of a little girl sitting down, facing away from him. He stopped for a moment, then continued forward. His stomach felt like it was fighting its way into his throat. "Ashley?" he said, his voice lacking any confidence.

The little girl didn't so much as twitch.

About two feet from the girl, Greg heard a *crunch* when he took a step. He stopped and looked down. Surrounding his feet were, what looked like, a pile of teeth. *What the fuck?* He moved his gaze back up to the little girl, and she now faced him. "Ashley. What *happened* here?"

The little girl smiled. Her long, pointed teeth almost shone in the dark. And then, for the first time, Greg saw her blink.

Afterword

I dedicated half of this book to the memory of two people I didn't know. Winham Rotunda and Jon Huber—better known as professional wrestlers Bray Wyatt and Brodie Lee/Luke Harper. I first saw them in 2012, on WWE's developmental wrestling show NXT and I was immediately drawn in by the charismatic low talking man in a floral shirt, standing in the woods with a larger, silent man in a dirty white tank top. I'm obviously a horror fan, and in a wrestling world full of jacked up former football players, I saw these two backwoods hillbilly characters that looked as if they were dropped straight out of The Texas Chainsaw Massacre, and they became favorites of mine before I'd even seen them wrestle. When I started writing the VERY first version of this book in 2014, the two had split up thier faction, but the original bayou characters had stayed in my mind. As a result, Abin Moses was inspired by Windham "Bray Wyatt" Rotunda, and his son, Ethan, by "the first son of the Wyatt Family" Jon "Luke Harper" Huber. Even if you're not a wrestling fan, I would recommend looking up some of their old Wyatt Family vignettes. I hope my characters make them proud, wherever they may be.

-Robert King II
　　April 20th, 2026

Acknowledgments

I'd like to give a special thanks to my mom, Sondra, for keeping the town of Snake Bight alive in my mind for over ten years and believing in it even when I didn't. I originally had a very different first draft of this book in 2014, and if she hadn't constantly bugged me asking, "What's up with that alligator story? I loved it!", I almost certainly wouldn't still be writing today.

Kayla—thank you again for being my guinea pig and reading the skeletons of my stories.

Thank you to my editor, Ramona, for not only fixing my errors, but for championing my story.

And finally, thank you to everyone that decided to pick this book up and give it a shot. I'd love to hear what you have to say, so find me on social media (@robkingfiction) and let me know!

And of course, please consider leaving a review on Amazon, Goodreads, etc. Reviews are crucial, especially to indie authors. They make it so more people can see our books and we can keep making them.

The Place Beneath The Dirt

About the Author

Robert King II is a horror/thriller author drawing inspiration from the likes of Adam Nevill, Ronald Malfi, and Stephen King. Robert lives in Michigan with his corgi, Raditz.

www.ingramcontent.com/pod-product-compliance
Lightning Source LLC
Chambersburg PA
CBHW051307130726
47987CB00004B/1702